The Lost Guardian

K. N. Timofeev

ISBN: 1495989887
ISBN-13: 978-1495989889

:

For everyone who said I could do this.

i

ACKNOWLEDGMENTS

To my husband, Dmitry, thank you for not only getting me the bracelet that inspired this story, but for being a constant source of encouragement. You mean the world to me and I couldn't have done this without you in my corner.

Nadine, you were with this story since the beginning, even though it's not something you normally would have read. Your confusion helped a lot. I knew what I was trying to stay it just didn't always make it to paper and you pointed that out to me numerous times. Ha-ha.

Acree. Where do I start? If it hadn't been for you, I don't think I would have written this story. I told you my idea and you told me to run with it. Thanks for the long phone calls that helped me to hash out what I wanted to say in this story and the ones to follow. Now all you have to do is start on yours.

Michelle. Thank you so much for all your words of wisdom. I owe you one. You helped me to figure out how exactly I was going to get this book out into the world.

A big fat thank you to my friends and family. Your continued support and enthusiasm kept me going till the very end.

A special thank you to you, dear reader, for picking up this book. While I may never meet you, please know that I am honored that you chose this book, my book, out of thousands to take home. I hope you enjoy reading it as much as I did writing it.

One

In the old westerns, the hero of the story rides off into the sunset, after doing something that was right for the hero but would cause other's to shun him. So they hightail it towards the horizon, maybe to a place where they would be understood and accepted.

But that only happens in the movies, right? Well, for one woman it was real life... sort of. Erin had just gone through a nasty divorce that left her with nothing, and to make matters worse, her *own* family had taken *his* side. They still welcomed him into their home with open arms—but they had never seen his dark side.

After her divorce, Erin tried to start over but John, her ex-husband, would show up at her doorstep, promising that he had changed and that things would be different.

And every time, she would give in and go back to him. Things would be alright for a while, but then would start to fall apart all over again. Finally, she couldn't —and wouldn't— take it anymore. She left for the last time and went to the one person who always seemed to be on her side: her grandmother, Elise.

Erin's grandmother had been the only one who seemed to notice the bruises that she had tried to hide. She was also the one who comforted Erin when she found out about the numerous affairs. Now her grandmother was there for her yet again, this time giving her a way out.

Elise took care of everything. She helped Erin to change her last name in secret and to get all her new forms of identification. She also set up the flight and all the other travel arrangements, giving Erin time to catch her breath. Elise even offered Erin the keys to her family home in Ireland.

Erin received a shock when her grandmother gave her information for a bank account. Elise told her that she had been putting money into the account since her parents— Erin's great-grandparents— had died. She explained that the account was substantial, so Erin wouldn't have to worry about money for a while. Erin tried to turn it down, but her grandmother wouldn't let her.

"How are you supposed to take care of yourself?" Elise demanded. "The money normally goes towards the house's upkeep. If you won't take it willingly, I'll have cash withdrawn and delivered to you." Erin finally relented and accepted the account information. She knew her reluctance was silly, but she hated taking money from anyone, and it irked her pride. But she really didn't have a choice— or so she kept telling herself.

Elise drove Erin to the airport, telling her about what to expect when she arrived. All the while, Erin fingered an antique, bronze Celtic Knot work bracelet. The bracelet was a goodbye gift from her grandmother.

"It's not easy doing the right thing," Elise told Erin when she gave her the bracelet, "but you come from a long line of strong women. Every time you feel like you can't go on, just remind yourself of that and draw on their strength, and remember that I am always with you too."

Erin boarded the plane without any mishaps and slumped into her seat with a heavy sigh. The whole situation had really taken a toll on her on a physical and emotional level. She had always been slender, but the stress of her divorce had left her unable to eat more than a few mouthfuls. This made her look like she was wasting away. She felt that way too. The bones of her face were more pronounced, making her face appear more angular than it actually was. Her clothes hung loosely around her body. But it was her eyes that truly showed how much she had suffered. Her hazel eyes were once full of fire and life, but were now dull and listless, surrounded by newly formed lines.

"Would you like anything to drink?" asked a flight attendant, breaking Erin out of her troubled thoughts. She had been zoned out and hadn't realized that the flight was underway. She wondered how long she had been lost in thought.

"Ah, yes...an ice water please." Erin answered softly. "When will we be landing?"

"We should land in Dublin in about two more hours," the flight attendant replied as she handed Erin a small cup of ice water from her push cart. Erin smiled, accepting the cup, and took a sip to mask her shock. She had been out of it for *five* hours. She shook her head, swearing to think of happier things until the plane landed.

After landing, Erin took a taxi to the hotel where she would sleep for the night. In the morning, one of her grandmother's old friends would come to pick her up and drive her to her new home.

Erin was still amazed at what her grandmother had managed to pull off in such a short time. She was extremely grateful. It was almost like Elise had known that Erin would need to escape. If Erin had to arrange all of this on her own, she wasn't completely sure that she could have, before being found out.

In the taxi, Erin emptied her mind and watched as the city faded into a blur of lights. She tried not to focus on how much of a failure she was in life. Sure, she earned her Master's in History but everything else in her life had completely fallen apart. This was not where she had envisioned herself to be at her age. She was supposed to be happily married, with at least one child, and teaching in her old high school. She wasn't supposed to be on the run from an abusive ex-husband and hiding out in a foreign country.

Erin sighed and pressed her head against the window. Her throat tightened and her eyes began to water. She took a few deep breaths to push the tightness down. She wouldn't cry, she told herself, or at least, not until she got to her room. It was better to cry in private.

An hour later, Erin's taxi pulled up to the hotel. It wasn't anything fancy like the ones that were closer to the airport, but it had a quaintness that she appreciated. She paid her fare, and then turned to examine the building. It was clearly old, built sometime during the late 1800s perhaps, but it had been well maintained.

Upon entering, Erin looked about the lobby and smiled again. The owners had tried to keep true to the building's heritage, the décor being all from the same time period, or at least close to it. The receptionist smiled kindly as Erin walked up to the desk. "Erin McManin," she said as she reached the receptionist's desk.

The receptionist quickly typed in Erin's name then smiled. "Ah yes here you are. Your room is 315. You just need to take the stairs to the top floor and take a left. Your room is at the end of the hall." She handed Erin the room key and had her sign in. "Do you need any help with your luggage?" she asked.

"No thank you," Erin said, taking back her identification.

"Alright then," the receptionist said with another smile. "Dinner has already been served, but you will find a list of restaurants in your room. Breakfast is served at six. Would you like a wakeup call?"

" No, but thank you," Erin said. "I'll manage."

"Okay," replied the receptionist. "Enjoy your night, and thank you for staying with us."

Erin smiled one last time at her before she made her way to her room. She passed a few other patrons on the stairs. They all gave her small, polite smiles. She tried to return them, but she was just too tired to care about being polite. Thankfully, the hallway to her room was empty, so she wouldn't have to force anymore smiles. The lock released with a click and with a tired sigh she entered her room.

When Erin turned on the lights, she noted that although the room was small, it was still nice. It had the typical beige walls and carpeting, common in hotels and other lodging establishments. The bathroom was to her right, just beyond the doorway. When she turned the light on in there, she noticed an old clawed-foot tub that had been fitted with a showerhead, along with the rest of the things one expected to see in a bathroom. Leaving the bathroom light on, she then turned on the rest of the lights. A habit she had picked up recently, thanks to her ex-husband.

On the far right wall, there was a twin bed that had a thick quilted comforter and two pillows. Next to the bed was a nightstand that held a lamp, which was quickly turned on, a phone, and a small clock. Across from the bed was a small entertainment stand that held an old TV. There were a few pictures on the wall that depicted the Irish country side, and at the end of the room was a window that had thick, green curtains. Dropping her duffle bag on the floor, Erin walked over to the window. She gazed out, looking at the city lights for just a moment before she pulled the curtains closed. She then plopped down on the bed, sinking into its softness. She rolled over, pulling a pillow into her body and buried her face.

Erin laid there for a few minutes, waiting for the tears that had threatened to fall in the taxi to come, but they never did. She sat up slowly and took a deep breath. For the past few months, she had lived with the constant fear of her ex showing up at her doorstep, or even more terrifying, actually inside her home. But half way across the world, that fear hadn't rear its ugly head, yet. She smiled sadly because, for the first time since her divorce, she actually felt free.

It was strange, this freedom, after feeling 'caged' for so long. She liked it. Deciding not to waste another second worrying about the past, Erin grabbed her duffle bag.

Erin had packed very little— no more than the necessities really. Her mood darkened when she realized that her entire life could fit into a single duffle bag. She shrugged. What was she supposed to do about it? She pulled out her pajamas and laid them on the bed. She checked to make sure that the door and windows were locked before she went into the bathroom. She contemplated taking a shower, but the desire for a good, long soak in the tub won out.

The steam from the water filled the small bathroom quickly, fogging the mirror. With a contented sigh, Erin sunk herself fully into the tub. She used the shampoo and soap that the hotel provided, since you really can't take anything like that on planes anymore.

The water was almost cold by the time Erin got out, but she felt so much better. She quickly got dressed, and then climbed into bed. Her mind started to go over every possible worst case scenario, which caused her to start freaking out. Her anxiety grew, threatening to become a full-blooded panic attack, but just then a sudden coolness washed over her. Without realizing it, she had put the wrist with the bracelet over her heart. It had glowed faintly but from her panic addled state, not to mention the brightness of the room, she had missed it. Her fears faded away, leaving her drained, and she soon fell into a safe, deep sleep.

The next morning, Erin woke up in a panic because she didn't recognize her surroundings. Once she did, her heart slowed down and she rolled over to look at the clock. The clock read six o'clock, giving her an hour before her grandmother's friend would arrive to pick her up. After a quick shower, she threw her belongings back into her bag. As she adjusted the strap of her bag, she took one deep breath. *This is it*, she thought. *Today I start my new life.*

The dining room was filled with the smells of porridge, sausage, and tea. Erin breathed it in and smiled. It reminded her of mornings at her grandmother's house. She grabbed herself a small bowl of porridge, adding lots of honey, and a few sausages. She really wanted coffee, but figured she would just have to make do with tea for the time being. As she ate, she tried to remember what her grandmother had told her about her friend.

"Her name is Moira Duncan," Elise had reminded Erin when she had handed over her ticket and passport. "She was my best friend growing up. I'm not too sure what she looks like now, but when she gets there, you won't miss her. Moira always had this knack for making an entrance." Erin smiled at that. Her grandmother, Elise, also knew how to make an entrance, so she knew Moira would be interesting.

"Erin!" someone shouted, startling Erin. She almost choked on the sausage she was eating. When she was able to breathe again, she turned and smiled, in spite of almost dying over breakfast. An elderly woman stood in the doorway to the dining hall, waving frantically. Moira Duncan had arrived. Once she was sure that Erin had seen her, she made a beeline towards her table.

Moira was wearing a pair of well-worn, tan slacks that looked like they were stained permanently with dirt. She also wore a man's buttoned shirt, and she carried an enormous bag. Her graying hair was pulled up into a bun, but there were several strands that had fallen out. Her eyes were a bright blue and sparkled with mischief as she practically marched her way over to Erin.

"Erin McManin?" she asked, but before Erin could answer, Moira started to speak again. "Of course you are! I knew it was you the moment I saw you. You look just like your grandmother, you know?" Erin just smile up at Moira, already liking her. "Ah, I see you're eating a good 'ol Irish breakfast. That's good. It will put some meat on your bones. I've never understood why Americans always want to look half-starved." Moira pulled out a chair. When she just sat there smiling, Erin realized that Moira was waiting for her to speak.

"Um...thank you for coming to get me," Erin said, not sure of what else to say.

"Don't you worry about it, my little birdie," Moira said, waving her hand. "I would do anything for one of Elise's children, or grandchild, in your case."

"All the same," Erin said with a small smile, "Thank you." Moira waved her off again and then proceeded to steal a sausage.

"Once you're done, we'll get underway. If we're on the road by seven, we should reach your new home around one," Moira said.

Erin almost choked again. "How early did you have to get up to come get me? Really, you shouldn't have troubled yourself so much. I could have taken a taxi or a train."

Moira raised an eyebrow then started to laugh. "There's no need to worry your pretty little head", she said wiping her eyes. "I was visiting my sister. She lives in the city, you see?" That bit of information made Erin feel better. She didn't want to be a burden to anyone. "Well, you'd best hurry up now, my little birdie. We have a long way to go."

With some help from Moira, Erin finished her breakfast in record time. The first thing Erin did when she walked out of the hotel was turn her face towards the morning sun. She wasn't sure if it was the good night's sleep or the prospect of a new life, but the early March morning seemed brighter than any she had remembered.

"Now, where in the world did I put my keys?" Erin smiled as she saw Moira digging around in her monstrosity of a bag. "Well don't just stand there gawping," Moira snapped playfully. "My car's over there. I'll find the keys soon enough. I always do."

Moira continued to walk towards her car, although her eyes never left their search for the elusive keys. Erin smiled in spite of herself when she saw Moira's car. Just like its owner, the car was old but still held its appeal. It was a simple hatch-back, whose yellow paint must have been bright in its early days, but was now a soft butter-yellow. When she came up to the car, she smiled bigger. The trunk and back seat looked like a mobile nursery. There were plant pots of all sizes, various gardening tools, bags upon bags of soil, and to top it all off, there were even a few flowers wrapped up like babies. "Found cha' you little buggers," Moira said triumphantly. In her hands was the largest collection of keys Erin had ever seen.

Once they were buckled in, and the flowers were checked to ensure their safety, they took off. "I can't tell you how excited I was when your grandma told me you were coming," Moira said. "It's been a long time since anyone's lived in that house. But don't you worry too much. Your grandma had me take over the caretaking. Once a year, I have my boys come by and make sure everything's working and tidy up a bit." Moira patted Erin's hand and gave it a small squeeze, which Erin appreciated. While she wasn't sure how much of her story her grandmother had told Moira, but apparently the old woman knew enough to have the gist of it.

The rest of the trip consisted of Moira talking and Erin listening. She laughed when Moira told some funny story about her grandmother, but it made her realize how little she knew about her grandmother's history. Her grandmother had never talked about her childhood, or even why she came to the states. "It was a sad day when your grandma left."

"Why did she leave?" Erin asked. "It couldn't have been easy to leave everything she knew behind?"

"Well, she met this nice American man, fell in love, and decided to start a life with him across the ocean."

"She met my grandfather here?!" Erin exclaimed.

"Sure did. He was this big shot business man, as I'm sure you know," Moira said, glancing at Erin who nodded. "Well, he was looking at building a new factory near the village. Now, most of us didn't like that, because we're just simple farmers; always have been and always will be. Some people were afraid of losing the land that their family had farmed for generations, and others didn't want all the noise or all the outsiders who would be brought in to work in the factory. Well, your gran managed to talk him out of it and somehow got a marriage proposal too." Moira chuckled a bit. "She left a string of broken hearts behind, but we've always kept in touch, more or less over the years."

Erin knew that her grandfather had made his fortune by building factories for various companies. Her dad took over the company and it was doing very well. She thought that it was strange that her grandfather had fallen for her grandmother because she had stopped him from getting what he wanted. She doubted that her dad would be that understanding. The business was everything to him.

That's why he constantly pushed her to get back with John. John was his business partner. *Well you're just gonna have to be disappointed Dad*, she thought, *'cause there's no way in hell I'm ever going back to him.*

As they drove, cities became towns, towns became villages, and villages turned into vast, open country sides. Erin was taken in by the beauty of the land around her and still couldn't believe that her grandmother could have left it. The rolling hills, deep woods, and open fields scattered with stones called out to her, almost as if in welcome. There was nothing like this back home. The nature they did have was highly landscaped. She thought that her grandmother must have loved her grandfather a lot, to have left the only home she had ever known. She hoped that one day she would find a love like that.

Sure enough, they reached the outskirts of the village around one o'clock. "Welcome to Dorshire," Moira said proudly. "Now we're stoppin' off at my house for a supper. Afterwards, I'll take you over to see the house."

"Thank you," Erin said, looking forward to getting out of the car. Her back was cramped and sore. "But you don't have to. I'd rather go on and get settled."

"Nonsense, there's nothing up there for you to eat, and there's no power either. I promised your gran that I'd look after you, and look after you I will!" That left no room for arguing, so Erin was going to be fed by Moira— whether she wanted to or not. Erin just shook her head and resigned herself to an afternoon of food being shoved down her throat, just like every time she visited her grandmother. She took comfort in that because she really needed a grandmother right now; someone to make sure that she was taking care of herself, and to pester her constantly if she wasn't.

Thirty minutes later they were pulling up to the main part of the village. Erin instantly fell in love. It looked as if time had stopped in Dorshire. The buildings looked like they had been repurposed several times, but some of the old painted signs still remained. Children rode their bikes in the street, heedless of traffic. Old men and women sat outside the pub or the beauty parlor, sipping drinks and laughing with each other. Dorshire almost seemed too good to be true for Erin, who was a bit old-fashioned herself.

"I live just on the other side," Moira stated, "but this is where all the shops, pubs, and official buildings are—banks, police station, library, and what have you. Do you need to stop and pick up anything while we're in town?"

"Actually, yes I do," Erin said quickly. "That is, if it's not too much trouble."

"You worry too much," Moira told her sternly, stopping in front of a nursery. "I have to drop off these flowers, so it's no problem at all. Go and get your things."

Erin blushed, and stopped herself from apologizing again. Moira was right, of course, but it really wasn't Erin's fault. The past year had been really rough, and she was always in a constant state of apprehension. But she promised herself that she would change that, and soon.

A bell jingled when Erin walked into a small convenience store. Grabbing a basket, she headed straight to the personal hygiene aisle. She filled her basket with shampoo, conditioner, soap, deodorant, shaving cream, and razors. As she made her way towards the register she decided to stop by the food aisle. She wanted to pick up some snacks, since there wasn't any food in her grandmother's house. Suddenly, there came a crashing sound at the other end of the aisle. Startled, she turned to see that an old man had fallen into a display.

"Oh my god," she cried. "Are you okay?"

The old man just stared at her as if he had seen a ghost. "I'm alright," he said shakily. He then started to pick up the display. He jumped again when Erin tried to help him. "I'm sorry," he said. "You just look a lot like someone I used to know a long time ago."

"My grandmother's from here," Erin explained. "Her name's Elise." The old man dropped the package he was holding. "I take it you knew her?" He nodded his head and then, once everything was picked up, practically ran out of the store. Confused, she returned to her shopping, picking up some chips and fruit. She paid for her items without any further incident, and then went to meet Moira. What happened in the store with the man was still bothering her.

"Moira," she said cautiously, "is there something about my grandmother that I should know?"

Moira glanced over at Erin with a confused look on her face. "Why do you ask?" Erin told her about what happened in the store. "Your grandmother was special to many people," Moira said with a sigh. "When she left, it hurt a lot of people. And it sounds like you ran into Jake Baker. He was always in love with your gran but never had the courage to say anything." Erin nodded slowly and wondered, for the tenth time that day, what else there was to her grandmother's past.

"I wouldn't worry too much over it," Moira said, kindly patting Erin's shoulder. "Imagine if your best friend just got up and left, never to come back, and then you see them looking exactly the same years later. You do look a lot like your grandmother, you know, so don't be too surprised if more people react the same way." They drifted into silence until they pulled up to a small house. "We're here," Moira said proudly.

Moira's home was a typical single-story Irish cottage— thatched roof and all. The white-washed exterior was just beginning to crumble, exposing the natural stone underneath. Vines had managed to creep their way up from the garden, but they did nothing to diminish the charming cottage. Erin had a huge smile on her face when she noticed that someone had painted the door a bright, canary yellow. To the right of the cottage she saw a large oak tree with a tire swing and a small garden to the left of the driveway. She noticed smoke rising from the chimney and took a deep breath, relishing the smell of wood smoke in the chilly air. Suddenly, her calm was shattered by squeals.

"Grandma's back! Grandma's back!"

From around the cottage three children came running: two boys and a girl. They paid no attention to Erin and threw themselves at Moira. They began to ask her questions at the same time, causing both Moira and Erin to laugh. It was only then that the children realized Erin was there, and fell quiet.

"Erin I would like you to meet my grandchildren," Moira said, beaming proudly. Both of the boys had dark—brown hair and blue eyes, while the little girl had blonde hair and green eyes. Moira laid her hand on the tallest boy. "This is Aiden. He belongs to my son Barry. And these two belong to my daughter Caelan. Tegan is the little girl and Devin is her brother." Erin smiled. "Say hello to Erin, my little birds." The little girl, Tegan, moved to hide behind Moira while the boys gave her shy smiles. "Well, I think supper should be ready; shall we?"

The children scurried to the back of the cottage, leaving Moira and Erin behind. She followed Moira towards the kitchen, where a woman with brown hair was placing biscuits on a baking pan. The woman turned around with a smile and dusted her hands on her apron. "How was your trip?" she asked.

"Uneventful," Moira replied. "Caelan, this is Erin, Elise's granddaughter." Caelan shook Erin's hand. Caelan still had bits of flour and dough on her hands. Erin didn't mind; she actually found it comforting.

"It's so nice to finally meet you. Mum's told me so much about you and your grandma."

"Thank you for inviting me to supper," Erin said shyly.

"Don't mention it," Caelan said, waving a hand just like her mother. "There's always room for one more. We'll be eating in about an hour, so just make yourself at home."

Erin thanked her again. She would have liked to help out with the cooking, but the kitchen wouldn't hold three people trying to work in it. There was barely enough room for two. She headed towards the living room; her eyes were drawn to the pictures on the wall. She walked over and was surprised to see a younger version of her grandmother smiling back at her. She really did look just like her grandmother. They had the same build, face, and hair color. She smiled and gently touched her grandmother's image. *Thank you*, she thought, *I will never be able to repay you everything you've done for me.*

"We're home," a male voice called out, followed by the sound of stomping boots.

"Barry, Murphy," Moira yelled back. "Wash up right away." Erin could hear the men chuckle as they walked past heading towards the bathroom. As she walked out of the living room, she ran into one of the men, who couldn't be anyone but Moira's son, Barry.

"Hello there," he said with a smile. He had brown hair, just like his sister and mother, and he had bright blue eyes. He was wearing worn clothes and smelled strongly of sheep. "You must be Erin."

"And you must be Barry," she said shaking his hand.

"I'm surprised my mum hasn't talked you to death yet." Erin laughed and shook her head. He leaned closer and said jokingly, "Don't worry; she still has time."

An hour later, the entire Duncan clan and Erin were settled around the table. Moira's husband, Murphy, was seated at the head of the table, with Erin on his right, and Barry on his left. Murphy was a man of few words. But Erin noticed the way his eyes sparkled as he watched the antics of his family. Caelan was next to her brother, and their children filled in the rest of the table, leaving Moira seated at the other end of the table. After a quick prayer in thanks for the many blessings in the family's life, including meeting Erin, they torn into the tender roast, biscuits, and vegetables on their plates.

"It's really too bad that James couldn't join us," Moira said in between bites.

"I know," Caelan said with a sigh. "But some things just can't be helped. James is my husband," Caelan explained to Erin. "He works for the Navy so he ends up missing a lot of family gatherings."

"It must be very hard on you," Erin offered.

"I knew when I married him that the sea is his first love. I miss him when he's gone but when he's on land, it makes it all worthwhile." Erin nodded her head mindful of her failed marriage. "So," Caelan said, breaking the silence, "what exactly brings you to this side of the world?"

Erin paused, not really sure if she wanted to tell them. After all she had just met these people, but on the other hand they had welcomed her so openly. She remembered that her grandmother had always said that talking about the painful parts in your life was the best way to mend the wounds. So she decided to open herself up a little and bleed out a bit of the pain.

"Things were all messed up back home," Erin said softly. "I got divorced, but things only got worse from there. It was like my world was falling down around me. I had nowhere to go, and no one to turn to. My grandmother offered her old family home to me to use while I try to sort everything out and get my feet back under me."

"I know that feeling," Barry commented. "After my wife Clair passed away, I was a complete wreck. I couldn't seem to be able to function even on the most basic level." Murphy placed a weathered hand on his son's shoulder while Caelan gave him a companionate glance. "I just had to get away," Barry continued. "Mum and Da took Aiden for a few weeks so I that could. I went to the coast and stayed in the cabin that we stayed at during our honeymoon. I cried and cursed. And eventually, the pain dulled to a point where I could think clearly again. I realized that there was someone who still needed me and was suffering just as much as I was. In my grief, I had completely forgotten about my son." Barry smiled at his son, who beamed up at his dad. "It's been a few years, but it gets a little easier each day."

Erin turned her attention back to her plate to mask the tears in her eyes. She wished with every fiber of her being that the same would be true for her. She hoped that, one day, she would be able to pull herself back together and get on with her life. She didn't like the person she'd become: weak and broken. She knew that she may never be the same again, but she hoped that, eventually, she would be able to bear her scars with a smile.

The children disappeared once again after desert, leaving the adults to converse amongst themselves. "Are you sure you want to spend the night at your grandma's house tonight?" Moira asked, for what seemed like the hundredth time that night.

"Mum, let it be," Caelan sighed, exasperated. "There's no room here for her to sleep, and maybe Erin wants some time to herself."

"But there's no power," Moira said, not giving up.

"It's alright," Erin reassured her, "I don't really mind. Plus you've already done so much."

"Are you sure?" Moira asked. Erin nodded her head and Moira sighed in defeat. "If you're sure, then we need to get out to the house before the sun goes down." With goodbyes and promises to get together again, Erin left the Duncan clan and got into Moira's car. The cottages got farther and farther apart as they headed towards Erin's new home. All the while, Moira was trying to convince her to spend at least one night back at her home. "Well, here we are," Moira mumbled.

It was clear that no one had lived in the house for a long time. A few shutters were hanging off-kilter. The grass was a little tall, and it probably would be even taller if Moira hadn't arranged to have it cut from time to time. In spite of all of that, it was still something to see. The two-story house seemed to loom over the women in the fading sunlight, but instead of feeling ominous, it was actually welcoming. Like Moira's home, vines covered most of the lower level; they even had grown over a few of the windows. On the right side, was a single story attachment with its own door. When they pulled up next to Erin's new home, she noticed there was a large barn in the back. Getting out of Moira's car, Erin lifted her gaze upward. She took in the dual chimneys.

"There's one fireplace in the main room and one in

the kitchen," Moira stated when she followed Erin's gaze. The two women stared silently at the house for a few moments, each lost in their own thoughts. "We might as well go in." They waded through the overgrown yard, Moira once again digging through her purse for the keys. "Last chance," Moira said as she pulled out the keys. Erin took the keys from her grandmother's friend with a brave smile and unlocked the front door.

When they entered, Erin immediately felt a presence. It the air inside the house was heavy and still. But it also carried the feeling of timelessness. The house seemed to welcome her. As she stood in the entryway, she was reminded of happier times. She closed her eyes, trying to absorb the good vibes of the house. Moira watched her carefully.

"The main room is on your left," Moira said pointing. "The kitchen is to the right." Erin nodded, pushing away the pull of the house. "Upstairs are the bedrooms, but I was thinking that it would be best for you to sleep down here," Moira said, walking over to the door on the left. "I'll get the fireplace started if you'll get some candles. They should be in the kitchen somewhere."

Erin struggled a bit with the sliding door that led to the kitchen, but she was eventually able to open it. Directly in front of her was a small table that was covered with a sheet and boxes piled high. To her left was a small china cabinet, and across from her was the fireplace. She walked up to it to get a better look. Unlike most fireplaces, this one was built up so that the opening was about waist high. She was intrigued because it held a cauldron and had herbs hanging around it. For some reason, it made her think of witches. She noticed that it had a small compartment, which looked like it was used to bake bread. She could almost picture her great-grandmother placing freshly risen dough into the compartment, as well as the aroma of freshly baked bread. For a moment, she actually smelled it. Startled, she shook her head and went back to looking for the candles, which she later found on top of the refrigerator. Grabbing them, she went to join Moira in the living room.

The door to the living room was also a pocket door, and just before Erin passed through, she noticed the frame. The door frame was craved with a Celtic Knot work pattern. A quick glance behind her showed that the kitchen door bore the same pattern. She was surprised and pleased to see these little details in the door frames. She ran her hand over the living room's frame. She could barely feel the tool marks in the wood. It was little details like this that made her love old homes. Modern homes just didn't have details like this anymore; they were all angles, and came off sterile more than anything. Her parent's house had mosaic flooring, stained glass, and carved columns, but they were more of a status symbol than for the simple joy of living in something beautiful.

There was a crash in the living room caused by Moira opening the flue. Feeling guilty about daydreaming while Moira was fighting with the fireplace, Erin walked into the living room, promising to explore the house once she was alone.

"I found the candles," Erin called out, holding up the boxes.

"Good," Moira said getting up from the front of the fireplace with a groan. She picked up a metal log carrier and held it out. "I'll get the candles set up but could you go out back by the barn and bring in some wood?"

"Sure."

Moira handed Erin a flashlight and pointed her towards the door that would lead her outside. Amused, Erin watched Moira bustling around the room, sticking candles in holders and lighting them. She moved quickly and confidently, despite her age and the growing darkness. Moira may be elderly, but she was as spry as a young girl. Maybe it came from living a highly active lifestyle, or maybe it came from her being from a good old Irish stock. When Moira ran out of candle sticks, she started towards the kitchen. She saw that Erin was still standing there watching her and waved her hands telling her to get a move on it.

The back yard was less maintained than the front yard. In the fading light, Erin noticed a cobblestone walkway that led to a well and to a small building that she guessed to be a storage shed or maybe an office; it was too small to be anything else. It wasn't hard for her to find the wood pile, which was next to the barn, and after filling the carrier, made her way back inside.

When Erin re-entered the living room, she was amazed at how beautiful it looked in the soft glow of the candles. It took Moira only a few moments to get the fire started, and in no time the fireplace added its light and warmth to the room. Erin held her hands out, relishing the heat from the flames. She went to take the dust sheet off the couch, but Moira shook her head and held out the carrier once more. Erin sighed and went to get another load of wood. Moira had her make three more trips before she deemed the wood pile sufficient. While she had Erin running back and forth, Moira had set up the couch to serve as a bed.

"I do hope you'll be warm enough," Moira said as she threw another log onto the fire and stirred up the coals. "It's still quite cold at night around here."

"I'm sure I'll be fine," Erin said as she walked over to Moira. She gave the elderly woman a strong hug. "Thank you. I really mean it, Moira."

Moira gave Erin a small smile and returned the hug. "You're very welcome, my little bird." She patted Erin's hand. "Now, I'll be back in the morning to check on you. The electrician will be by as well. He just needs to check the wiring in a few places before they will turn on the power."

"What's wrong with the wiring?"

"Nothing now," Moira said nonchalantly as she gathered her things. "I had it fixed a few months ago but never turned in the paperwork proving that I did. Now I can't find it, so they have to come back out just to check." Erin followed her to the front door to bid her goodbye one last time. Moira made it as far as the bottom step before she turned around. "Are you sure?"

Erin laughed as she said, "Yes, now go home and get some rest. You've earned it." Moira sighed and went back to her car, shaking her head the whole way. Erin waved goodbye, then closed the door.

Erin leaned against the door and breathed deeply. She tried to push all thoughts from her mind and just allow the house to welcome her like it seemed to do before. But nothing came. She felt neither sorrow nor fear. She was surprised to find that she was calm and at peace. She locked the front door with a small smile and returned to the living room.

The living room looked extremely welcoming, bathed in the light of the candles and the fireplace. Erin took off her shoes and enjoyed the feeling of the thick, plush carpet that nearly covered the entire floor. Earlier, she had noticed that on both sides of the fireplace were two built-in bookcases. They ran from the floor to the ceiling and were completely filled with not only books but knick-knacks too.

Walking over to one of the bookcases, Erin looked at the titles. A few were so old that she couldn't even make out the writing on the spine, but one caught her eye: *Last of the Mohicans*. She pulled it out and smiled. That book was always her favorite in school. She even had a copy back home. The moment the word 'home' crossed her mind, her face fell. She missed her home in spite of everything. She missed her family, even though they were part of the reason why she had to move half way across the world. She missed her books and her favorite reading chair. She even missed the few friends she'd made while hiding from her ex. She'd lost so much to regain her freedom, but if she was able to rebuild her life here, it would be worth it.

When Erin was turning towards the couch, something about the mantel caught her eye. She smiled when she saw that someone had carved Celtic Knot work into the mantel as well. What was really interesting was that it wasn't a simple design like the door frames. It was an elaborate carving that when she took a step back, she saw that it resembled two dogs, or maybe wolves, running towards each other. She tilted her head, eyebrows knitted. She could have sworn that she had seen the exact same image somewhere before.

Erin went to scratch her head, but stopped when her bracelet reflected the firelight. She took off the bracelet that her grandmother had given her and saw that it was the same design. She was surprised and not surprised to see that it was the same symbol. Most of Ireland was a mix of the new and the old.

"Must be a family symbol," Erin said out loud, running her hand over the carving. As she did, a strange feeling took washed over her. It felt like her entire family—

generations beyond count— were standing in the room with her, welcoming her home at last. She could almost see their faces and feel their embraces. Their presence filled her with strength and a sense of belonging that she had never known, even before her life was torn down around her. It brought tears to her eyes and peace to her shattered heart. She swore that she actually felt her heart mend a tiny bit.

The feeling faded as quickly as it had come, leaving Erin extremely tired. She was barely able to keep her eyes open as she blew out all the candles. She was so tired that she didn't even change out of her clothes. She just threw her body onto the couch and instantly fell asleep.

Two

The next day, Erin was up before the sun. Normally she wasn't that early of a riser, but there were two things that caused her to get up at that ungodly hour. First, with the fire out, the house had gotten cold; extremely cold. Second, she had a strange dream. In the dream, she was walking up an impossibly long staircase in total darkness, save for a light that was coming from behind a door at the very top of the staircase. She climbed the stairs all night, but she never reached the door. No matter how many steps she took, the door always remained the same distance from her.

Erin shook her head, trying to expel the last fragments of her dream, while blindly searched for the candle and matches she had seen on the coffee table the night before. After fumbling around in the dark, she struck the match and lit the candle. The single flame created deep shadows in the living room, giving it an eerie feeling. Pushing her unease aside, she walked over to the fireplace, silently cursing her own thoughtlessness. If she had remembered to bank the fire the night before there would be some embers that she could use to restart the fire, but all that she had was cold ash.

Erin pushed the metal screen out of the way. She was surprised to find that when she reached to remove the grate, there was a bit of warmth still coming from the ash. Carefully, she pulled the grate out and held her hand over the ashes. Yes, she thought, there were still some embers burning. Using the poker to move the ash around, she discovered three embers still red hot. She took a bit of kindling and laid it on the embers. She blew on it until it created a flame, then quickly added more twigs, blowing constantly. As the fire grew, she put the grate back and added more small sticks. With the caution of a bomb diffuser, she added some of the smaller logs to the fire. She held her breath as the flames licked the wood. Slowly but surely, the logs caught and the fire roared to life.

Erin sat back on her heels, pleased with her work. She dusted her hands as she stood up and looked around the living room. She noticed that everything had a thick layer of dust on it. If she was going to live in this house, it definitely needed a serious, top-to-bottom cleaning. She replaced the fire screen, then looked about the room and contemplated where she should start. The obvious choice would be the bedroom, but she had no idea what state the mattress was in. She may have to replace it, so the bedroom would have to wait, for now. The kitchen was another good choice, but without power she could only clear away the dust, and that wouldn't take too long. Her attention returned to the living room. The couch was comfortable enough to sleep on, at least for a while longer. Moreover, as of right then, it had the only source of heat or light.

"The living room it is then," she said, her voice echoing slightly in the quiet house.

The first order of business was to remove the dust covers from the rest of the furniture. Each sheet was pulled off with a flourish, revealing two plush sitting chairs, a small table with an antique radio, and a few more tables that were probably used once to hold lamps or potted plants. She even uncovered an old record player, much to her delight. She enjoyed uncovering everything, but she wished that had been a little gentler when removing the sheets because the air was filled with dust. She coughed and ran towards the windows to throw them open. She leaned out of the window, gulping the fresh air. The cold morning air slapped her face but she relished the feeling. She had been numb to the world for far too long. Dust still danced in the air, so she decided to explore the rest of her new home.

Erin suddenly wondered if her great grandparents used machines or if they did their laundry by hand. Some of her friends in college had told her horror stories of grandparent and great-grandparents who refused to come into the modern age. *To each his own,* she thought, but shuttered at the thought of washing her clothes, linens, and everything else by hand. She then remembered that there looked to be another room on the other side of the kitchen, and desperately hoped it was a washroom.

Erin figured that there was no time like the present so she went to investigate. She grabbed a candle and matches because, if her memory served, the vines had grown over the windows on that side of the house. Sure enough, when she opened the door on the other side of the kitchen it was pitch black. She lit her candle and carefully walked in, only to run smack dab into a spider web. She screamed, but managed to hold on to the candle, spilling only a little wax on her hand.

"Just a spider web," Erin told herself. When she looked up to see the offending web, she noticed something strange on the beams above her. "What is this?"

Erin squinted trying to see the objects better but it wasn't until she held her candle a little higher that she noticed what they were. "Hooks," she said tilting her head in confusion. "Why would there be hooks in the ceiling?" The answer became clear a little later as she continued her search for the possible location of the washer and dryer.

Erin screamed again when something brushed against the top of her head. She swatted at it, knocking it off its hook. When she bent down to pick up the object, she saw that it was only a bundle of herbs. She looked at the bundle amused. She held it to her nose, curious to see if it still held a scent. It didn't. To her, it only smelled like long dead plants. She shrugged and tossed the bundle aside. A few more steps brought a large cabinet to her attention. When she opened the doors, she saw several mason jars filled with herbs.

"Basil," Erin read aloud squinting to see the faded handwriting, "rosemary, thyme, lavender, and belladonna." The last jar caused her to pause. From what she understood, belladonna was a poisonous herb. She wondered why her great-grandmother had it in her pantry. Shaking her head, she turned around and noticed another door just to the right of where she was standing. She offered a silent prayer, to whoever would listen, that behind the door was the wash room.

Erin smiled as the light from her candle revealed a washer and dryer. Granted, they were very old and probably didn't work but at least the house was set up to have them. She left the drying room, to only pause when she reached the kitchen.

"Might as well get one going in here as well," Erin said looking at the fireplace.

The flue was almost impossible to open but it eventually gave way, leaving Erin's hands covered in soot. She went to the sink and turned the tap but nothing came out. She wondered if the water was even on. Then there came a groaning and clanking as water flowed through the pipes for, what could have been, the first time in decades. It was brown and foul smelling at first, and then became clear and odorless. She let it run for a few more minutes before she stuck her hands under the running water. She made a mental note to do the same for all the other faucets later on.

Erin was able to find a few rags and used one to dry her hands. She dampened the rest so that she could get at least some of the dust that had accumulated on the bookcases. Just as she was about to leave the kitchen, she spied an old broom that was propped up against the wall near the door. She grabbed that too. She placed her simple cleaning instruments near the couch and then turned her attention to the record player.

"I think some music is in order," Erin said to herself. The record player sat on a small table, near the door that opened to the backyard. She was pleased to see that underneath was a compartment that held an assortment of records. She smiled as she pulled out a jazz record. She loved jazz. There was something about it that just soothed her soul. Carefully she removed the record and placed it on the player. She turned the handle on the side then gently placed the needle on the record. At first, she thought the player was broken because there was no sound. She kept staring at the player until she noticed a small knob in the bottom left corner.

"Ah ha," she cried triumphantly when she turned it and an upbeat jazz song came through.

The music banished the silence of the house and filled it with energy. Erin remained standing, her eyes closed, letting the music wash over her. "Oh I forgot about the fire," she said to herself. "I'd best take care of that and then start cleaning." She remembered how her mother always got on her about talking to herself.

"I never know if we have company or not," Erin's mother would always say. The thought of her mother brought a frown to her face. She knew that her mother was probably worried sick because of her little vanishing act. She hated doing this to her, but honestly, she was left with no other option. It was either take this opportunity or spend the rest of her life as a hollow shell, constantly on guard for the next assault. She sighed. She hated hurting her mother, but she had to take her life back.

"I'm sorry Mom," Erin whispered.

It only took Erin a few moments to get a decent fire going in the kitchen. She left the doors to the living room and kitchen open. She hoped that the heat from the two fires would, at least, make the down stairs warm. But she realized that she would need more wood to keep both hearths going throughout the day. The day was in full swing, so seeing her way out to the barn wouldn't be a problem. She snatched up the carrier and then headed out to the wood pile.

The early spring dawn was truly beautiful. The sky filled with reds and golden yellows. Erin took a few moments to appreciate the dawn before she continued her trip. As she put logs into the carrier, she started to get the feeling that she was being watched. However, when she looked around she didn't see anyone, nor was there a car in her driveway. The feeling didn't go away; it only grew stronger. She quickly gathered as much wood as she could carry and practically ran back inside.

Back inside, Erin felt better and even laughed at her own foolishness as she grabbed a rag. She decided to tackle the bookcases first. But she didn't get much cleaning done. The books on the shelves kept distracting her. More often than not she was pulling a book off the shelf, flipping through the pages or reading the back cover, than actually dusting.

"It's nice to hear music playing for once," commented a deep, male voice from behind her. Acting on pure instinct, Erin turned around and threw the book she was currently holding. She observed what appeared to be a tall man duck and retreat back into the hallway. "What you do that for?" he shouted.

Erin grabbed the nearest thing, the fire poker, and held it like a bat. "What are you doing in my house?" she demanded glad that her voice sounded calm and assured.

The complete opposite of what she felt.

"My job," he replied dryly from the safety of the hallway. "Look lady, I'm not looking for any trouble."

"Then you should have thought about that before you broke into my home!"

"He didn't," replied a familiar voice from the hallway.

"Moira?" Erin asked cautiously. Sure enough, it was. She came around the corner with an apologetic smile on her face.

"I gave my spare to Caleb," Moira said pointing to the man behind her. Erin then noticed the bags at the man's feet and that Moira was holding a mop and a broom, plus several buckets holding cleaning supplies.

Erin glared at Caleb, still brandishing the poker. "I knocked on the door," he said, "but with the music playing, I didn't think you heard me."

Erin slowly lowered her impromptu weapon. Caleb smiled kindly, but she still wasn't sure of him. He looked nice enough. He had the permanent tan of someone who worked outside all the time. His brown hair was shaggy. But it framed his large, brown eyes perfectly. Any other girl would have fallen for those eyes and the slight smirk on his lips, but other girls hadn't been through what Erin had. She knew first hand that dark souls tended to wear pretty masks.

"What are you doing here," Erin demanded again.

"Caleb is the electrician I told you about yesterday," Moira replied. Erin replaced the poker back on its rack, but didn't move from her spot. "How 'bout some hot tea and some breakfast?" Moira asked. Caleb knelt down, picked up the bags, and then took them to the kitchen. Without a word, he walked back out of the house. Through the living room window, Erin watched him reach into the back of his truck to get the tools of his trade.

"I'm really sorry about that," Moira said when Erin followed her into the kitchen. "I wasn't thinking... and with everything that you've been through."

"It's okay Moira," Erin reassured her. "I was just taken by surprise, that's all." That wasn't completely true but Erin didn't have the heart to scold the old woman especially when she looked so contrite.

"I should have come in first," Moira insisted. Erin just shook her head as she picked up the bags. On top of one of the bags were two Tupperware containers that held warm porridge. Moira pulled two thermoses from her massive purse and set them on the counter. "We can clear off the table and enjoy our breakfast."

The porridge was rich with honey, almonds, and a bit of fruit. On the first bite Erin closed her eyes, savoring its flavor. Moira smiled over her own bowl. The two women ate in silence.

"So, do you know Caleb well," Erin asked as she sipped her tea.

"Oh yes," Moira said enthusiastically. "He used to work in his uncle's repair shop as a boy and then he started working for the electric company after he graduated from high school. He also helps out his brother from time to time when he needs it."

"What does his brother do," Erin asked.

"Construction," Moira said, and then laughed a bit. When Erin gave her a confused look, she elaborated. "You see, the McKinley's, Caleb's family, are the ones who keep this town running. They fix our cars, our homes, and they maintain the water and the power. They're also some of the best farm hands you will ever hire." Erin sat back in her chair amazed at the versatility of the McKinley clan. "They're also the most reliable folk you'll ever meet", Moira went on. "If you ever find yourself in need, 'call on a McKinley' as the saying goes around here."

"So they say," Caleb stated from the doorway. Erin turned around startled. Once again, she hadn't heard him walk up. "Everything looks good." Caleb smiled and Erin forced herself to return it. Her upbringing would only let her be rude up to a point.

"Your power should turn on in a few hours, but if it doesn't call this number," Caleb held out a yellow piece of paper to Erin. "The number at the top will connect you to the service desk." Erin expected Caleb to leave once she took the paper, but he remained in the doorway staring at her. It was starting to make her feel uncomfortable. She was just about to tell him off, when he finally spoke. "Sorry about scaring you earlier," he said.

"Don't worry about it," Erin found herself telling him. Caleb smiled and Erin found herself smiling back. He nodded his head, and then left with a wave to Moira.

"Shall we get started," Moira asked suddenly, making Erin jump. When she turned around Moira had a knowing smile on her face. Erin rolled her eyes as she cleaned off the table.

The kitchen was spotless an hour and a half later. The floor had been swept and mopped. The counters and cabinets had been wiped down and the dishes had been put back into the cabinets. The only thing that was left to clean was the refrigerator and Erin was nearly done with that.

"I do hope the power comes on soon," Moira said looking at her watch. "I was hoping to make a grocery trip today." No sooner were the words out of her mouth, when the light in the fridge came on. Erin and Moira let out a cheer. "Wonderful," Moira said clapping her hands together. "Now if you just get cleaned up a bit, I'll take you into town."

Erin grabbed her bag from the living room and headed upstairs. She didn't take a shower, only washed her face, after letting the water run for a bit, and changed her clothes. She stared in the mirror while she brushed her teeth. She was still getting over her jet lag, but her old sparkle was coming back. Maybe her grandmother was right; maybe this place was just what Erin needed.

"All set," Moira asked as Erin walked down the stairs.

"Just about," Erin replied as she dug around in her duffle bag. "I also need to stop by the bank, if that's alright with you?"

"No problem at all," Moira said with a wave of her hand. "Bridget, the lady who runs the nursery, asked if I could cover her for about an hour, so there's no need to rush your errands."

The ride into town was filled with talks about plants and the coming of spring. Erin smiled and nodded when appropriate, but as usual, Moira rattled on hardly taking a pause. They parked in front of the nursery and Moira gave Erin her car keys so that she could place her purchases inside and take her groceries home if needed.

Erin's first stop was the bank. It was small, like she had expected, but what surprised her was that it didn't have an ATM machine. She wondered why as she waited for a manager and when she was finally seen, she got her answer. Apparently, Dorshire was one of the few places left in the world that ran on cash or checks only.

Erin walked out of the bank with enough cash to take care of herself until her checks came in. She looked up and down the main street, taking it all in. Moira said she would be busy for an hour, so Erin planned to get as many things done in town as she could. Until she got a car, she would have to depend on either taxies, if there were any, or Moira. A small appliance store caught her eye. Now, Erin had no problem with tea, but she was American and coffee was a highly required substance for daily life. With any luck, the store would have at least one coffee maker, or so she hoped.

The clerk smiled when Erin walked in. "Is there anything that I can help you with," he asked.

"I'm looking for a coffee maker," Erin asked fingers crossed.

"They're at the back," the clerk said pointing. "Don't get much call for them. You must be American."

"Guilty," Erin said with a smile that the clerk returned.

The store was pretty well stocked for one so small. Erin passed refrigerators, dishwashers, laundry units, and just about everything that a home could need. When she came upon the coffee makers she smiled. They all had a layer of dust on them that was at least an inch thick. She grabbed one and was about to head to the register, when she neared the laundry units. She wondered if she should wait until after she checked out the ones at the house before buying new ones. But the ones back at the house had been sitting for so long that she was pretty sure they wouldn't run.

"Those are our basic models," the clerk said as he walked up. "All of our units come with a one year warranty."

"I have an older set back at the house."

"When we deliver the new ones, we also take away the old. Most of the time there are still a few good parts." The clerk smiled, but he didn't make Erin feel pressured into buying anything. She decided that she might as well go on and get a new set. If there wasn't anything wrong with the old ones, at least they would get some good parts from it. Fifteen minutes later, Erin placed her newly purchased coffee maker in the back of Moira's car. After checking her watch, she saw that she had just enough time to hit the grocery store before Moira was free.

Erin was pleasantly surprised when she entered the grocery store. While it had products that one would expect to find, it also had a whole section of homemade goods, a real bakery, and a butcher. She filled her cart with enough food to feed her for a month. She also was excited about trying some local food. She planned on asking Moira for a few of her recipes to try.

So engrossed with her own thoughts, Erin didn't notice a young man watching her from the shadows across the street. His mouth was pulled into a sneer and his cold, blue eyes were filled with contempt as he watched her place her groceries in the back of Moira's car. His eyes narrowed when Moira came out of the nursery. He watched the two women as they drove away. Just as the car was out of sight, the man let out a cruel chuckle, then drifted down the street.

March gave way to April before Erin had finally deemed the house clean. Every inch of the house had been dusted, polished, washed, and wiped within an inch of its life. She also tackled the ivy a bit, cutting away the vines from the windows, but other than that, she had left it alone. She liked the way it made the house look and she never tired of looking at it from the driveway. Overall, things were progressing nicely.

Erin had even repainted. The living room and hallway were a rich cream color, which complemented the sunny yellow in the kitchen. She only painted one of the bed rooms, the master bed room. When she saw that it too had a fireplace, she knew that she just had to sleep there. The walls were now a warm shade of green, like leaves in summer. The master bathroom was also nice and spacious; plus, it had a skylight over the tub. She spent many a night soaking and staring out at the stars.

While it was a lot of work to get the house livable, Erin relished every moment. By keeping her hands busy, she didn't have time to dwell on the pitiful aspects of her life. Slowly, with each passing day, she was becoming more like her old self. Her anxiety was all but gone, and she was starting to put some weight back on.

Erin also had explored the grounds and found an old truck in the barn. It even worked. She knew that, at some point, she would have to go through everything that her grandmother and great-grandparents had left behind but she couldn't bring herself to do it just yet; although, she had claimed some of the left over clothes as her own.

Erin had yet to explore the attic, but again, she could not bring herself to go up there. It may have had something to do with the dreams that had been plaguing her every night since her arrival, or because she always had a fear of attics. She blamed it on one too many horror movies. She was starting to wonder if the dreams had a hidden message. Never in her life, as far as she could remember, had she ever had the same dream over and over again.

Erin sipped her morning coffee, enjoying the sunrise. She had come to love the sunrises and sunsets. The country side seemed to explode with rich colors at these times. As she glanced out the window, she grimaced at the disaster that was otherwise known as the front yard. Even though Moira had done her best to keep the yard from going completely wild, it was still neglected. The grass was in a serious need of mowing. The oak tree in the front needed to be cut back. The bushes needed to be trimmed too. And as for the little garden that was next to the washroom, she would need Moira's help to fix that. She also knew that the back yard was just as bad, if not worse, than the front. She smiled having, found her task for the day.

After breakfast, Erin went to gather some firewood. Even though the heat worked, she loved to curl up on the couch at night and read a book with a fire going. Ever since that morning when she had felt watched, she always made sure that she gathered all of the firewood during the day that she would need for the night. She didn't want to be out after dark. Once that chore was complete, she went into the garage to see if there was a lawnmower.

The barn was old and dusty, just as old barns should be. It may have once held livestock but had been converted into a workshop later on. After a few minutes of digging around Erin found a mower, and after a few more minutes, she managed to get it out of the barn. She smiled when it roared to life on the first attempt. The grass was still too wet from the morning dew to actually mow, but at least she had a working mower and after further exploration, she also found a weed-whacker. In fact, the barn held what appeared to be everything she needed to get the yard under control again.

Erin had just placed everything back into barn when Moira pulled up. "Morning," Moira called out, "and what are you getting into so early?"

"I was planning on tackling the yard today," Erin

replied

"While I won't argue that it needs it," Moira said with a frown, "you're spending too much time alone. You've turned down three suppers, and you don't want to go to the Spring Festival with us."

Erin sighed. She knew she couldn't hide away in the house forever, but she just wasn't ready to deal with a large crowd of people. "Would you like some coffee or tea?" Erin asked, changing the conversation. Moira sighed but accepted a cup just the same.

As Erin heated up the water, Moira dug around in her bag. "I have some letters for you." Erin turned around surprised. "They're all from your grandmother," Moira said holding them out. "She figured it would be safer to send them to me first."

Erin took the letters with trembling hands. She wondered what the letters contained. Had her family discovered where she was hiding, or worse John? If that were the case, Erin figured her grandmother would have called instead of sending letters.

"Well I just stopped by to see how you were getting along and to drop off the letters," Moira said after she finished her tea. "If you want to reply, just give them to me and I'll send them along. See you on Sunday?" Moira had made it a point to invite Erin over for Sunday dinner every week.

"Actually why don't you guys come over here," Erin suggested. She was pleased to see Moira's surprised expression and was rewarded with a large grin.

"What a lovely idea," Moira said clasping her hands together. "If memory serves, I remember that they kept a large picnic table in the barn." Erin nodded, letting her know it was still there. "Great! I'll send the boys over early to bring it out." Moira reached to get her things, when she turned back around. "What would you like us to bring?"

Erin thought about it before she replied. "I'll take care of the main meal and dessert, if you'll bring the sides." Moira agreed and gave Erin a bone crushing embrace before leaving. Erin smiled and waved as Moira pulled out of the driveway. She still had a few hours to go before the grass was dry enough, so she used that time to plan Sunday's dinner. After combing through her great grandmother's recipes, Erin decided to go with a roast chicken —simple and hearty— for the main meal and a coffeecake for dessert.

Erin waited patiently for the sun to dry the grass, because she had a lot to do if she wanted it to look presentable by Sunday. She walked upstairs and to her room. She dug through her great-grandfather's clothes and dug out an old work shirt. She put it over her tank top and exchanged her pajama bottoms for a pair of gym shorts. She pulled her hair back into a messy bun. She was ready to work. On the way out she grabbed her mp3 player. Music always made hard labor easier.

Erin went slowly, because the mower was old and she had a lot of yard to cover. She would have to do it in two parts, due to the sharp hill that went down to the road. By noon, the yard in front of the house was mowed, and all that was left was the hill that went down to the road. But halfway through mowing the hill, the mower suddenly stopped. She tried to restart it, but the engine wouldn't turn. She checked the fuel and saw that there was still a good amount, so she turned it over to see if maybe it had clogged, but she couldn't figure out why it wouldn't start.

"Maybe I can help." said a male voice in the silence between songs. Erin jumped up and came face to face with a man about her age. Although he was dressed causal, his clothes were expensive. He had a slight tan and golden, well-kept hair. His eyes were an icy blue that caused Erin to shiver. She couldn't place it, but there was something about the man that made her nervous. "My name is Connor Ferguson. I live four miles east at Castle Broad."

"You live in a *castle*?" Erin asked, unsure if she had heard him right the first time.

Connor shrugged. Apparently he was used to such reactions. "It's been in my family for generations. Do you live here?" Erin remained silent and Connor went on, turning towards the house, as if he didn't notice her silence. "Or perhaps they're finally selling this place. It's been abandoned for so long. I always wondered why they hadn't torn it down yet."

"It belongs to my grandmother," Erin said hotly. Sure, the house had been semi-neglected, but it was still a beautiful home. Especially now that she had put some much needed work into it.

"Your grandmother?" Connor said turning his attention back to Erin.

"Yes," she said carefully. "I was thinking about moving to Ireland and she offered her home," Erin lied smoothly. "I figured the least I could do was straighten the place up for her."

"And you are doing a wonderful job," Connor said turning his cold eyes on Erin causing her to shiver again. "Well, let's have a look at this shall we?" As he bent down to look at the mower, Erin highly doubted that Connor even knew what he was looking at. She was surprised when he turned it over and got it to start. "There you go," he said with a smile. "That should hold you over for a while."

"Thank you," Erin managed to say, amazed.

"You know I never caught your name..."

"Erin McManin." Connor took her dirty, sweaty hand and placed a kiss on top. Erin blushed and snatched her hand back. She fought the urge to wipe his kiss off.

"It's been a pleasure," Connor said. He walked over to his car, which Erin hadn't noticed until that moment. "If you're in to old homes, Miss McManin, you should stop by my home. Family lore says that it's been around since Roman times."

"Perhaps," Erin replied. Connor smiled at her one last time before he drove off. It was only when she couldn't see him that she was able to breathe again.

Thanks to Connor, Erin was able to finish mowing the yard. She raked up the clippings and moved them to an area near the road so she could burn them later. She had just started trimming the bushes when the wind began to pick up. When she looked to the sky, she saw storm clouds rolling in. She quickly wrapped up the bush she was on and then rushed to put everything away.

Erin had showered and made a late lunch by the time the storm hit. "April showers bring May flowers," she said to the rain pelted glass. She sighed; disappointed that she had to stop working on the yard. But there was no helping it. She sighed again and grabbed the letters from her grandmother. "I might as well read these now."

The storm continued into the night and Erin was grateful again for the fireplace. It's hard to feel scared during a storm when there's a roaring fire. She had the record player going, only this time it was playing classical music. She had curled up on the couch with a quilt and an engrossing mystery novel. She had made herself some coco and couldn't have been more content.

By nine-thirty, Erin was ready for bed, but when she went into the kitchen, something caught her attention. At first, she thought it was the wind, but as she listened, it sounded more like crying. She followed the sound to the drying room. She turned on the light, but saw nothing. Then she heard scratching coming from the door. She grabbed a flashlight and cautiously opened the door. She screamed when something ran over her feet. When she whipped the light around, she saw that a cat had run inside.

The cat could have been white, but it was difficult to determine under the mud that covered its fur. Its ears looked like they were red and it had bright green eyes. The cat just stared at Erin, meowing, looking completely pitiful.

"Where did you come from?" Erin asked the cat who only meowed again. She smiled at the little cat. She never had any pets growing up. Her father wouldn't allow it, but she had always loved animals. "I guess you can stay the night." The cat allowed her to pick it up and she noticed how scrawny it was. It was most likely a stray. "Would you mind if I washed you up a bit?" She knew that cats supposedly hated water, but the cat allowed her to rinse off all the mud. Erin toweled the cat off. She smiled as it started to purr. "I bet you're hungry too," Erin said, pulling out a can of tuna.

Three cans later, the cat was purring loudly and rubbing itself against Erin's leg. Yawning, she went upstairs, followed closely by the cat. As she brushed her teeth, the cat made itself comfortable on one of the pillows, earning another smile from Erin. "Okay little one," she told the cat as she climbed into bed, "you can stay for just one night."

The cat only purred louder. Erin drifted off to sleep with a smile.

The next morning, Erin was startled by a pair of green eyes staring at her. She sat up quickly, causing the cat to jump away. "You scared me," she scolded but the cat didn't seem to care; it only sat on the floor looking at her. "I bet you want to be fed again?" The cat meowed, causing Erin to smile. "As you wish your majesty," Erin said mockingly as she threw off the covers.

Once they reached the kitchen, the cat was yowling loudly for tuna, which only made Erin smile more. As she watched the cat eat, she once again noticed how thin it was. She could make out the rib cage, and its spine was visible as well confirming her suspicions that it was a stray. She guessed that the cat couldn't be more than a year old, but it was difficult to be certain. She thought about keeping the cat. If she did, she wouldn't be in the house by herself. Her mind was made up. When she went into town today, she would get things for the cat as well.

The dinner with Moira and her family went well. The children were excited about being able to tell all their friends that they had been in the McManin house, which apparently was rumored to be haunted, and they fawned over the cat. In fact, it was the children who decided on its name— Fae.

Things at the house were going well, except for the lawnmower, which had stopped working again. Despite that, she was still making progress with the yard. She had the trees and the bushes trimmed back. She had cleared out all of the dead plants and weeds from the garden. The little garden fence, sadly, had to be torn down but there wasn't much left of it anyway. The inside of the house still needed some work though. She still hadn't put away the things that were left by her grandmother and great-grandparents. She was saving that for a rainy day.

Ever since Erin arrived in Ireland, she had been rising early. This morning, however, she had actually slept in a bit. She stretched out, then curled into a ball, not wanting to leave the comfort of her bed. She contemplated staying in bed all day but quickly dismissed the idea.

Erin flung the blankets back and got up. There was still too much to do around the house for her to laze about. Although, she did promise herself a day of relaxation once everything was done. Downstairs, she fed Fae, who happily munched on his breakfast making noises that caused her to smile. Just as she sat down to eat her own breakfast, she heard the sound of a car coming up the driveway. When she glance out the window, she smiled as Moira's yellow hatch back pulled to a stop. She figured she had another letter from her grandmother.

"Good morning," Moira called out as she came in.

"Morning," Erin replied with a smile. While Moira didn't touch the coffee, she did help her self to a small bowl of oatmeal. "How are you doing?"

"Well enough," Moira said before stuffing a spoonful of oatmeal into her mouth. "What are your plans for today?"

"I thought I'd work on getting the barn cleared out and then I might work on the study," Erin said.

"You really are working yourself too hard," Moira said concerned. "This house has been here since long before you were born. Yeah, it's a little worn down but it still stands strong. You should really be spending more time out there socializing, not hiding away."

Erin held back a groan. She was so familiar with Moira's argument that she could recite it word for word. While Erin knew she was just trying to be helpful, she wished that Moira would just drop it and let her re-enter the world when *she* was ready. "I'm fine. Really I am. It's just that I'm not quite ready to mingle. I need time to figure some things out for myself."

"I know," Moria sighed. She was familiar with Erin's counter argument. "I'm just worried about you, that's all. I promised your grandmother that I would look after you."

"And you're doing a wonderful job," Erin said placing a hand on the old woman's arm. "I just need more time." These words didn't seem to comfort Moira at all. "And I promise, once I have everything worked out, I will get out and live my life." Moira placed her weathered hand on top of Eein's and gave it a small squeeze.

"Well, I'm sure you have plenty that you need to do, so I'll just be on my way. See you on Sunday?"

"Sure thing Moira. And thank you."

Moira gave her one last fleeting glance before leaving. Erin sighed the moment that the door closed. She tore open the letters that Moira had brought, desperate for information from home.

Her grandmother's letters came weekly, keeping Erin up to date with all the drama back home. Her mother was making herself sick with worry. Her dad had thrown himself into his work and John was still hanging around. Erin frowned. She had hoped that her disapearence would finally open her parents' eyes to the fact that she, under no circumstances, was going to go back to John. She really wanted her parents to be on her side. While her parents stubbornly held to their ideals, it looked like her disappearance had caused more of a scandal than she realized. Laura, her sister, pissed at their parents, had finally started to rebel.

Laura always had a love for fashion, especially revamping retro looks. However, their parents said that it was an impractical career and pushed her towards law school. Growing up, Lauren had always idolized Erin, but she often bended to their parents' expectations. But Laura wasn't playing by their rules anymore. Laura, according to the letter, had abandoned a possible career in law and was pursuing one in fashion. Erin smiled at that. She was glad that her little sister was going for her dreams.

Another surprising bit in the letter had to deal with Erin's old school friend, Amara. Apparently, she had heard about Erin's disapearence and flew from Australia. Once there, she had stirred things up even more primarily by calling Erin's parents out on their failure as parents and punching John when he tried to talk to her.

"Well Fae," Erin said when she was done reading, "it looks like things are getting interesting back home." Fae responded by meowing and running to the door.

After letting Fae out, to do whatever it was that he did all day, Erin headed up the stairs to change into her work clothes. She had just finished changing, and was about to walk outside, when there came a loud thunder clap. She let out a squeal in surprise, turning quickly towards the sound. She gasped again when she caught her reflection in the mirror. She looked exactly like someone who had just given up on life completely, with her disheveled hair and baggy clothes.

"No wonder Moira's been so worried," Erin commented as she tried to smooth out her hair. The thunder crashed again, this time bringing in the rain. Apparently, the universe thought she needed some personal time too. She figured it was time to go through the abandoned clothes, if only to find better fitting ones, until she got some of her own.

Including Erin's, there were three bedrooms and two bathrooms that made up the upper floor. One room clearly had belonged to her grandmother, and it looked like her parents hadn't touched it since she had ran off. Erin ran her hand over the cross-stitched plaque with the name 'Elise'. The fabric was faded and dingy, but it was still beautiful. Suddenly, Erin had a vision of her great-grandmother sitting in a rocking chair, pregnant and sewing. Her great-granmother smiled and ran her hand over her belly, as if she had felt the child inside move. Erin's vision blurred, and when it cleared again, she let out a small gasp, because this time it was *her* mother who she saw.

Her mother was in Erin's room, present day, holding a small stuffed animal, crying softly. Erin pulled her hand back from the plaque as if it had burned her. She was having a hard enough time dealing with the thought of her mother suffering, but seeing it made it ten times worse. She quickly walked away from the door. Her grandmother's room would have to wait.

Erin turned to the room nextdoor instead. It was the smallest of all the bedrooms. It looked like her great-grandparents had used it for storage. She could barely get the door to open, because the room was packed with boxes and furniture.

"I guess I should just work my way in," Erin mused as she stared at the massive pile of stuff. The first few boxes held more books; clearly, her great-grandparents were avid readers. Unfortunately, the down stairs book case was full, so Erin couldn't put the other books out. "I guess it's up to the attic with you," she said to the books. "Just for a little while... I promise."

Erin was surprised at how empty the attic was but she guessed that her great-grandparents couldn't get up the narrow ladder in their golden years. The few pieces that were already up there looked as if they had been there for a long time. Shurging, she searched for a light switch or light bulb. As she was searching,she heard what sounded awfully like whispering. She froze.

"Hello," Erin called out, but heard nothing. She strained her ears, but didn't hear anything else. She just shrugged and pulled the string that she had found for the light. The bulb flickered a bit, but it lit the room up well enough. When she turned around to descend from the attic, the whispering started again. This time she remained silent. It sounded as if several people having a conversation, but she couldn't make out the words. Slowly, she walked towards the back of the attic. As she neared the middle, and shifted to avoid a large chest, the whispering stopped. She remained still, waiting for it to start up again. Fae chose that moment to meow loudly, causing Erin to scream.

"Dammit Fae," Erin shouted as she placed her hand over her heart. "You nearly scared me half to death!" Fae just stared at her, blinking. She could have sworn that he was smiling. "Do that again and no more tuna for you, mister." Fae just continued to stare at her, and then strutted out with another meow.

Erin looked around the attic once more, but the whispering never came back. She shrugged, then proceeded to move the boxes from the spare bedroom into the attic. Attics always creeped her out. She figured her mind was playing tricks on her. There was a storm brewing, afterall.

After a few hours, the room had been cleared out and cleaned. Erin smiled at her handy work. While moving boxes, she had discovered a small bed and a dresser. She decided to leave them there. She even put up a few pictures on the wall. She had also left a few knick-knacks out to make the room look less sparse. Even though the room was small, it was still rather cozy.

Erin's growling stomach told her she had missed lunch. The rain was still coming down, although not as heavy as before. She closed the door to the small bedroom and came face to face with her grandmother's old room. She was still unnerved by the vision she'd had earlier. She quickly walked past the room, heading downstairs for a late lunch.

Erin stared out the window as she ate, trying to come up with a good reason not to touch the door again. She wasn't sure why she was so reluctant—supposed vision or not. Fae meowed at the back door, wanting to be let out. She shook her head at him. He was the most unusual cat she had ever met. She reluctantly let him out and watched as he streaked right past the small building that was right behind the house. She hadn't ventured out there once. She smiled. A mystery building was better than going through her grandmother's past.

Erin threw on a rain coat, grabbed the keys, and then braved the rain. She nearly slipped on the stone walk way a few times, but managed to make it to the building in one piece. The wind picked up, making the rain pummel her mercilessly. She struggled to find a key to fit the lock. The lock was old and none of the skeleton keys she had seemed to work. She groaned and was forced to return to the house. Now she *had* to go into her grandmother's old room. When she turned to head back, she was surprised to see Fae waiting for her by the door.

"Too wet for you, huh?" she asked him with a smirk. He meowed in reply. "Yeah, me too. Let's get inside where it's nice and dry."

It took Erin nearly five minutes to actually open the door to her grandmother's room . She scolded herself for being so silly. She took a deep breath and opened the door as quickly as she could. At least there wasn't anything she had to do to the room, she noted as she stood in the doorway. The only thing it really needed was fresh sheets and a good dusting. But she didn't do either of those things. She just sat on the bed and looked around. The walls were covered with magazine clippings and pictures of her grandmother's life before she had left for America.

One picture caught Erin's eye. It was a picture of Elise with her mother, Erin's great-grandmother, standing in front of a building. Erin recognized it as the small building in her backyard that she had just tried to get into. They seemed to be wearing long robes, and her grandmother was holding a large book. Erin tried to get a better look at the book, but the only thing she could make out was a black circle in the middle of the cover. She wondered what the book was, because she hadn't seen anything like it in the house so far. Fae rubbed himself against her legs, demanding to be picked up.

"I wonder when this picture was taken," Erin said to Fae. "It looks like it was taken during Halloween, but Grandma looks so young, and their faces are so serious." Fae just purred loudly, then leapt out of Erin's arms and ran over to the closet.

"So you think I need new clothes too?" Erin smirked. She turned her attention to finding some clothes that actually fit her. She wasn't surprised when she saw her grandmother's old, fashionable clothes. Elise, apparently, always had an eye for fashion.

Erin pulled out several pairs of slacks, but she didn't see any jeans. She hoped that there were some in the dresser, or else she would have to go out and get some jeans. She smiled as she pulled out sweaters, blouses, and a few dresses. Despite being made decades ago, they still looked nice, without looking old fashioned. She wondered if any would fit her.

Somehow, Fae had managed to get onto the shelf that was in the closet and was sniffing around. Erin wasn't really paying him any attention so she failed to notice the way he was looking at her from his perch, to the green box next to him. When her head was directly under where the box was, Fae bumped it, causing it to fall on her head. Erin yelped, rubbing her head. She went to shout at Fae, but he had already disappeared, so she picked up the green box instead.

The box didn't look like anything special. Other than its bright green color, it didn't have any embellishments, except for a rusty latch. Still rubbing her head, Erin placed the box on the dresser. She was going to go back to the closet, but then she heard something—whispering. She spun around, looking at the room then ran into the hallway, but just like before, there was no one there. She slowly walked back to the bedroom and the whispering started again. She slowly walked back into the room. She was sure that the whispering was coming from inside. She looked around the room, trying to find the source of it, when her eyes fell on the green box. The whispering stopped as soon as she did. She continued to stare at the box, but the whispering didn't start up again.

Cautiously, Erin reached out to the box and held her breath as her fingers gently touched it. Nothing happened. She pulled her hand back and then touched the box again.

Again nothing. She repeated the action a few more times but the result was always the same. She stared at the box, then picked it up carefully. She turned it this way and that, trying to see if there was anything that would explain the sounds she had heard. Finding nothing, she was forced to finally open it. She was surprised to see that the only thing that the box held was an old key.

"That's strange," she said to herself as she picked it up. The key didn't look special in anyway; in fact, it looked no different than the other keys that were on her key ring. "That's it," she exclaimed, suddenly making a connection. "This must go to to that building!"

Erin skipped down the stairs excitedly, grabbing her flashlight along the way. The storm had started to ease up again, but she was so excited that she barely noticed. Sure enough, the key unlocked the door. She let out a huge smile.

The first thing Erin did was feel along the wall for a light switch, but she found none. She had to use the flashlight instead. As she shone the light around the room, she was slightly disapointed. The building was indeed a study, but for some reason, she had expected it to be more. One the far wall across from her was a bookcase, and a large desk with a comfy looking chair sat just in front of it. The only other furnishings were a few small tables that held oil lamps, another chair, and some decorative pieces.

Luckily, someone left matches, so Erin was able to

light the oil lamps. She felt a little cheated now that she was standing inside the study. She really had expected it to be something more than what it was. Her eyes were drawn to the books—some looked quite old. She picked up one of the books and sat down at the desk. As it turned out, it was a journal. She soon realized that it was a really old journal with the last entry being sometime in the mid-1900s. She carefully placed it back on the shelf and reached for another. That one contained a self-written history of Dorshire. That excited her. Intrigued, she sat down and flipped through the pages. She was so engrossed in the history that she nearly knocked the lamp off the desk when Fae jumped up unto the shelf above her. She hadn't realized that he had followed her in.

"You've got to stop doing that," Erin scolded, her hand over her heart. "I could have burned this place down." Fae meowed, sat down, and then set about cleaning himself. She muttered under her breath about entitled cats and then returned to her reading.

Erin loved history. That's what she majored in, and apparently it was a family trait. Whoever wrote this history was very thorough. The way that he or she wrote seemed to draw her in so deeply that she actually felt like she was there. She almost smelled the baked goods from the 'best harvest festival' and heard the Roman legions as they marched against rebels. She was so dead to the living world that she didn't notice that Fae, once again, was about to knock something onto her. Only this time, instead of a small box, it was a wooden statue.

"That's it!" Erin yelled, snatching Fae from the shelf as she rubbed her head. "I don't know what's wrong with you, but I've had enough!" She stomped across the study and chucked him unceremoniously into the rain. "You can get wet for all I care!" Still rubbing her head, she walked back to the desk and noticed the wooden statue had broken. "Dammit," she cursed as she picked up the pieces. "The head came off." When she turned the statue around to see if it could be fixed, something fell out. "Another key?"

When Erin went to pick it up, the whispering started again. This time, she didn't ask who was there—this time she listened. With her eyes closed, she tried to understand the words but she only caught a couple: chest and book. After a few minutes, the whispering faded away, leaving her in silence and extremely confused.

"What chest?" Erin asked out loud. "What book?" She felt a little silly asking the air for answers, but what other options did she have? Today had been, without a doubt, the strangest day of her life.

Erin didn't feel quite so safe in her grandmother's house anymore. Something was going on here and she didn't like it. She braved the storm to get back to the house. Silence pressed against her and she felt the beginnings of a panic attack. Her heart raced. She broke into a cold sweat. Terrified, she fled up the stairs, but instead of going to her room, she went to her grandmother's. She threw herself onto the bed, clutching a pillow tight to her chest. She closed her eyes and slowly counted to ten. Her heart slowed and she released her death grip on the pillow. She focused on her breathing, making sure she took deep, even breaths. Exhausted from the attack and the day, she drifted off to sleep. It was dark when she awoke.

"I've slept the day away...great." Erin walked back downstairs and heard Fae meowing outside. When she opened the door, he ran in, completely wet and covered in mud. "Serves you right," she told him with her hands on her hips. The two stared at each other. "You shouldn't have tried to give me a concussion." He hissed at her and then started to clean himself, pretending not to care. "Well, if that's how you're gonna act then I guess you don't want your dinner?" He instantly stopped licking and started to rub himself around her legs, meowing gently. She couldn't stay mad at him when he looked up at her with those big green eyes. "Alright then, let's eat."

Later, Erin was curled up on the couch with a cup of hot chocolate and a book. This was the fifth book that she had read since arriving, and she realized how long it had been since she was able to enjoy one of her favorite past times. After her divorce, she had moved around so much that she didn't have time to read; she could only survive. Most of the time, she was barely in one place long enough to unpack what little belongings she had. Even more often, she had to flee without packing anything at all.

Erin's impromptu afternoon nap meant that she

was in for a long night, but she didn't mind. She promised herself that tomorrow her only job was to go clothes shopping, and you didn't need a lot of sleep for that.

When the clock struck twelve, Erin decided that she should at least try to get some sleep, but her mind went back to the strange happenings of the day. Why was the key to the study tucked away in her grandmother's old closet? What did the other key—the one from the statue—go to? What was up with the whispering? She felt like she was in the middle of a mystery novel and she didn't like it.

"Chest and book? What do you think it means?" Erin directed the question at Fae, but he was sound asleep. "You're a big help, you know." She sighed and stretched out on the couch. The two keys were sitting on the coffee table and her gaze was drawn to them.

There was nothing overly special about them. They just looked like skeleton keys, but Erin couldn't shake the feeling that there was more to them than met the eye. There had to be some kind of connection between the keys and the whispering. She tried to remember where else she ha heard the whispering, hoping to find a connenction. She then remembered her earlier freak-out in the attic. There were a number of chests up there and if what the whisperers said was true, the second key should open one of them.

It was a tanalizing thought. Erin was tired of being jerked around by disembodied voices so the sooner she solved this the better. She snatched the keys from the coffee table and vaulted over the couch to get to the stairs. When she reached the base, she stopped. She felt like she was being watched. She turned and saw Fae sitting on top of the couch, staring at her.

"Come on then," Erin beckoned, motioning to Fae. He leapt eagerly off the couch and sprinted past her. When he reached the top of the stairs, he sat waiting for her to catch up. She wasn't sure why she wanted him to come along, but he had been there, and was the cause for most of the strangeness of the day. If she was going to settle this matter once and for all, it would be with him. Perhaps he would show her the way.

"Now, which chest is it?" Erin asked herself as she fumbled with the light. There were several chests in the attic. None of them screamed *I'm the one*, so she started with the first one. It didn't open. She heard Fae meow, and when she looked up, she saw him sitting on a large chest towards the middle of the attic. The chest was separate from the rest of the stuff in the attic, almost like someone wanted you to see it.

"I think this could be it Fae; good job." Erin held her breath and inserted the key. It fit. "So far so good," she told him, and then turned the key. She was rewarded by the sound of the tumblers clicking into place.

Erin placed her hands on either side of the lid. Still holding her breath, she pushed it up. Nothing happened.

She felt rather foolish. After everything that had happened throughout the day, she sort of expection something to happen—a flash of light, whispering; anything really. Since nothing happened all, she could do was go through the contents of the chest, looking for answers.

Right on top was a shelf that was divided into sections. On the shelf were dozens of pieces of jewlery; some looking quite old. There were rings, bracelets, necklaces, earrings, and a few tourques. Those really surprised her. When Erin picked up one of the tourques, she noticed that it bore the same design as the bracelet that her grandmother had given her. She put it back and picked up a few more pieces. These ones bore eagles, plants, and arrows.

If Erin's assumption about the wolf design was correct, then the other symbols must also be family emblems. She sat back on her heels, amazed at how little she actually knew about her family history. Back in the states, most people din't seem to know or care about their ancestors, beyond their arrival to the U.S. Her grandmother had never told any stories about herself, her parents, or anyone from her side of the family. But then again, no one ever asked.

Erin removed the shelf and laid it carefully on the floor next to her. The rest of the chest contents were equally as strange as the shelf's. There were bundles of sticks, several crystals, and some colorful stones. There was also several large bundles of cloth that turned out to be robes. She thought that they looked similar to the ones that her grandmother and great-grandmother wore in the pictures. But so far no book.

Erin was just about to give up, but then she noticed another bundle. This one was different. Instead of being plain, it was colorful and bore the same wolf design that she was familiar with. When she picked it up, she knew that beneath the wrapping was a book. Her heart started to race as she sat down, slowly loosening the knots that held the fabric together.

The book looked no different from any other old book; leather-bound with silver clasps. The only strange thing that Erin noticed about it was that it had no title and there was a large stone in the middle of the cover. The stone wasn't anything special, just your every day gray stone, but it looked like it had been stained with something dark.

Erin flipped the clasp open and carefully opened the book. The spine creaked and crackled, as if it protested being opened. The first thing she saw was an envelope. She opened it and pulled out a letter. She placed the book down and read the letter.

I hope that this letter finds you well, whoever you are.

I must start out by saying that I am sorry. I am so sorry for placing this burden on you. But I have good reasons, I assure you. You see, for centuries our family has been locked in a never-ending war with another. The family that we have been fighting for centuries is similar to ousr, except they have chosen to walk the dark path. When my time came to lead the fight I am ashamed to admit that I fled.

You see, I never had a real childhood. My entire life was filled with preparing to fight this other family. I saw things that I would never wish anyone to see—especially a child. So I made my choice. I walked away. I met a gentle man and I fell in love with him. He was pure, unlike me, unaware of the darker side of life. I would sacrifice the world to protect him and our children.

I returned here only after the death of my mother. My last act in the war is this. I have placed wards around this home and this book. Only one within our family would be able to get to this book. I hope that you are. After all, who knows how long it will be before someone reads this letter and maybe time will wear away the wards. I do not know, and honestly, I do not care. But if you are one of my family, your fate is out of my hands.

Please accept my sincerest apologies for everything that has—and will—befall you. I wish you the best and offer one bit of advice: You are not alone. All of those who have gone *before you will be there, if you listen hard enough.*

Elise Jones

Erin stared at the signature for a long time. This letter had been written by her grandmother. She reread the letter several times, but it made no sense at all.

"What war is she talking about?" Erin asked out loud. As she sat there, on the floor surounded by strange objects, she began to really wonder about her family. These weren't things that a normal family would have experienced, and what was with all the secrecy?

Erin let out a huge yawn. She stretched her stiff body and decided that she should get some sleep. She told herself that she would tackle this mystery in the morning. It was just too absurd to deal with right now. As she got ready for bed, she was blistfully unaware of the wheels that had been set in motion, all because she had found the book.

Three

That night, Erin had a new dream. She found herself standing on a grassy hill, looking out over a valley. On the far side, there was another hill, with a person standing on it, like she was. However, she couldn't see who it was. The person was just a dark spot on a distant hill. The sky darkened and two armies appeared in the valley below. The one that was near her wore white, while the other side wore black. With a furious roar, the two sides charged each other. She could hear the clang of swords and the screams of the dying. She watched, terrified, and unsure of what to do. She tore her eyes away from the carnage below and turned them to the shadowy figure. She squinted, trying to make out the person. The other hill rushed towards her. She could almost see the figure, when a pressure on her chest woke her up.

The pressure turned out to be Fae, sleeping on her chest. Erin's heart was still racing, and she could swear that she could still hear the screams from the battlefield. She regretted all of the times that she had wished she could have dreams other than the staircase one, but if this was what she was going to get, then she's take the stair dream any day.

The effect of the dream stayed with Erin all morning, no matter what she did. She heard the screams echo in the silent house. The smell of smoke and blood hung around like a bitter perfume. She hugged Fae close to her body, seeking comfort, and even though he was purring, the dream still held her. She wondered what had triggered the dream, when she remembered the book that she had found the night before.

"I don't think it was from the book," Erin told Fae as they walked up the stairs. "It has to be because of the letter that my grandma left. Of course, that's it. She had mentioned a war."

The book was exactly where Erin had left it and so was the letter. She stared at the book, picked it up, and flipped the pages. It didn't seem special, but she couldn't shake the feeling that it was no ordinary book. It seemed to call to her, begging to be read, and when she held it, it almost felt like it was humming. She wondered what stories the book held. Obviously, they were important, or it wouldn't have been protected so much.

"Maybe I should..." Erin started to say, and then shook her head. "No...not today...I don't have time for this!" But in all honesty, she had nothing but time. She had no job to go to, she didn't have to meet up with any friends —not that she had any— and there were no pressing errands that she had to run.

Erin turned away from the book and tried to think of something that she had to do, but came up with nothing. She was a historian through and through and was addicted to the thrill of discovery. She turned back to the book and ran her hands over the leather binding. At the very least, the book could hold the answers to some of the questions she had about her family.

"A small look won't hurt," Erin murmured, more to herself than to Fae. She decided that the best place to do research would be in the study, so that's where she went.

The book sat in the middle of the desk, looking innocent and forbidden at the same time. Erin sipped her coffee. She sat down and fiddled with a pencil, and stared at the empty notepad that she had found in one of the drawers, wondering where to begin.

"A journey of a thousand miles begins with a single step," she whispered, and then turned to the first page of the book.

The first thing that she noticed was that it was

handwritten and not printed. The words were faded and written in some form of Old English. However, as she squinted to make the words out, she found that she could read them easily.

I, Amelia Smith, Guardian of the land, and head of the Mactíre Clan, sanction this book as the guiding hand for all of those of my bloodline. I am not the first to have collected and documented our heritage, and I certainly will not be the last. The knowledge within these pages has grown over the centuries as things of this nature tend to do. And while I have painstakingly and lovingly transcribed everything into this book, I have left blank pages for the future generations. I hope that this book stands as a testament to my family, until the end of all things.

While Erin read the passage, she pictured a woman, not much older than she, sitting at the same desk, writing by candle light. She blinked a few times and the image faded. On the notepad, she wrote down Amelia's name and the word 'guardian' with a question mark beside it.

"What does it mean?" Erin asked herself hoping that the answers would appear further on in the book. She turned her attention back to the book.

The history of the family is long and prestigious. Our roots extend all the way back to the arrival of the Tuatha Dé Danna; although, this is purely speculation and familiar lore. Our family has always defended this land, by our sword or by our gifts —thus, earning the name 'Guardian'.

However, before one delves into the magic within this book, there needs to be a good understanding of our history. While some of the stories are most likely exaggerations of the truth, but they do give the reasons why we are the way we are and why we do things the way that we do. My mother always told me that the best place to start is at the beginning, and so, that I where I begin —at the beginning, the very beginning, during a time before the written word.

It all started with a woman named Kieran...

Erin was soon drawn into a time before the written word —a time when the gods walked the earth alongside man. She was there when the woman who was credited with starting Erin's lineage was born. She was there when Kieran started her training as a Druid, and when she abandoned her training, all because of a vision of doom. Erin then followed her family through the ages as they developed their gifts that they used to protect the people of Dorshire, always mindful of Kieran's prophecy. Erin was also there when the prophecy came true and her family

80

began their century long conflict with the family who sought to destroy everything that they held dear.

Erin let out her breath as she read the last line of her family's supposed history. "What in the world?" she asked out loud.   She hadn't been entirely sure what to expect from this book when she had first opened it. It read more like a fantasy novel than a family history. She knew that some families embellished their history and Ireland was the land of myth, but what she read bordered on ridiculous. The idea that her family had magical powers was laughable to say the least, and the other family, who apparently ate the magical abilities of other families...come on.

"Maybe there's some truth..." Erin wondered, tapping her pencil against her lips. She started to take the story apart bit by bit, trying to discern the truth. Whenever she came across something that looked promising, like names, dates, and deaths, she wrote it down. Unfortunately, there wasn't much.

Erin sat back in the chair, arms folded, and frowning. There were no last names, except for Amelia. The other family was only referred to as the Dark Family. She spun around in the chair, lost in thought. There had to be more information somewhere. Her eyes landed on the journal that she had picked up yesterday. She sat forward in her chair, eyes wide. Of course —that was where her information would be. Quickly, she scanned the rest of the bookcase, noting several journals.

Erin smiled and was about to reach for one, when her stomach growled. Startled, she placed her hand on her stomach and realized that she was hungry —terribly hungry. A quick glance at the window told her that she had spent most of the day lost in the book.

"I guess I can start again tomorrow," Erin reluctantly said as she turned off the lights.

Over the next few days, Erin immersed herself into the past lives of her family. She was relieved that none of the journals that she read were as interesting as the first few pages of the big, leather-bound book. All in all, the journals were just everyday musings of the authors. They talked about their lives, the people they helped, and crops. None of them mentioned anything about the Dark Family or the supposed war. She soon had a stack of names and events to check out at a later date, but nothing she had read vindicated what was in the first book.

However, Erin rather enjoyed reading about the daily lives of her ancestors. Of course, the journals weren't from every member of the family, but still, they were interesting. She made notes of when her family transitioned from a matriarchal family to a patriarchal. She wasn't surprised to see that it coincided with the witch trials. She suspected that many families had made the change to protect their lives and their family.

As Erin continued to read, she was reminded of something that one of her professors had said back in college. "History is more than just kings and queens, more than battles won and lost, more than conquests. It's largely about the everyday lives of the people. Most historians spend their lives studying the common man. Their discoveries tell us more about a period than anything else. Remember the big events, but focus on the little things."

Erin had to agree with him. While the events hinted about in the leather-bound book were fascinating, they really didn't provide a clear picture of her family. The journals did. She was delighted over these small discoveries. It made her want to learn more, and not just about her family. Dorshire had a rich history that would never be written down into any history book.

Erin was reading an entry about the worst drought in thirty years, when her mind drifted back to the book that she had found in the attic. During her initial examination, she had flipped through the pages and had seen that they were filled with recipes that looked suspiciously like spells. She wasn't quite sure what to make of them but they did make her a little nervous; not that she believed in things like that, but that also meant that she wasn't going to indulge in it either. Her sister would have, but Erin liked to err on the side of caution. Just because you don't believe in something, doesn't mean that it can't be true.

Erin continued to comb through the journals in the study. Moira applauded her efforts to learn more about her family, but still urged her to get out more. Erin, however, still didn't feel comfortable enough opening herself back up to the world. She pleaded with Moira to give her more time, but she knew that, eventually, she would have to come out of hiding. This terrified her. She tried not to think about it too much. She would cross that bridge when the time came, and not a moment sooner.

Erin was preparing for another day of minor yard work and research when she noticed a taxi pulling up in the driveway. She froze. Her heart was racing and her eyes widened in alarm. Was it John? Had he found her? How? She broke out into a cold sweat and started to shake. Mentally, she tried to devise an escape route. She clenched the curtains tightly as the taxi came to a stop. She held her breath and waited to see who got out.

The person in the back seat opened the door and got out. Erin was elated to see that it was a woman and not a man. She was a tiny thing, with dark skin and short, dark hair. She looked at a piece of paper in her hand and then back up at the house. Erin remained by the window to watch the woman. She didn't know who this woman was or what she wanted.

Slowly, Erin realized that she recognized the small woman, who was starting to get her luggage out of the trunk. It was Amara Jones, her best friend since middle school. All of her fear was gone and happiness took over. With a huge grin, she flung herself from the window and ran out into the yard.

"Amara!" Erin shouted. Amara turned and broke out into a smile of her own. They ran towards each other, and when the two women met they gave each other a bone-crushing hug. Tears fell from Erin's eyes, but they were happy tears. The last time she had seen her friend was shortly after her marriage.

"You are one hard Sheila to find," Amara joked. Erin could only smile, ignoring her hurting cheeks. "Well, are ya gonna invite me in, or are we gonna stand in the yard all day?"

Erin laughed. She picked up one of Amara's bags and, arm in arm, they walked back to the house. She didn't care how Amara had found her; she was just so happy to see her. From the first day they had met Amara and Erin were inseparable. They took part in the same activities and sports. They had the same classes all the way through to college, and during the summer they rotated between each other's houses. The thing that Erin loved the most about Amara was the fact that she always filled any room that she walked into. Amara was so full of life that it seemed to spill over, and Erin needed that right now.

Amara fell in love with the house as soon as she walked in. Her brown eyes were sparkling as she took in every detail. She squealed in delight when Fae came out of hiding and he took to her as quickly as she took to him.

"I know you're trying to be all *incognito* right now," Amara joked, using air quotes, "but I'm a little hurt that you didn't send me something to let me that know you're okay." Erin grimaced. "I hopped the first flight to the states, barged into your house, and tore your parents a new one. John was there, spewing shit like he always does. I couldn't stand it, so I broke his nose."

"I know," Erin laughed. "My grandma sends me letters through a friend. I still can't believe you did that."

"You bet your ass I did," Amara smirked. "I told your dad that if he cared more about his family than his money, he would be a half way decent person. Your mum tried to calm me down, but I wasn't having any of it. Although, I did softened up when she started to bawl." Amara gave Erin an apologetic smile, and Erin reached over and squeezed her hand. "I didn't mean to hurt her, but I found out through your sister that you had been missing for months and no one thought to tell me!"

"I'm sorry," Erin said hugging her friend.

"It's okay," Amara reassured her. "Oh, and speaking of your sister...did you know that she dyed her hair blue!" Erin laughed and shook her head. "She's doing alright, just to let you know. She told me that if I were to ever run into you to let you know that whenever you're ready, look her up."

"How did you find me exactly?" Erin asked.

Amara leaned back on the couch and placed her feet on the table. "You know your grandma's one stubborn woman." Erin laughed and slumped back herself.

"Yeah, she is."

"Don't be mad with her for telling me," Amara pleaded. "I hounded her for days before she finally told me."

"I'm glad she did," Erin said with a smile. Honestly, she was. Even with everything she had been doing to keep herself busy, she still missed her friends and her family. She knew that Amara would never betray her, and now she had someone to talk to from her old life.

"I figured that this was the best time to go looking for ya, since I'm meeting potential donors in Dublin on Monday," Amara said. She had a pharmaceutical degree, but instead of working for a hospital, she became a 'bush doctor'.

Amara was part of a non-profit organization that drove around the Australian outback and provided medical assistance to the Aboriginals and those who lived far away from any town — earning them the nickname 'bush doctors'. The Australian government gave what they could, when they could, but if it wasn't for the financial donations they received from outside sources, the bush doctors wouldn't be able to do their jobs as well as they did.

"I think you owe me a night out on the town," Amara said, flinging herself off the couch. Erin started to object, but Amara wasn't having any of it. "This is nonnegotiable. We are going out to see what this little village has to offer, and that's that."

"I don't have anything to wear," Erin countered.

"Well then, I guess it's a good thing I came prepared," Amara replied with a wicked grin. She opened her suitcase and pulled out a smaller bag. "Here," she said throwing it at Erin. "I think I got your size right."

Erin started to grumble, but Amara just smiled and pushed her up the stairs. "You'll thank me tomorrow," Amara reassured her. Erin had her doubts. It had been so long since she'd done something like this. Even so, Amara had her washed, dressed, and styled in under an hour and on the road.

"There's only a pub," Erin said almost apologetically.

"Perfect!" replied Amara. "I love small town charms!" Erin sighed and resigned herself to a night dealing with her friend's whims.

The pub was busy, with the sounds of music and laughter pouring out every time the door opened. Erin started to breathe quickly, feeling like she was on the verge of a panic attack. Amara must have felt it too, because she took Erin's hand and gave it a squeeze. Erin closed her eyes and forced her breathing to relax. *Nothing can happen to me*, she told herself. *I have Amara and she will always watch my back.* Erin gave her friend a small, unsure smile and then got out of the truck.

There was almost no room to move around in the pub. The patrons were packed around the bar and the tables. A few looked up when Erin and Amara entered, then turned their attention back to their own tables. Amara took Erin's hand and dragged her friend towards the bar. She smiled at the bartender and asked if there was a menu. The bartender looked slightly offended, because what Irish pup worth its salt didn't offer food. Amara ordered fish and chips and pints for them both. She then pointed towards a window table that was miraculously vacant. They wove their way through the crowd and claimed the seats before they could be taken by someone else.

"Lively bunch, aren't they?" Amara commented smiling. Erin nodded, trying not to freak out over the crowd and the noise. "Do you see anybody you know?"

Erin looked around the crowded pub. The majority of the faces were strangers, and just as she was about to shake her head, she saw Caleb. He was sitting at the bar, laughing with some friends. She felt her heart jump. He wore a cream colored, cable-knit sweater that made his tanned skin look even darker. She felt a twinge of sadness as she watched him converse easily with his friends and other patrons. He belonged here. She didn't — not really. She hadn't belonged anywhere for a long time. She was startled to find that she wanted to belong here. Dorshire had crawled under her skin and rooted itself into her. There was no escaping it now. She vowed to get out and see the town and its people more. She knew, if she wanted to belong, she would have to open up to people.

Sensing that he was being watched, Caleb turned and looked right at Erin. She felt her face grow hot and quickly turned back to Amara, who had seen everything and had a smirk on her face. To Erin's horror, Caleb left his friends to worm his way through the pub towards her, but just before he reached their table he stopped and raised his hands.

"Are we going to throw anything?" He was smiling. Erin knew he was just joking with her. She shook her head, and he joined the two women. "So what brings you out and about on this fine night?"

"That would be me," Amara stated, assessing Caleb. She apparently liked what she saw, because she extended her hand with a huge smile on her face. "Amara," she offered. "I've been Erin's friend since middle school. And you are?"

"Caleb McKinley," he replied. "How're things at the house?" he asked Erin.

"Well enough," Erin replied. "The only problem I'm having is with the mower. It keeps dying on me."

"No, no, no," chided Amara. "We're here to have fun, not to talk about work."

Caleb laughed. A server brought their food over.

Amara tore right into it. Erin watched her friend and could only shake her head.

"I'll leave you to enjoy your evening," Caleb said, still chuckling. "When you're done, if you like, come join me and my friends over there." The two women looked over and saw that Caleb's friends raised their glasses in a greeting. He patted the table and then walked back to his friends. The moment that he was out of ear shot, Amara turned to Erin.

"My, my," Amara said. "And how did the two of you meet?"

Erin blushed and looked down at her food. "He's an electrician. He came by to check on some wiring."

"Sure he did," Amara teased. "What exactly did he mean by 'throwing something'?"

Erin's blush got even redder, but she knew better than to ignore her friends questioning. "When I first met him, I threw a book at him and threatened him with a poker." Her embarrassment grew when Amara busted out laughing. "It's not funny!" she snapped, but that only made Amara laugh harder. "He startled me and...and it's a perfectly normal response!"

Amara now had tears streaming down her face and she was holding her sides. Erin threw a fry at her in frustration and Amara threw one back. Erin reluctantly smiled and then started to laugh herself. It felt good to laugh. It felt good to just let go and be. When Amara left to take their baskets back, Erin looked out the window and smiled; everything was perfect.

"Hello Erin," said a cool voice from behind her. "What a pleasant surprise."

Startled, Erin turned around to see Connor standing behind her, smiling slightly. "H-hello," Erin stuttered. "It's nice to see you again too."

"Erin?" She turned and saw that Amara was back and she was scowling at Connor.

"And who just might you be?" Connor asked, extending his hand.

Amara's scowl deepened and she didn't take his hand. "Jones," she replied shortly. Erin raised her eyebrows. Amara only made people she didn't like refer to her by her last name. Connor smiled, unaware that he had been jibbed.

"Well, Ms. Jones", Connor stated coolly, "I hope you two have a wonderful evening." He turned to Erin and gave her a small nod. "Erin." And then he walked out of the pub.

As soon as he was gone, Erin scolded her friend. "What is wrong with you?" she asked. "He was just saying hi."

"Something about him reminds me of a dingo." Amara rubbed her arms, not taking her eyes off the door.

She shook her head and plastered a smile on her face. "Shall we?" In true Amara fashion, she didn't wait for Erin to answer, and just dragged her over to Caleb and his friends.

Pretty soon, Caleb and his friends had Erin and Amara laughing so hard that they were in tears. The group talked about just about everything, but the main topic was the upcoming May Day Festival. A few of Caleb's friends asked Amara if she was going to stay and if she would like to go with them, but she turned them down. Erin didn't care that no one asked her, because she had no intention of going.

Erin sipped her beer, looking around the pub. She noticed Caleb was looking at her strangely. He seemed nervous and his eyes were filled with something that she couldn't quite place. Her heart started to beat erratically and she felt her face grow hot. He just smiled his good ol' boy smile and edged closer to her.

"Are you planning on going to the festival?" Caleb asked carefully. Erin found that she couldn't speak, so she just shook her head. "That's a shame," he replied. "It's actually a lot of fun with all the music, food, and rides." He took a sip and regarded her thoughtfully. "I really hope you'll change your mind. Moira and her family will be there...and so will I."

"What are you talking about?" Amara asked startling the two of them.

"The May Day Festival," Erin squeaked out.

"Oh, you are *so* going," Amara stated frankly. Erin glared at her friend, but Amara just smiled back at her. "How 'bout you, Caleb?"

"I'll be there", Caleb said with a small smile. "I was actually wondering if Erin would like to go with me." His question hung in the air. Erin was too shocked to do anything but sit on her stool and breathe.

"Of course she will," Amara answered, elbowing Erin. "What time would you like to meet?"

"The morning is usually just for families with young kids, but the real festival starts at sundown. I could meet you at your house around three and we can go from there?"

"Perfect," Amara said, answering for Erin again. "Well, gents," she said, pulling out some cash, "it's been fun, but it's time for these ladies to call it a night." A few of Caleb's friends groaned but said good bye all the same.

Just as Erin turned to leave, Caleb placed his hand on her shoulder. She tensed and turned to face him. "You don't have to go if you don't want to," he told her. "But I'd like to think that we could be friends."

Erin found herself smiling. "I think I'd like that too," she said. She was rewarded by another smile from Caleb. Her faced flushed a bit as she smiled back. Amara watched the two with a smile of her own. She hoped that Erin wouldn't back out at the last minute. Erin needed to have fun, but she also needed to see that not all men were like John. After leaving bad relationships, many women viewed every man like their ex. This caused them to miss out on many good opportunities and good men; the ones who would be the balm to their wounds. Amara didn't want that for her friend.

Erin woke up early the next morning surprised that she didn't have any dreams. She had one nearly every night since her arrival, but last night she didn't, or just didn't remember. Amara mumbled something in her sleep and rolled over. Last night they had slept like they had when they were young girls: facing each other and holding hands. Erin smiled. Amara was never a morning person and would sleep the entire day away if she could. Quietly, Erin got out of bed and went downstairs to make breakfast. She was reading the morning paper when she heard a shout from upstairs.

"Damn cat!" Amara shouted. "What you got against sleeping people?" Erin couldn't help but laugh. Fae came running into the kitchen, looking rather pleased with himself. Amara came down a few minutes later, glaring at the feline.

"Coffee?" Erin offered. Amara grumbled something in reply. About a half a pot later, Amara looked awake enough for Erin to risk speaking to her.

"Sleep well?" Erin ventured carefully.

"Until your devil cat woke me up," Amara retorted, glaring again at Fae, who was busy cleaning himself.

"He's the best alarm clock I've ever had," Erin joked. "Actually there are some things that I want to talk to you about." Amara raised her eyebrow. "You know that I don't believe in any of that supernatural stuff, right?" Erin had debated with herself all morning about whether or not to tell Amara about all the strange occurrences that had happened to her. But her feelings of unease in her own home won over her fear of sounding crazy.

"Yeah..." Amara said slowly.

"Well, since I've been here..." Erin's face started growing hot, "...strange things seem to keep happening." She told Amara everything — the dreams, the whispers, the book. By the time she was done, Erin thought her face was actually on fire and hoped that her friend didn't think she was nuts. Amara didn't say anything for a long while.

"I wouldn't worry too much about all of that, if I were you," Amara finally said. "You've been under a lot of stress lately, so it's normal for you to have strange dreams every now and again." Erin must have looked doubtful, because Amara smiled reassuringly. "Trust me on this. And I wouldn't worry too much about the book. It's nothing really to worry about. Like you said, it's probably highly embellished. Just focus on getting yourself right again."

"I'll try," Erin said.

"I think I know how you might stop these dreams," Amara offered. Erin looked at her hopefully. "You need to get out of this house and have a life."

"What?" Erin asked.

"Get out," Amara urged, "make new friends, get a job...whatever you want... but live again. For too long you have been living on edge, and now you have a chance to be at peace, so take it." Erin started to scowl but Amara reached for her hand. "Please? For me? You are my best mate and the closest thing I'll ever have to a sister. I want you to be happy." Erin's scowl faded but she was still irritated.

"I'll try," she grumbled. How many more people were going to tell her what to do and how to live her life? It was starting to get on her nerves. Sure, she was more reserved than she used to be, but she wasn't the same woman either. If and when she decided to get back 'out there' in the world, it would be on her own terms and no one else's.

"That's all I can ask for," Amara replied. "And you can start by not backing out on your date with that tall, dark, and handsome Caleb." Erin shot her a dirty look. "He's a nice guy," Amara said with a shrug. "But it's up to you."

Erin grumbled about meddling friends throughout

the rest of breakfast. Despite that, the two friends spent the rest of the day talking, joking, and laughing. Erin savored every moment, because that night she had to drive Amara to the train station. She hugged her friend fiercely and tried to fight back tears.

"Just promise me you'll try," Amara urged. Erin nodded and waved goodbye until she could no longer see the train.

The house seemed emptier without Amara to fill it with her life force. The walls that seemed so comforting before now felt like they were closing in. Erin realized that she couldn't continue to hide away from the world. She had to rejoin it.

"Great," she sighed as she crawled into bed.

Four

All of the things that once gave Erin comfort now were suffocating. Even Fae was on edge. Two days after Amara's departure, Erin couldn't take it anymore. She had to get out of the house. She decided that morning she should explore Dorshire a little more and drove her truck into town. She parked in front of the nursery, which was still closed. She got out of her truck, and looked around unsure. She didn't know what to do next.

Most businesses were still closed for another thirty minutes. She was surprised to see that the pub was open so early. She quickly crossed the street heading towards it. Curious, she read the sign next to the door. Breakfast Every Day 6-9. Erin's stomach growled, reminding her that she had left without eating. *Might as well*, she told herself as she pulled the door open.

After her breakfast, Erin decided to stroll up the main street. As she strolled by the buildings, she saw a woman dash down an alley way. The woman was carrying several heavy bags. Intrigued, Erin decided to follow. She had nothing else better to do. When she peered around the corner, she saw the woman fumbling with her keys.

"Do you need some help?" Erin asked. The woman dropped both bags and her keys with a startled cry.

"Bloody hell!" the woman exclaimed, looking up towards the sky.

"I'm sorry," Erin apologized.

"No, it's not you," the woman replied. "It's just..." The woman stopped and tried to smile at Erin. "Would you like to come in?"

"In?" Erin questioned. The woman pointed to the door she was trying to open. Painted on the glass was the name 'Haven Books'. Erin realized she had just found the local bookstore, but it wasn't due to open for another hour. "You're not open yet. I don't want to bother you."

"Don't worry about it," the woman countered picking up her keys. Erin picked up the bags, earning her a grateful smile from the woman. "My name's Kayle," the woman said.

"Erin."

"Well Erin, welcome to Haven Books," Kayle said opening the door. The smell of old and new books hit Erin the moment she in. She smiled as she breathed deeply, relishing the scent. Kayle nodded approvingly. Haven was filled to the brim with books, and not everything was organized. There were boxes filled with books all over the place, and the shelves were crammed full.

"I've been meaning to catalog and organize everything for a while now but, you know..." Erin couldn't help but smile at the chaos of the store.

"I could help you," Erin offered. Kayle scrutinized her carefully.

"We also deal with antique books," Kayle said.

"I've dealt with them before," Erin replied. Kayle seemed unsure but Erin felt charged. "I could help you start the catalog." She hadn't started the day looking for a job, but if one was going to fall into her lap she wasn't about to turn her nose up at it. Kayle shrugged and ushered Erin towards the back of the store.

"Here's the horde," Kayle said with a sweep of her hand. The back office was small and nearly every inch of it was covered with stacks, boxes, and bags of books. Erin could only just stare at it, mouth slightly opened.

"It's just me and Stephen," Kayle said, defensive

and apologetic. "I would like to hire some more people but…I'm a little…" She seemed to be at a loss for words.

"It's not going to catalog itself," Erin said cheerfully. She wove her way through the piles and cleared a spot for herself at the desk. She flashed Kayle a confident smile and stared at the books around her. She sat down at the desk, unsure of where or how to begin. She just sighed and grabbed a stack of books that were still on the desk, and got to work.

Three hours later, Erin's eyes were tired and sore from staring at book titles and the computer screen. Around her were new piles, but they were organized piles. While, to her it, looked like she wasn't making any progress, Kayle, who checked in on her, was very impressed. She thought that Erin should take a break, but the look of determination on her face made Kayle stop. She would let Erin work for another hour and then make her take a break. Then she would offer Erin a job.

The front door jingled, drawing Kayle back to the front. "Stephen, you won't believe this!" she exclaimed.

"You found an extremely rare book, on an extremely rare subject, from an extremely rare period?" Stephen joked. Kayle stuck out her tongue.

"Ha-ha. No, this woman came in today and right now she's cataloging and organizing the books in the back!" Stephen snorted. Kayle grabbed his hand and marched him towards the back. She didn't notice the blush that crept into his cheeks. Stephen had a monster crush on Kayle. He stared in disbelief when he saw Erin diligently working away on the computer. He offered Kayle an apologetic smile, and then followed her back to the front.

"Told you," Kayle smirked. "Now go run to the pub and get some fish and chips for lunch. I think I got some pop here...but hurry."

Thirty minutes later, Stephen returned. Erin smelled the food and realized that she was famished. Kayle flipped the sign to 'close', then ushered Erin to a small eating area outside. Kayle beamed at Erin, while Stephen stole glances between bites.

"Do you still want the job?" Kayle asked Erin.

"Oh yes," Erin replied eagerly. "I know there's quite a bit to go through," she said diplomatically, and Stephen chuckled, "but I would like to help, because you have some amazing books that would most likely never make it to your shelves."

Kayle's face stilled. Erin was afraid that she had offended her but Kayle just smiled and nodded her head. Erin was right. There were many books that had never been put on display, because Kayle didn't have the time. She also knew that an inventory would prevent her from buying too many multiples. She really needed someone else to work in the shop, one who didn't have any other responsibilities. Kayle found all the books and buyers for the older ones. Stephen handled of the antique dealers, because they didn't like to work with a woman. This meant that they spent more time out of the shop than in it. Erin would be an asset.

"Fantastic!" Kayle said clapping her hands together. "I just need you to fill out some paperwork and you can start first thing tomorrow!" Erin grinned so hard that her cheeks hurt. *What a funny turn the day had taken*, she thought to herself. Now she had a new job and quite possibly, some friends.

The next few weeks flew by for Erin. She felt like she had finally found her feet at long last. Every morning, dreams or no dreams, she woke up smiling at the prospect of the day. She had become fast friends with Kayle and Stephen. She had also started to put a dent in the horde of books that crowded her office. She was so wrapped up in her work that she had completely forgotten about her supposed 'date' with Caleb. He hadn't, and a few days before the festival, he walked through the door of Haven Books, much to Erin's surprise.

"Caleb," she squeaked, "what a surprise!"

"Moira told me that you got a job", Caleb answered the question that she didn't ask. He gave the book store a quick go over and smiled. "It fits you."

Erin blushed. "What brings you by today?" she

asked, wanting to change the subject.

Caleb looked a little embarrassed. "I was wondering if you still planned on going to the May Day Festival with me?"

"Oh!" Erin said shocked. "I completely forgot." Caleb tried to hide his disappointment. Erin was just about to apologize, when Amara's voice rang through her head: *promise me.* "But if you still want to go, I would love to." She was rewarded by Caleb's bright smile. "We're working a half-day that day. What time did we agree on?"

"Three," Caleb replied. "Do you want me to pick you up or do you want to meet there?"

In her mind, Erin was already saying that she would meet him there, but when she opened her mouth she found herself saying, "You can pick me up." She was so stunned that she didn't hear Caleb's reply. When he left, she heard a chuckle behind her. Kayle was leaning against the office door frame.

"It's about time someone got that boy smiling again", Kayle remarked. "How'd you two meet?" Erin blushed and busied herself with straightening up a stack of books. "You don't have to tell me a thing. Anyways, I have to run to the bank and I probably won't be back by closing. Would you mind shutting up the shop?"

Erin shook her head, relishing any escape from further questioning. She didn't know why, but everyone seemed to think that there was something going on between her and Caleb. It was ridiculous. They hardly knew each other. *But he wants to,* said a small voice in the back of her mind. She shook her head to dispel the voice. It was much too soon to think about something like that.

The rest of the day went smoothly for Erin. There weren't many customers, so she sat in the back, working on the inventory, but she kept an ear out for a ring at the door. Her mind kept going back to Caleb, making her blush. She shook her head and berated herself for acting like a high school girl with a crush. *I just got out of a bad relationship,* she mentally reprimanded herself. *I shouldn't throw myself into another relationship.* *But you shouldn't let the past prevent you from having a future,* countered another voice in her head, one that sounded suspiciously like Amara. The sound of the bell saved her from getting into an argument with herself.

"Be right there," Erin called out. She plastered a smile on her face and walked out to greet the customer. For the second time that day, she received a surprising visitor, this time it was Connor

"Hello," Connor said, looking about the shop just as Caleb had. The difference with Connor was that he looked at the shop with mild distain.

"Connor," Erin stammered out, "what can I do for you today?" He started to walk towards her, but Erin positioned herself behind the counter.

"I was wondering if you had any plans this weekend?" Connor asked her. Erin's heart sped up. "Would you like to go to the festival with me, and then maybe have dinner afterwards?"

"Thank you, but no," Erin answered quickly. She was probably just as surprised as Connor, although for a different reason. Connor looked like a man who never got turned down before. She noticed a brief flash of anger in his face, but it only lasted for a second before his was back to its normal expression. "I already made plans," she explained, "with someone else."

"I see," he said carefully. "Some other time then?" Erin nodded, but she already knew that she would never accept any invitation from him. Connor flashed a quick smile before leaving. Erin was confused by the whole ordeal.

Why was she jumping towards one man while practically running from another? She had no idea. She tried to get some work accomplished, but after an hour she knew that it was hopeless. She closed the book store a little early, but she knew that Kayle wouldn't mind.

On the way home, Erin began to worry about May Day. Should she really go? Or should she back out? What in the world would she wear? Then she remembered something that she had seen in her grandmother's closet; a green dress. *It could work*, she thought, but wouldn't know until she tried it on.

When Erin got home, she went directly to her grandmother's old bedroom and tore through the closet, looking for the dress. She found it in the very back, squished between some winter coats. The dress was simple, but in a classic sort of way. She thought the green was a lovely shade. When she tried it on, she was surprised at how well it fit.

It was a little too snug around the chest, but it wasn't really noticeable. It hit her just below the knees. When she looked at herself in the mirror, she was pleased to see how well it formed with her body. She couldn't help but smile and twirl around. The dress made her feel pretty, and that was a new feeling for her as of late. While the days were getting warmer, the nights were still pretty chilly. She tore through her closet and dug out a cream colored shawl.

"Perfect," Erin told her reflection, turning this way and that. The only thing that she needed now was shoes. Unfortunately, shoes were the only thing from her relatives that she couldn't claim as her own. "It looks like I have to go shopping after all," she told Fae.

The following day, Erin drove to the next village over, simply because there wasn't much in the way of shopping in Dorshire. She found a nice little boutique. She ended up leaving with some more pants, a few more shirts, a couple of sweaters, and of course, shoes. As she placed her purchases in her truck, she happened to notice that she had parked in front of a hair salon. A smile broke across her face, and without a single bit of hesitation, she walked right in.

"Looks like my sister was right," Erin told Fae as she put away her purchases. "Shopping is good for the soul!" Fae just tilted his head as Erin laughed at herself. "I know that sounds awfully shallow, but it's true." She ran her hands through her freshly cut hair, enjoying the way it felt. She only lost a few inches, but it felt like she lost ten pounds. She also had the stylist add some layers. She felt like a million bucks and more like her old self.

Sadly, the high from her day of shopping didn't last long. When Erin woke up on the day of the festival, she was filled with dread. She tried to lose herself in her work, but that proved to be useless. Before she knew it, it was time to go home. She sat in her truck for five minutes when she got home. Her mind was whirling. She was questioning her sanity for the twentieth time, putting her head in her hands, when coolness washed over her, just like it did on her first night in the house.

To Erin, it almost felt like someone telling her that it would all be alright. Most of her anxieties faded away. What was left, she felt like she could handle. "I promised," she reminded herself. "I promised." She took several deep breaths and got out of the truck.

She was ready by a quarter to two. She had braided

her hair to the side, and had even put on some makeup. She stared at herself in the mirror, panicking. Would Caleb think that she dressed up for him? She wondered if she should change her clothes into something different, but quickly dismissed the idea. She had dressed up for herself. She wasn't going to change just because some guy might like the way she looked. But then again, this wasn't just any guy. This was Caleb, the man who was making Erin feel things that she wasn't ready to feel yet. She found that she didn't want to hide from these feelings. She was tired of hiding. She was startled when she heard someone knocking. A quick glance at the clock told her she had been arguing with herself for fifteen minutes.

Caleb greeted her with a warm smile that caused Erin to blush slightly. "You clean up real nice," he joked.

"I could say the same 'bout you," Erin countered, and she was right. Caleb's charcoal sweater suited him nicely, and so did his dark jeans.

"Ready?"

Erin nodded and locked the front door. As she walked past Caleb, she caught a whiff of his cologne. It was mildly smoky, with a hint of spice. She thought that it was a nice smell and it made her think of fall.

Caleb walked Erin to his car and opened the door for her. She thanked him with an easy smile. But underneath, she was a nervous ball of emotions. If he noticed, he didn't say anything, which she was grateful for.

As they drove, he filled her in on his past experiences of going to the May Day Festival. By the time they reached the field where the festival was, she was sitting on the edge of her seat, as excited as a kid at Christmas.

It was everything Erin had hoped for and more. Families were running around, going to each colorful booth, purchasing food, playing games, or getting a souvenir. The music from the stage was a lively mix of new and traditional music. A few children were running around, handing people little paper baskets with spring flowers, and much to her delight, there was a real life May Pole. She had wanted to be a part of a May Pole dance since she was little, and now she was going to get her chance. Erin turned to Caleb with the biggest smile on her face.

"It's amazing!" she squealed.

"Just wait 'til you get in," Caleb laughed.

They spent the next hour just wandering around, having the time of their lives. Erin made a point to try at least one thing from every booth she passed, which made Caleb laugh at her. She didn't mind though. She was having so much fun. Caleb tried his hand at a few games and managed to win Erin a prize— a flower crown. She was all too happy to wear it. Caleb told her that she looked like a fairy princess. She gave him a playful shove and then dragged him off towards the May Pole. As they got near, Erin noticed that Moira and her family were waiting to dance as well.

"Erin, Caleb!" Moira shouted as she noticed the pair. "I was wondering if I was going to see you here." They exchanged hugs and excitedly talked about their own day. Finally, it was their turn to dance. Erin could barely contain herself. Caleb declined, and settled along the side lines with the other men, to watch.

Erin was completely beside herself as she danced. She laughed hard as they wove around the May Pole with their ribbons. Her smiles nearly broke her face, but she couldn't care. By the time the dance was over, she was breathless. She was grateful when Caleb offered to get her something to drink. Moira and her family promised to meet up with them later on. Erin took her brief moment of solitude to prepare herself for the rest of the fair.

"You seem to be having a good time," said a cool voice behind Erin. She spun around and saw a slightly irritated Connor. "I see that you came with Caleb. Not exactly the best choice, if you ask me."

"Not that it's any of your business," Erin retorted, "but why do you say that?"

Connor just shrugged. "If that's your type, then who am I to argue?"

However, before Erin had a chance to put him in his place, Caleb returned with their drinks. He was visibly angry. The two men stared at each other. Erin swore that she could taste the testosterone in the air.

"Let's go," Caleb snapped at Erin grabbing her by the arm, dragging her away from Connor.

Erin was so surprised by this sudden change in character that all she could do at first was comply. But as they got farther from Connor, her surprise turned into anger and she yanked her arm free.

"Who the hell do you think you are!" Erin snapped.

"You have to stay away from him," Caleb replied. "He's nothing but trouble."

"It's none of your business who I choose to associate with, McKinley," she growled. "I'll be damned if I'm gonna let someone I *just met* tell me how to live my life! Never again!" She turned and ran through the crowd, desperate to get away before she started to cry. She could hear Caleb calling after her, but she didn't stop.

No one really paid Erin any mind as she ran. She didn't even know where she was going, but trusted her feet to take her where she needed to be. She ran until she couldn't run anymore, and collapsed to the ground. The tears she had held back now fell and great, racking sobs shook her body. She cursed herself for dropping her guard and putting herself into another bad situation.

"Stupid!" she called herself over and over. "You're just a stupid little girl!"

"No you're not," Caleb said softly behind her. Erin

froze. With an inward grown, she slowly pulled herself up off the ground. She brushed away Caleb's attempt to help her, and put some space between them. "I am sorry," Caleb said after several tense minutes of silence. She wrapped her arms around herself, refusing to turn around and look at him. "I shouldn't have grabbed you. But you're wrong. I *do* get some say in your life." That caused her to turn around, her face alight with anger and her hands clenched into fists at her sides. "As your friend, I don't want you to get hurt, and with Connor you will."

"How do you know that, huh?" Erin snapped, crossing her arms again.

Caleb sighed and ran his hand through his hair. "Can I show you something?"

"Right now?" Erin sighed.

Caleb nodded, and then turned to walk back towards the festival. Erin followed, but made sure to stay out of arms reach. As it turned out, he led them to a small standing stone, just on the outskirts of the festival grounds.

"They say that this stone has been here since Ireland was created. Legend says that whoever touches this stone can only speak the truth." Caleb placed his hand on the stone then turned to Erin. She looked at him skeptically. *Is he serious*, she thought.

"A long time ago, when I was a teenager, I was in love with a girl named Molly. She was a year younger than me. We were childhood sweethearts. She was the most beautiful person I had ever known — inside and out. After I graduated, I worked for my uncle until I got my certification to work for the electric company, all the while saving for an engagement ring." Erin wanted to stay mad at Caleb, but the sincerity in his voice, coupled with the pain in his eyes cooled her temper. She wondered what had happened to Molly, and what in the world did it have to do with Connor.

"Molly had big dreams, you see. She always wanted to get away from here, go on to bigger and better things. She wanted to be a doctor. I, on the other hand, couldn't imagine leaving Dorshire at all. This was my home. I was happy here. I should have faced the truth that it wasn't going to work between us, but I couldn't think of my life without her. I had bought an engagement ring just as Molly graduated high school, and I was going to propose that night at her graduation party. But when we were alone, she told me that she had gotten her acceptance letter to her first choice college...in Dublin.

"I knew that if I had asked her then, she would have said yes. It wouldn't have been because she wanted to but because she would have felt like she had to. We had been together so long that it was only natural for us to get married as soon as we could. That's just how things tend to work here. You're born here, you marry here, and you stay here. Few people leave. And if I had asked, that would've meant she would have to give up on her dreams. That wouldn't be fair to her, so I put the ring back in my pocket and congratulated her."

"What happened?" Erin asked softly.

"At first, we talked every day, then it became every week, and then months would go by without a word. I tried to tell myself that she was just busy with her studies, but I couldn't shake the feeling that something was wrong. So one weekend, I drove to her school, only to find out that she had dropped out. No one knew where she was. I searched for days before I found someone who had seen her with Connor a few days before. I tracked them down to a shady hotel. But she was no longer the Molly I knew. She had lost weight, and she looked like she hadn't washed or combed her hair in months. She had a needle in one arm and a bottle by the other."

"I'm so sorry," Erin said knowing those words wouldn't give much comfort. "What about Connor?"

"He was there too," Caleb replied, "sitting in a chair, smiling, as the woman I loved destroyed herself."

"Where is she now?"

"At first, rehab, but then she started to talk about demons in the shadows and satanic rituals. So now, she's in an asylum. I visit her from time to time, but she no longer recognizes me anymore."

"I am so sorry Caleb," Erin said taking his hand. "I know you were hurt, but you can't completely blame Connor for what happened to Molly."

"It's not just her", Caleb said urgently. "There are other women who have gotten involved with him and his family as well. They either end up like Molly or they disappear. There's something wrong with the whole family."

"Caleb..."

"I know," he replied tiredly, "it's your life. I get that; I truly do. I just don't want to see you end up like that. I don't want to see anyone end up like that."

Erin wrapped her arms around him and laid her head on his chest. She was still a little irritated at his macho man display, but understood it now. She could barely imagine the pain that he had gone through losing his first love like that. He would probably hate Connor until the day he died, but she didn't know enough about the man to form an opinion yet. However, Caleb really didn't need to worry about her falling victim to anyone, because hell would freeze over before she let herself become a victim again.

Five

Erin knew that the Irish weather was supposed to be unpredictable, but she had hoped that by July it would have tempered out a bit. Her hopes seemed to be in vain, because here she was, for the third consecutive day, locked away inside due to the cold and rain. She was starting to feel the effects of cabin fever.

"When will it stop, Fae?" Erin asked solemnly as she stared out the window. Fae just rubbed his body against his mistress's legs. Erin sighed and turned from the window. She sat down on the sofa and watched the flames in the fireplace dance. She picked up a book that she was reading, hoping it would chase away her restlessness, but after reading the same three sentences over and over, she gave up with a groan.

Erin gently tossed the book onto the table and fell back on the couch. She looked at the window again and sighed. She got up and walked into the kitchen, opening cabinet doors and the refrigerator. She sighed again and walked upstairs, looking into each bedroom, but finding nothing to do. Defeated, she walked back downstairs and slumped on the couch, staring at the ceiling. She had originally thought that she could do without cable or the internet, but now she was regretting that decision.

"If only the shop was open," Erin mused. The recent rain and a bad roof meant that the bookstore had to close down for repairs. Unfortunately, the contractor couldn't start until the rain stopped. Until then, the store was closed, and the books in danger of getting wet had been moved to safer locations. Kayle checked in on the store daily, so there was no need for Erin to make the trip.

Erin suddenly sat up —an idea forming in her mind. While she couldn't work on the catalogs, she did have something just as interesting. She smiled as she launched herself off the couch, grabbing a rain coat as she ran out the back door. She had books upon books of family history she had yet to thoroughly go through. They would at least give her something to do until the weather improved.

Erin spent the next few rainy days creating a rough family tree. She started with her grandmother, and then worked her way up. She wrote down every birth, death, and marriage. She hoped that Dorshire's genealogy records would have everything she would need. In the back of her mind, she wondered how her grandmother would feel about her digging into their family's past.

Finally, there came a break in the rain. Erin took the opportunity to travel to town. Her first stop was the bookstore. She wasn't the least bit surprised to find Kayle, already there, talking with the foreman.

"'Bout time," Erin said when she walked up.

"I know," Kayle replied enthusiastically. Her eyes narrowed as she watched the construction crew like a hawk, or a very protective mother. Erin threw her arm over her friend's shoulder and pulled her in.

"Don't worry," she reassured Kayle, "they know what they're doing, and in no time we'll be open again."

"I hope so," Kayle said softly. Erin gave her another reassuring hug before she left.

Erin crossed the street and headed towards the nursery to ask about some funny-looking flowers she had noticed growing next to the study. When she got to the other side of the street, the sun came out from behind the clouds. She smiled and closed her eyes, tilting her face towards the sun relishing its warmth.

The warmth from the sun chased away every ounce of sloth left in Erin from the rainy days. She knew she was going to have to live this brief sunny day up. With a literal skip in her step, she strode down the sidewalk, smiling at the other members of her community who, like her, were revitalized by the sun.

"Good morning, Moira," Erin called out cheerfully, and then frowned. Normally, Moira was dashing about the shop like mad, taking care of the plants, but she was nowhere to be seen. Erin thought that she might be in the greenhouse, which was normal too. But what wasn't normal was the heaviness in the shop. It was starting to give Erin a headache and the feeling that something bad was about to happen. She walked through the nursery, calling out for Moira, but got no reply. She finally found Moira in the office, sound asleep at the desk. Erin smiled as she placed her hand over her heart. She had been afraid that something had happened to her adoptive grandmother.

"Moira," Erin ventured, walking towards the sleeping woman. Moira didn't stir. Erin gave her a small shake, calling her name at the same time.

"What?" Moira said groggily. "Oh, Erin dear, I must have fallen asleep; silly me."

"Are you alright?" Erin asked with a small smile.

"Oh yes," Moira replied, pushing away from the desk. "I must be coming down with a cold or something."

"Well, with the way the weather's been lately, I don't doubt that."

"It's a shame your great-grandmother isn't around anymore," Moira said, adjusting her clothes.

"Oh?"

"She was the best herbalist for miles around," Moira boasted. "She could cure just about anything with the herbs she grew in her garden."

"I never knew," Erin murmured sadly. "I've been researching my grandmother's side of the family. But all I have right now is a list of names and dates that I collected from some old journals I found lying around. I really don't know much else."

"I'm pretty sure that she had a journal," Moira offered kindly. "Well then, I think I better pick some mint and chamomile for tea." Erin smiled and offered to get the herbs for her friend.

As Erin gathered the clippings, her mind wandered. There was so much that she didn't know about her family. In the past, this wouldn't have bothered her, but now it did. Maybe it was because she didn't know who she was anymore. She thought that, by shedding some light onto her family's past, she could discover who she was meant to be. While it was a pleasant thought she still had more questions than answers.

Erin spent the rest of the morning helping Moira. Although the older woman argued that she was capable of running her shop, Erin couldn't help but notice how tired she looked and how much Moira was starting to cough. Erin didn't leave until lunchtime, when Moira's shift was over, and decided to stop by the pub for a bite to eat.

Erin ran a few more errands in town. After that she headed home. The restless air that had filled the house was now gone, as if the sun had chased it away from the house, like it did to Erin. She actually had a pleasant evening. The next morning was just as nice as the previous one. She smiled at the sunrise when she went out to get the paper. She inhaled deeply, relishing the smell of good, wet earth. She took the paper and her coffee and sat on the back porch. She wanted to be outside as much as possible. She flipped through the paper, just scanning headlines, when she saw one that made her smile. Later in the week, along the coast, there was supposed to be a festival.

"Sweet," she exclaimed to Fae. "I think this could be fun. What do you think?" Fae meowed, wanting his breakfast. "You're completely right," Erin replied taking his meow as agreement.

The sea air whipped Erin's hair the moment she exited her car and she didn't care one bit. She always loved going to the beach, and this time was no different. The air was a wondrous mix of brine and festival food. It lifted her spirits and put color into her cheeks. She thought that this was the best thing to chase away the dreariness of the past few days.

The colorful flags that hung everywhere flapped violently in the wind from every building and phone pole. Huge swarms of people walked up and down the streets, sampling from the venders, while just as many flocked to the docks to examine the various boats in the harbor. Erin stood by her car and took it all in —the smells, sights, and people— loving every minute.

While there were many people milling around the streets, Erin had no problems navigating around. She easily wove her way through the crowds, smiling at the other people. She laughed when excited children pushed their way through the crowds, practically bursting, to see everything that the fair had to offer. Just seeing them made her want to run around like, well, a kid in a candy store.

Erin was delighted when she found a gyro vender. She used to eat them all the time in college and missed them. She purchased one, found a semi-quiet curb, and settled down to enjoy her gyro and a little bit of people watching. Her peace was soon interrupted by someone shouting her name. When she looked up, she saw Caleb waving, amidst a gaggle of people who bore a strong resemblance to the tall, dark Irishman. She was so startled that she wasn't aware of the fact that her mouth, full of food, hung open. The moment she did, she tried to swallow what was in her mouth and nearly choked herself to death.

"Caleb," Erin coughed as she tried to breathe.

"Easy there," Caleb laughed, thumping her on the

back. He handed her a water bottle, which she gulped down. "Better?"

"Yeah thanks," she replied, blushing. "Are you here with your family?"

"The whole clan," Caleb said, beaming. He then proceeded to introduce her to his family. They all greeted her warmly and as if she was a long lost friend, not someone they had just met.

"I've been dying to meet you," Caleb's mother exclaimed as she hooked her arm around Erin's. "Caleb's told me so much about you and I just had to see the woman who made my boy smile again." Erin could only blush. When she opened her mouth to tell her that they were just friends, Caleb's mom brushed her off.

"I know you two say that you're just friends, but that's how all good relationships start. That's what happened with me and my husband. Friends for years, and then one day we saw each other; I mean *really* saw each other." Caleb's mother continued to smile up at Erin, but thankfully, she didn't press the topic again.

After that brief, embarrassing moment, Erin actually had a good time laughing and joking with Caleb and his family. She was starting to feel comfortable around people again. She was also becoming comfortable in her own skin. This made her happy. She was starting to heal, starting to come alive again.

As the sun began to set, Erin bid Caleb's family farewell. Caleb offered to walk her to her truck, which caused her heart to flutter.

"I feel like I should apologize for my family," Caleb stated shyly as they walked pass the other cars. "They can be a little overbearing sometimes."

Erin laughed him off. "They were fine, and I had a great time."

Caleb smiled his crooked smile, causing Erin's heart to beat faster. She mentally chided herself that she mustn't allow herself to lower her guard. "So..." Caleb ventured as they neared the truck. "What have you been up to lately?"

"Family research mostly," Erin replied. "Haven's roof sprung a leak, so until it's finished, the shop's closed."

"Is that it?"

"Well, yeah," Erin replied. "What's wrong with that?"

Caleb raised his hands and took a step back. "Nothing really. It's all well and good to know your past, but you shouldn't forget that you're living in the present."

"I'll keep that in mind, Confucius," Erin reported, folding her hands into a prayer position, bowing slightly.

Caleb sighed and rolled his eyes as he ran his hand through his hair. "Why do you always do that?" he demanded. "Why is it that whenever I, or anyone else, tries to get close, you throw up a wall?"

"I don't do that," Erin snorted. "And even if I did, it's none of your business!"

Caleb groaned and turned to walk away, throwing his hands up. As he turned, his phone went off. He flipped it open and the light illuminated his face. She watched his face darken and then he let out an angry laugh. "That's just great. Fantastic."

"What?" Erin asked, even though she was still angry at him.

"It seems like my family has already left. Don't worry, I'll find another ride."

Erin watched as he walked away, and for some reason, she felt tears forming as she watched him. "Wait," she called out. He stopped. "I'll take you." Caleb slowly turned around and then walked back towards her.

"Here," Erin said, holding out her keys. Caleb took them, and without a word, got behind the wheel. Erin followed his example and climbed into the passenger seat. The cab of the truck was tense. She turned on the radio, but it didn't help.

The drive seemed to go on forever, especially with the two of them not speaking. Erin stared out the window, thinking about what Caleb had said. He was wrong, she kept telling herself. She wasn't keeping people at bay. She had friends. But the more the thought about it, the more she saw that he was right.

From the moment she landed, Erin had done everything possible to keep herself separated from everyone. Sure, she went to Moira's every now and then, but she rarely went out of her way to join in the conversations. She only spoke when someone asked her a direct question. The same was true for her job. She would spend hours working away, saying no more than a few words at any given time. Whenever Kayle and Stephen asked her to join them for drinks after work, she would always turn them down. She did this so much that they had stopped asking her. She wasn't friendly; she was polite, and that was a huge difference.

Erin looked at Caleb's reflection in the glass and wondered about him. As much as she hated to admit it, but she had started to develop feelings for him, and this frightened her. It had been a year since she'd been involved with a man romantically. Just that thought was enough to stop her heart. Her breathing became short and shallow and her vision began to blur.

"Stop the car!" Erin shouted, opening the door at the same time. Thankfully, Caleb complied without a fuss. He had barely pulled the truck off the road and stopped when Erin threw herself out. She ran a few feet and then fell to her knees, vomiting. When she tried to get up, Caleb was there to give her a hand and a half empty bottle of water to wash out her mouth. He then took a few steps back, which Erin was extremely grateful for, allowing her to regain some control. "I have anxiety attacks," Erin offered weakly, once she had a handle over herself.

"He must have hurt you real bad," Caleb said softly. Those kind words pushed Erin over the edge again. Tears poured from her eyes and huge sobs broke from her mouth. Her feet gave out again, but this time Caleb was there to catch her. He knelt with her in the grass, gently rubbing her back and offering words of comfort.

"That's it, lass. Let it out. You'll feel better. I promise." This only caused Erin to cry harder, but Caleb didn't seem to mind. He just pulled her closer, enveloping her with his strong, warm body. Her sobs began to subside, but Caleb didn't let her go. Erin slowly looked up at the man who was trying so desperately to find a place in her life. She realized then and there, that she wanted him in her life too. He helped her to her feet, and then gently led her back to the truck.

"I'm taking you home," Caleb said. "If I don't, I'm afraid that you'll drive yourself into a ditch." Erin let out a weak laugh. He offered her a half smile, and then started the truck back up. This ride was as silent as the first, without all the hostility. When they pulled up to Erin's house, they got out and walked to the front of the truck. "I'll call a friend," Caleb said, handing Erin her keys. "Don't worry."

"You could stay," Erin whispered, not looking up.

"No, it's alright," Caleb said.

"Please?" Erin asked, looking up. Caleb searched her face for any uncertainty. When he found none, he nodded, followed her inside. He steered Erin towards the couch, and then went into the kitchen to get something for them to drink. He joked about her 'American' tea selection. She wrapped her hands around the steaming mug and stared into the empty fireplace. Fae jumped up on the couch and rubbed himself against his mistress, purring.

"We met in college," Erin said after a while. "He was studying engineering and I was studying history. We fell in love." She then proceeded to tell Caleb everything about her marriage: the good and the bad. He said nothing the entire time, which she was grateful for. She didn't know if she would have been able to start again if she stopped talking. For hours, she poured out her story, only crying a little this time. Once she was done, her tea was cold and she was empty.

"You are a remarkable woman," Caleb finally said. "I don't know of anyone who could have gone through what you did and still be able to talk to anyone, let alone another man, ever again." Erin let out a huge yawn. Caleb took her cup out of her hands and placed it on the table. "Go on. Go to bed. I'll clean up."

"There are two spare bedrooms upstairs," Erin said tiredly.

"You still want me to stay?" Erin nodded, and pointed towards the clock, which showed that it was three in the morning. "I'll sleep down here," Caleb said.

Erin shrugged, waved goodnight. However, she stopped just before she hit the stairs. "Caleb?"

"Yeah?"

"Thanks for listening."

Caleb walked over to Erin and gave her a tight hug. "Anytime," he replied. She looked up at him, and before she could change her mind, gave him a kiss on the cheek. She smiled at Caleb's surprised face, and then walked up the stairs. She threw on some pajamas and fell into bed, falling asleep almost instantly.

The next morning Erin woke up late. She felt better than she had in ages. She had been holding on to the pains of her past for so long that she had forgotten what it felt like to not have them. The downstairs was so quiet that she thought that Caleb was still asleep. But when she went into the living room, she saw that he wasn't there. He wasn't in the kitchen either. She did notice that someone had made coffee and had left a note.

Erin,

I didn't want to wake you so I called a friend to pick me up. Why am I not surprised that you don't have a phone? Here's my number. If you ever decide to get one,

131

give me a call. I'll come by later to check on you. I was also thinking that we could have dinner some time. All up to you though.

See you soon,

Caleb

Erin broke out into a huge smile. In this note, this little note, there was so much promise, so much hope. She couldn't wait to experience it.

Summer may have been in full swing, but for Erin, it was like spring. To the people around her, she seemed to have blossomed over night. She laughed more, smiled more, and finally started to let people in. She and Caleb had gone on a few dates since the festival by the sea. They enjoyed each other's company, but both still carried too much baggage from their past for their relationship to truly develop into something more. But they were happy with what they had right now. Erin was actually surprised at just how happy she was. She often found herself wondering how much happiness one person could hold before they exploded. Little did she know that she was about to receive another surprise, only not as nice.

It was a fine summer morning and Erin was working out in the yard. She was on her knees, tilling up the earth for the new flowers Moira had given her. As she worked, she hummed to herself enjoying, the warmth of the sun on her back and the feel of the earth between her fingers. Fae was enjoying the nice weather as well. But he spent it curled up asleep on the front steps.

Erin was in the process of removing the flowers from their trays when she thought she heard someone call her name. She stood up and looked around, but saw no one. She shrugged and turned back to her gardening, but then she heard it again. This time, her name came with a tingling sensation in the back of her head. She tightened her grip on the spade when she heard the sound of tires crunching up the driveway. She slowly turned around and saw a cab pulling up. She slowly stood up, heart pounding, and mouth dry. Her heart stopped when the cab door opened and a figure stepped out.

At first, Erin was confused. The figure getting out of the cab was a young woman with blue hair, and for the life of her, she couldn't remember if she knew someone with blue hair. That is, until the person fully exited the cab. "Is this any way to greet your sister?" the young woman said.

Erin threw herself at her younger sister with tears in her eyes. "Oh god, Laura," she cried, "I've missed you!" Laura too was crying and nearly crushed her sister in her embrace. Crying and laughing, the sisters removed Laura's luggage, and after paying the cabbie, walked arm in arm towards the house. "How on earth did you find me?"

"Amara sent me a letter, shortly after I went to

college," Laura replied with a smirk. "Honestly, who still writes letters?"

Erin laughed and mentally made a note to thank Amara. They dumped Laura's bags in the living room. Erin watched as her sister took their grandmother's childhood home in, just like she did when she had first arrived, all those months ago.

"How are you here?" Erin asked again.

Laura gave her sister a devilish smile. "I already moved into the dorms," Laura explained. "I'm going to the New York Institute of Fashion. They offer a summer tour for a few of their more promising students." Laura could barely contain her pride at being counted amongst those few privileged students. "I'm actually supposed to be in Paris right now."

"You aren't missing any classes are you?" Erin demanded.

Laura laughed. "Classes don't start for a week. We're supposed to be exploring the city, but I thought a visit with my sister was more important." Erin still looked concerned. "Don't worry," her sister reassured her. "I have some friends posting pictures on Facebook as me. Mom and Dad will never know."

Erin pulled her sister in for another embrace. The two stayed like that, taking in the feel of the other's body and their scent. Tears fell from their eyes as they pulled away. A thousand questions hung in the air between them, but they never asked them. Fae jumped up on the couch and squeezed himself in-between the sisters. Erin laughed and gave her sister a quick tour of the house.

Just like Erin, Laura is taken aback by the essence of the house. They talked in whispers, like it was a church or museum. Laura handled objects like they were priceless artifacts. For some reason, this bothered Erin. *Why are we acting like this*, she wondered. She dragged her sister up to the attic and showed her all the vintage clothing. Needless to say, Laura was ecstatic, and her mind turned from the pull of the house to the various ways she could alter the clothing.

"So are you going to tell me, or do I have to ask?" Laura asked.

Erin sighed, unsure of where to begin. Laura reached out and clasped her sister's hand, giving it a squeeze. Erin opened her mouth a few times, but nothing came out. She took a deep breath and started to tell her sister everything. Laura's eyes widened as Erin told her sad story of love gone wrong and her final escape. Erin didn't tell her about the dreams, whispers, or the book. She was taking Amara's advice and trying not to think about it.

"I'm so sorry," Laura sobbed, throwing herself at Erin. "I wasn't there for you. I'm a horrible sister."

"No, you're not," Erin reassured her.

"Yes, I am!"

"You were just a kid," Erin reminded her. "There was nothing that you could have done, but you're here now and that's what counts." Laura wiped her eyes and tried to smile. Then Erin told her about her new friends and job. She also told her about Caleb. Laura squealed and gave her sister another hug.

"Come on, there's someone I want you to meet," Erin said, hoisting her sister up.

Moira practically exploded when Erin introduced Laura. She pulled Laura into one of her bone-crushing hugs and then proceeded to fuss over her. Erin and Laura smiled as the older woman fluttered about her kitchen like a trapped bird, turning down any offers for help.

Moira placed a tray on the kitchen table filled with biscuits and freshly steeped tea. Once again, she turned down the sisters' offers of help and poured the tea. "I can't tell you how happy I am to finally get to meet you, Laura. Your grandmother has told me so much about you."

Laura looked surprised. "I wish I could say the same."

"Well, your grandma has her reasons for not talking about her past."

The trio of women sat in silence for a few moments. The only sounds were their tea cups hitting their plates.

Erin found the silence comforting, but her sister, being young and rash, fidgeted. She bounced her leg and looked around. She also nibbled continuously on the biscuits. Erin and Moira saw this and shared a smile. Finally, Moira let out the laugh she had been trying to hold back.

"You are so much like your gran," Moira laughed. Laura stopped fidgeting and beamed.

"Really?" she asked breathlessly.

"Oh yes," Moira replied. "She couldn't sit still to save her life. She lived each moment as if it was her last."

"Tell me more about her," Laura insisted. "I want to know more."

The rest of the afternoon was spent with Moira telling the sisters stories about their grandmother. They laughed so hard that tears ran down their faces.

On the way back to Erin's house, Laura was silent and spent most of the drive looking out the window. Erin glanced at her sister from time to time and saw that something was bothering her younger sister. Erin waited until they pulled into the driveway to broach the topic.

"Are you alright?" Erin asked. Laura said nothing. She just stood there and stared at the house.

"Do you ever wonder why grandma never talked about all of this?" Laura asked. Erin had wondered. "Why did she keep this a secret? What was she hiding?" Erin had no answers for her sister.

The next day, Erin took her sister to work with her. She wanted to leave her at home, but Laura insisted. "You don't have cable or internet," she pointed out. "What am I supposed to do with myself?"

In the end, Erin relented and she was glad she did. Laura lit up the little shop with her larger than life personality. She sat behind the counter and chatted up Kayle and Stephen. When Erin pointed out that there were a few old-fashioned pattern books in the back, Laura spent the rest of the day copying the old designs.

"You have a good life here," Laura told her sister as they shared a pint in the pub later that day.

"I think so too," Erin replied. The sisters clanked their glasses.

As they ate their food, Erin watched her sister. Laura was still the sister who Erin had grown up with, but now she seemed more like herself than when they were living at home. Erin was grateful that Laura had broken free from their parents' interfering before she had gotten too deep into something that she didn't want for herself.

Unbidden, Erin's thoughts turned back to all the strange occurrences that had happened in the house. Her sister's initial reaction, and continued reaction, made her nervous for her sister. Erin didn't want to tell her sister, because she loved those sorts of things and would want to try something. But she felt compelled to tell her sister about the strange, supernatural things she had experience. Amara had waved them off, but maybe Laura would understand it better than Erin and give her a more concrete answer.

"There's something that I haven't told you yet," Erin said. Even though she had said it barely above a whisper, Laura had heard and gave her sister a questioning look. "It happened shortly after I arrived. Strange things started to happen to me." There in the pub, Erin told her sister the rest of her story. Laura just sat there, wide-eyed, as she listened. When Erin finished, she half expected her sister to laugh it off. Instead, she leapt up, excited.

"You *have* to show me," she demanded, throwing the rest of her beer back.

Erin still wasn't completely sure about showing her sister the book, but Laura wouldn't have it any other way. Erin took her sister to the study and placed the book on the desk. Laura ran her hands over it and looked up at her sister.

"This is it? It looks so ordinary but not, you know?" Erin nodded. She too had thought the same thing when she first saw the book.

Laura sat down and slowly opened the old book.

For a moment, Erin thought that she heard whispering, but it faded so fast that she couldn't be sure. Unlike Erin, Laura didn't actually read the book. She just flipped through the pages, taking it all in.

"This looks like a spell book," Laura said as she flipped another page. Erin nodded, but where as she had been alarmed, her sister looked excited. "We gotta try something!"

"No," Erin said sternly. "Anyway, there's no such thing as magic."

"Maybe or maybe not," her sister retorted.

"Are you serious?"

"Of course," Laura countered. "When you went missing, a lot of people thought that you were dead, because you wouldn't just disappear like that. Well, I kept having dreams about you. I saw you here; I just didn't know where here was exactly." Erin didn't know what to say. "I know that not all magic is real," Laura went on. "Many of the old spells are just superstitions." Erin raised her eyebrows.

"What, you're the only one who can like history?" Erin had nothing to say to that. "Anyway, we don't have to do a *spell*, we could always try something else." Laura flipped back a couple of pages in the book and smiled. "How 'bout this?" She turned the book towards Erin. The page her sister pointed to looked like some kind of meditation. "So how 'bout it, Erin? Can we try this?"

Erin wanted to say no and snatch the book away from her sister. It wasn't that Erin believed in witchcraft or anything; it's just that she didn't want to tempt fate. But the look on Laura's face killed Erin's refusal.

Erin sighed. "I guess so." Laura squealed in delight and snatched the book up. She ran towards the house, not caring that her sister hadn't moved. "What's the worst that could happen?" Erin asked to no one in particular. But to be honest, she really didn't want to know.

By the time Erin made her way back inside, Laura had set everything up. The coffee table had been pushed flushed to the couch, candles had been lit. Laura was bent over an unlit candle, carving into it with a butter knife.

"What are you doing?"

"You mean 'what are *we* doing,'" Laura corrected. "We're going to try and talk to our ancestors. The book says that we need to burn some weird incense and anoint a white candle with some special oil and carve runes into it. Well, you don't have any of that other stuff, so we'll just have to do with this candle and the runes." Erin reluctantly sat on the floor in front of her sister. When Laura was done, she placed the candle on a small plate and smiled up at Erin.

Erin sighed again. "Okay so what's next?"

Laura quickly consulted the book. "We have to light

the candle and think of the person who we are trying to reach. Do you know anyone?"

"Kieran," replied Erin.

"Who's that?"

"She's supposed to be the first…" Erin wasn't sure how to refer to her.

"Witch?"

"For lack of a better word," Erin said with a shrug. Laura nodded and lit the candle.

The sisters stared at the candle's flames. Erin knew that she was supposed to clear her mind, but she was having a hard time. Everything seemed so loud: the clock, Fae, even her own heart. She glanced up at Laura and saw that her eyes were vacant and her breathing had slowed. Erin mentally sighed and focused again on the flame. Her eyes began to water, so she closed them for just a second. When she opened them again, she was alarmed to see that she was no longer in her home. Instead of sitting in her living room with her sister, she found herself standing in a mist-filled plain, completely alone.

"Laura!" she cried out franticly. There was nothing around her —nothing but the mist. "Laura!" Her voice sounded strange, muffled; it echoed in the vast waste land around her.

"Over here!" Erin spun around and nearly cried

when she saw her sister walk towards her. "Where are we?" Laura asked, taking her sister's hand. Erin shook her head. She had no idea.

"Kieran," Laura called out cautiously. Erin tried to shush her. "There's nothing here but us," Laura snapped. "And you already shouted."

"We don't know that for sure," Erin snapped back. She couldn't see anything, but she felt like they were being watched. It sent chills up her spine and all she wanted was to get out of wherever they were and go home.

"Erin," Laura whispered, pointing off into the distance.

Erin felt her sister grip her hand tightly, as she followed her pointed finger. Erin's heart stopped when she saw that something was coming towards them, hidden by the mist. They couldn't make out its shape, but judging by the way the mist flowed over it, it had to be huge. It stopped a few feet from the terrified sisters, and then sunk back down.

Erin was about to ask her sister if she had any idea how to get back, when the thing exploded from the mist. The sisters screamed as a huge, black, smoke creature reared over them. The only clear features it had were its long and deadly-looking claws and teeth. Without thinking, Erin ran away from the creature, pulling her sister behind her. The creature gave a deafening roar and pursued them.

The sisters ran frantically, zigzagging all the way. Erin spared a quick glance at Laura and saw that her face was contorted with fear, tears streaming from her eyes. When her eyes met Erin's, they were apologetic. 'I'm sorry for getting us killed,' they said, and that caused something to shift in Erin.

She wasn't going to let some shadow creature get her little sister. Then Erin got an idea. She mentally pictured her living room, and slowly it started to come into focus. The mist retreated gradually and the sounds from the creature began to fade. She focused even harder, and almost cried out when she saw an image of her and Laura sitting on the floor. Then, they weren't being chased, but actually sitting on the floor in Erin's living room. They both fell back, panting, as if they had just run a marathon.

Erin jumped up and turned on a lamp. The light hurt their eyes, but they were too grateful for the light to care. "Never again," Erin said breathless. Laura, still on the floor, nodded and blew out the candles.

They slept in the same bed that night. They also had every light in the bedroom on and had locked the door to their room. They crawled into bed, facing each other, clutching the other's hand. They didn't fall asleep for a long time.

The next few days were blessedly uneventful. Laura

went to the bookstore with Erin and helped out. They visited with Moira, who knew something had happened, but didn't ask. They continued to share the same bed at night. Neither was willing to talk about the misty plain or the creature that tried to attack them. Erin had taken the book back into the study and placed it in a locked drawer and locked the study as well. There was no more talk about magic. Instead, the sisters talked about their plans for the future. Laura teased Erin over Caleb as often as she could. Then the time came for Laura to leave.

Erin helped her pack and tried not to cry. She would miss spending time with her sister. "Here's the number and address of the hotel that I'm staying at," Laura said as she wrote in a notebook. "And I'm giving you my dorm info too. I can't take all of these clothes with me, so you can just mail them later." Laura smiled at her sister. "I'm sorry."

Erin knew what Laura was apologizing for and gave her sister a reassuring hug. They didn't speak as Erin drove to the station. There were so many things that Erin wanted to say to her sister but couldn't find the words. They had always been close growing up but now things were starting to change, and Erin was going to miss out on most of it.

"You should really see about getting internet or something," Laura told her sister after getting her tickets. "Then we could at least email, or maybe even Skype." Erin laughed.

"I'll look into it," Erin promised.

"See that you do," Laura said, laughing as well.

Six

Erin's thoughts were troubled as she drove home from the train station. She had put on a brave face for her sister, but the misty plain and the creature deeply disturbed her. So many questions flew through her head. She was afraid that the only way she was going to get any answers would be to take a closer look at the book. Just the thought of touching it again made her blood run cold. She was afraid that she and her sister had unintentionally opened a door that should have remained shut.

Erin shook her head vehemently. There was no way on god's green earth that she would ever open that book again. But she had to. The book was the largest collection of her family tree. It had names, dates, marriages, and births all conveniently in one location. Even though she was afraid of the book, it held too much valuable information to ignore.

The feeling of being watched came over Erin, the moment she crossed the threshold. It wasn't threatening. It felt more like someone was watching to see what she would do. The feeling only made her angrier and more determined to put all of this behind her. This was *her* home and she was not about to let some book make her feel like she wasn't welcome or didn't belong.

"This is *my* home!" Erin shouted. "If you don't like it then *you* can leave, 'cause I'm not running anymore!" The feeling of being watched faded away. Instead, she swore that the house now seemed smug or proud of her outburst. "This is ridiculous," she muttered.

The next few days were so quiet that Erin soon forgot about the misty plain and the creature that had tried to attack her. She got up, went to work, hung out with her friends, and went on a date with Caleb. She relished the normalcy of it all, but not for long. Even though she had forgotten about the supernatural, the supernatural hadn't forgotten about her.

Erin knew that something was up the moment she

walked through the door to her home. The air was heavy and charged. It made her hair stand on end and goose bumps form on her arms. It reminded her of when she would come home to find John in a foul mood. When he got like that, she waited for all hell to break loose, which it always did. Fae was in a foul mood, hissing at her whenever she went to pick him up, and yowling at the door to be let out. When she finally complied, he took off into the night screaming like a banshee.

Erin's night only got worse. She burned dinner beyond all salvation. She developed a headache of epic proportions and couldn't find the aspirin. She walked into a door and stubbed her toe on the edge of the coffee table. The book she was reading fell apart in her hands. Frustrated, she decided to just go to bed, only to nearly fall down the stairs once she reached the top. She wondered if she should risk attempting a bath and thought better of it. With how things were going, she would most likely end up drowning. She hoped that a good night's rest would be the end of her misfortune.

Unfortunately that wasn't the case. In the dead of night, Erin was awoken by a terrible dream. Her body was covered in a cold sweat. Her heart raced. She gulped the air, frantically looking around her bedroom. The shadows were deep and dark, but there was nothing in them that would harm her.

Still shaken, Erin turned on her bedside lamp. The light banished the shadows to the farthest corners of the room, but it didn't chase away the effects of the nightmare. She got out of bed and cautiously walked down the stairs to the front door. At first, there was only silence bearing down on her. She then heard the faintest of meows from outside. She quickly unlocked the door and scooped Fae right into her arms. Just the act of holding his warm body against her chilled one was enough to calm her down.

"It was awful Fae," Erin told her cat, clutching him tight to her chest. "That creature from the misty plain was hunting down my family. His claws slashed them apart. Mom, Dad, Laura, Gran..." Erin shuddered and pulled Fae in tighter. "I think the worst part was when it turned on Moira. Instead of disappearing like everyone else, her veins turned black and she fell to her knees in pain. She screamed my name and asked why I wasn't helping her." Fae meowed and licked her nose. "I know it was only dream, but..." Her voice faltered and she started to cry. She felt like the dream was a warning, but for what she had no idea.

Erin made herself a small cup of chamomile tea. She sipped it slowly, drawing comfort from its smell and the warmth from the mug. Bit by bit, she began to feel better, until she was ready to attempt to sleep again. Her luck had finally turned. There were no more dark dreams to haunt her, or any dreams for that matter.

Erin awoke the next morning a little worse for wear, but whatever had hung over the house the night before was gone. Either way, she was grateful to walk into Haven.

There were still piles of books that waited for her attention. She reminded herself that dreams didn't mean anything. They were just random images from her subconscious. With her mind made up, she turned her full attention to her real world problems and left the rest in the shadows where they belonged.

"So your sister's back in France?" Kayle asked during their afternoon break.

"She should be," Erin replied. "She's probably running all over Paris right now, dragging her friends into obscure second hand shops." Kayle smiled. She had really taken to Laura during her short visit. "Which reminds me... I should probably go on and send that package."

"Well, when you do, can you add this for me?" Kayle reached into her bag and pulled out copies of antique dress patterns. "She had mentioned that she really wanted to buy these when she was here but didn't have the money."

Erin graciously took the patterns from her boss and friend. "Thank you," she said.

"Don't mention it," Kayle said with a wave of her hand. "I just made some copies."

"Thanks all the same though," Erin said.

"Hey, what are friends for."

Erin smiled and placed the patterns in an envelope.

When she got home she would add it to the clothes her sister had said she wanted. Erin was adding a book on gardening to the computer, when she realized she hadn't seen Moira in a while. It was odd because the old woman checked on her constantly. After work, Erin decided to make a quick stop by Moira's home to check on the old woman. When she got there, she knew something was wrong.

There were more than usual cars in the drive way. No children were running about the yard. Everything seemed eerily quiet. Erin slowly turned off her truck and got out. Something inside of her screamed that what she saw was all wrong. Images from her nightmare came unbidden, making her heart freeze in alarm. Terrified, she ran towards the house. When she went to turn the doorknob, she was startled to find that it was locked. Moira never locked her door, ever.

It took only a moment for Erin to recover from her shock. She knocked on the door loudly, waiting for some response— any response— but none came. With mounting fear, she peered into the windows but saw no one. She then ran around to the back of the house, only to see more cars.

"They're at the hospital," a gravelly voice explained. Erin turned to see Moira's neighbor leaning on his rake.

"What happened?" Erin demanded.

The neighbor shook his head. "Moira was late

coming home from work the other night. When her son went to look for her, he found her collapsed in the greenhouse. They took her to the hospital, but last I heard, she was in a coma or something."

Erin's stomach dropped. Words escaped her. The only thing that she could do was stand there with her mouth opened in disbelief. When she regained some control over her voice, she asked for directions to the hospital, and then ran back towards her truck. She struggled to not speed the whole way there, reminding herself that she would be of no help if she got hurt herself.

Thirty white-knuckled minutes later, Erin walked through the doors of the hospital. Still dazed, she looked around the lobby, hoping to see someone from Moira's family. Seeing no one, she made her way towards the receptionist desk and inquired about which room her friend was in. The receptionist was polite but told Erin that only family members were permitted to visit at the moment. Unable to persuade the receptionist, Erin sat down in one of the many uncomfortable chairs in the lobby. She placed her head in her hands and started to cry.

How could she have been so unaware of how dear Moira had become to her? True, they weren't blood related, but for Erin, Moira was as much a part of her family as her own grandmother. A thousand questions whirled around in her mind, and she couldn't help but to think the worst.

"Erin?"

Erin's head shot up to see Caelan walking towards her. Erin jumped up and wrapped her arms around the other woman. The severity of the situation was reflected in the way Caelan's arms tightened around Erin and the way her body shook as she tried to hold back tears.

"I've been meaning to call you," Caelan said when she finally pulled back. She wiped away a stray tear and tried to put on a brave face.

"How is she?" Erin whispered.

"Not good," Caelan replied. "The doctors can't find the cause. The only thing they can tell us is that she's in a great deal of pain."

Erin raised her hand to her mouth. "Can I see her?"

"Of course," Caelan said. She took Erin by the hand and led her to Moira's room.

Moira's room was filled to the brim with family. A few looked up when Erin and Caelan entered, but most kept their eyes towards the woman lying on the bed. The only sounds came from the machines that were monitoring Moira's vitals. Barry was sitting on a couch with the children piled on top of him. He gave Erin a small nod when she entered the room, which she returned. Murphy was sitting by his wife's side. It broke Erin's heart to see him so defeated. He looked as if he had lost his whole world. They all did. Moira was the rock of their family. No matter what happened in their lives, Moira was always there. She was always the strong one, but now her frailty was exposed.

Erin took a seat on the other side of the bed and gently took a hold of Moira's hand. She was shocked to find it so cold. Erin let her tears fall. Caelan placed a hand on her shoulder. Tegan woke up and crawled into Erin's lap. She held the little girl close, trying to comfort her, but that was hard to do when all Erin wanted to do was break down herself. She would do that later when she was on her own. Until then, Erin would have to keep herself together and help out in any way she could.

They remained by Moira until a nurse came in to inform them that visiting hours were over. Erin followed the Duncans back to Moira's home and started to cook dinner for everyone. She stuck with the comfort foods that she knew well. Caelan smiled gratefully and set the children up at the table to do their homework. Barry and Murphy were sitting in the living room, quietly discussing everything but the woman they had left in the hospital. Other family members found tasks to keep themselves busy. But as the evening wore on, many of them left for their own homes, with promises to return the next day or the next chance they got.

Once the children were in bed, Erin sat down with the remaining family members. Caelan was busy pouring whiskey into tumblers, which they all accepted. It burned their throats and bellies, but helped to numb the pain of the day a little.

"How long are you going to be able to stay?" Erin asked Caelan.

"A few weeks", Caelan replied. "John will be here tomorrow, and the rest of the family, who live farther away, will be coming in as well."

"If you need a place to put some of them up I have plenty of space," Erin offered

"Thank you," Barry said. "Most of our family lives nearby. Only a few live far away. We'll manage."

"Well, if you need me for anything, please let me know," Erin said. They thanked her again.

Erin visited Moira several times over the next few weeks. The doctors were still unable to shed any light on her condition, which only added to the family's concerns. Erin had taken to reading to Moira whenever she visited. She was unsure if Moira heard any of it, but it was better than just sitting there, watching her unmoving body and listening to the beeps from the heart rate monitor.

Erin was on one such visit when she received a surprise. While approaching Moira's room, she heard a male's voice coming from inside the room. She had just talked to Caelan, and knew that none of the family would be there. She thought it could have been one of the doctors, but if so, who was he talking to? When Erin peeked through the crack in the door, she was startled to see that it was Connor. As far as she knew, Connor didn't know Moira at all. So why was he there?

His back was to the door so he didn't see Erin, but that also meant that she couldn't see what he was doing. She heard him muttering something, but his words were too soft for her to make out. She then noticed that he was waving his hands over Moira's body. Erin remained in the doorway, trying to summon the courage to ask him what he was doing, when he straightened and started to turn around. Erin panicked. She quickly walked down the hall in the opposite direction, hoping that he wouldn't recognize her from behind. A quick glance over her shoulder told her that he hadn't. She watched Connor walk away, but didn't make a move towards Moira's room until he had entered the elevator and the doors closed.

Erin cautiously peered into Moira's room, looking for anything out of place. When she didn't see anything, she shook her head and chided herself on being so silly. What reason would Connor have for harming Moira?

Erin placed her bag on the floor next to the chair she usually sat in, and was just about to settle down when a machine started to beep frantically. She saw Moira's face as it contorted in pain. The doctors had tried various pain killers, but they only worked for a short time. Erin reached out to grasp Moira's hand. She wished with all her heart that she could do something to ease the old woman's pain.

When Erin's hand touched Moira's, pain coursed through her body like fire. Every inch of her screamed and begged for the pain to stop. It felt like she was being burnt alive. She clinched her teeth to hold back her screams. Somewhere in the back of her mind, she thought that this must be what Moira was feeling, and she was glad that the old woman wasn't conscious for any of it. She tried to push the pain away, but that only caused the fire under her skin to burn more.

From somewhere, a cool hand touched Erin's head. It dimmed the pain in her head somewhat, allowing Erin to breathe easier. *Give it to the earth*, said a voice in her mind. *Take the darkness out and give it to the earth. If you do not, you both will die.* Briefly, she wondered what the voice was talking about. What darkness?

The coolness spread throughout Erin's body, making her feel lightheaded, but at least the pain was subsiding. Soon, she felt well enough to try to open her eyes. When she did, she received the biggest shock of her life. Somehow, she was above her body, looking down. The only thing that she could do was stare and wonder if she had, in fact, died. The voice in her mind only chuckled and urged her to keep watching. Her eyes grew as a white light enveloped her and Moira's unconscious bodies.

In her current state, Erin knew that the light was their life-force. She was alarmed to see that Moira's was slowly being extinguished by black vines. Erin's blood ran cold, because it was so similar to her nightmare. What frightened her even more was that the black vines were slowly making their way up her own arm.

Give it to the earth, the voice urged again.

"How?" pleaded Erin. "I'm three stories up and in a hospital!" The voice chuckled.

Maybe this will help you.

Erin's brief release from the pain was over as she was placed back into her own body. It still wasn't as bad as before, but it was still strong enough to bring tears to her eyes. So focused on the pain, she didn't notice that her surroundings were changing. The floor was no longer cold, hard linoleum; it had become soft, lush grass. Trees appeared out of nowhere, and she swore that she felt heat from the sun and the wind across her face. The only thing that remained the same was Moira's bed. Erin was so amazed by the room's transformation that she momentarily forgot her situation, but the voice in her mind pulled her back.

Do not try to force the darkness, the voice told Erin. *I will help you guide it to where it needs to go. We may yet save your friend.*

Before Erin could ask the voice what exactly it meant, the black vines began to move rapidly up her arm. Panicked, she tried to stop them, but nothing worked. As the vines neared her heart, she prepared for death. Instead, the vines flowed around to the base of her skull, then down her spine to the ground beneath her. Relieved that she wasn't going to die after all, she relaxed, allowing her body to be a conduit. It hurt though. The more black vines in her body, the more pain she experienced. A few times, she lost her concentration, which caused the vines to spread out. But the voice stepped in at those times to rein them in. She risked a glance at Moira. What she saw gave her hope. The vines were releasing their hold over her. That gave Erin the determination to hold on for as long as it took.

An eternity seemed to pass before the last of the black vines flowed from Moira, through Erin, and down to the earth. As soon as the last of them were gone, she let go of Moira's hand and collapsed, exhausted. A quick glance at the clock told her that only a few seconds had passed. She stared at the clock in disbelief. How could that be?

"Erin?" Moira croaked.

Erin's head shot up to stare at Moira's smiling face with a mix of joy and disbelief. She still looked weak, but she was awake. Erin couldn't believe her eyes and cried.

"I knew you would save me," Moira said weakly. "But his hold over me isn't broken. I know this doesn't make any sense, but you have to use the book...your family's book. Please."

"What do you know about the book?" Erin exclaimed but Moira had passed out. Try as she might, Erin could not wake her. When she saw the contented look on

Moira's face, she decided to let the old woman sleep. Moira had been through a lot, and needed rest. Still a little disoriented, Erin gathered her things and went back home. Driving proved to be challenging. She could barely keep her eyes open. Twice, she nearly crashed when she fell asleep behind the wheel.

Erin didn't even bother to take off her shoes when she finally got home. Like the zombies in the movies, she shuffled straight to the living room. She threw herself onto the couch and passed out as soon as her head hit the cushions.

For days, Erin tried to rationalize the events that had happened in the hospital. She had never been a believer of the supernatural. There was always a logical explanation for everything, but she was having a hard time finding one this time. At first, she thought she had hallucinated the entire event, but she had done nothing to cause such a vivid hallucination. She wasn't on any medication, she didn't do drugs, and she hadn't injured her head. What unnerved her most was that Moira knew about the strange book that was still locked away. Erin's grandmother could have told Moira when they were younger, but Erin thought that was unlikely. Erin knew Moira well enough to know that she would have told Erin about it, because she shared everything. *Perhaps not everything*, said the reasonable portion of Erin's mind. She sighed. Whatever had happed was over, so there was no reason for Erin to keep worrying about it.

Moira was still in the hospital and still unconscious. The doctors had told the family that she didn't appear to be in pain anymore. But it now appeared that her body was shutting down. More and more machines had to be attached to her to keep her body going.

The thought of Moira no longer being in the world brought Erin to tears. She hated feeling helpless and that is exactly what she felt. More and more, her thoughts turned to the book that was still locked in the study. While Erin wanted to save the woman who had welcomed her like family, she was still afraid of the book. She was afraid of what would happen if she failed, but more afraid of what it would mean if she succeeded.

Erin stopped by Moira's house on her way home from work one day. Kayle had brought back some pastries from her latest book hunt. Erin hoped that the kids would like them, and for a few minutes, forget that their grandmother was dying slowly in a hospital bed. Erin was greeted by silence, common these days, but she thought that she could hear someone crying softly.

Erin placed the pastries in the kitchen and went in search of the crying. What she found nearly caused her to cry herself. Murphy was sitting on the bed that he and Moira had shared for sixty years, crying softly over a picture of him and his wife on their wedding day. Erin sat down next to him and reached out for his hand.

Instead of taking her hand, Murphy threw his arms around her and sobbed. His frail body shook violently as he clung to Erin for dear life. She rubbed his back and made comforting sounds, but inside she was steeling herself to do whatever it took to save Moira and her family. To hell with the consequences!

Once home, Erin went straight to the study. She didn't want any time to talk herself out of what she was about to do. She unlocked the drawer, and for the first time in weeks, came face to face with the very thing she had been avoiding. Reminding herself of why she was there, she took the book out. She placed it on the desk and sat down. She stared at it for a few moments. She then closed her eyes, held her breath, and opened it.

Quickly, Erin flipped through the pages, looking for anything that she could use. After several minutes, she found something promising: *To Remove an Affliction.* She ignored the rational part of her mind that protested the ridiculousness of it all and continued to read.

The removal of an affliction is one of the fundamental arts of a Guardian. This is best done during a full moon, but if the caster's will is strong enough, it can be done anytime. To perform this spell, the caster will need the following ingredients: an image of the afflicted person; a bowl filled with water;

salt; one candle preferably green or white, and lastly, paper.

First, place the salt in the bowl of water to purify it. Write the affliction the person is suffering from on the paper and burn it with the candle, scattering the ashes to the wind. Then take the image of the afflicted individual and dip it into the bowl. Afterwards, take the water and dump it near a wooded area.

Intent is important here. As you burn the paper, you must 'will' the illness to burn away. As you wash the image, you must want to wash away the illness. If the caster's will is strong, and if the afflicted has a strong will to live, the individual should recover quickly. If not, then it may be the ill person's time. Guardians **cannot** change a person's destiny. Everything has its time and place, and all things must die eventually.

Erin read the passage several times to make sure that she didn't miss a thing. She tried to ignore the part about how, if it was a person's time to die, nothing could be done. She had to remain positive. As she ran towards the house, she glanced quickly up to the sky. She was relieved to see that there was a full moon out. If the spell said a full moon was best, she was happy that she had it; every little bit helped. She tore through the kitchen, gathering the items, and then ran back outside.

"Please let this work," Erin pleaded to the universe.

Erin jotted down everything that the doctors had told her about Moira's condition. As she wrote, the wind picked up, but she didn't care; she wouldn't allow herself to get distracted. She followed the directions from the book, and once she had burned the last piece of paper, turned to the bowl. The wind now whipped her hair around her face. Electricity seemed to course through the air, making the hair on her arms stand up. Any doubts she had about magic being real were fading fast. She took a picture of Moira out of her back pocket and held it over the bowl. She smiled sadly. It was from the May Day Festival. She traced the image of Moira with her fingers lovingly. With one final prayer, she dunked the photo into the water.

Erin half expected the picture to dissolve, but it held up to the multiple dunking it received. She kept her thoughts on Moira: her smile, her laugh, how she loved everyone and was loved by everyone. She realized that the picture was starting to get hot. Every time she lifted it out of the water it steamed. It burnt her fingers and started to boil the water in the bowl. She paid no attention to the pains she received every time her fingers hit the water. She couldn't stop. She wouldn't stop.

Just when Erin thought she couldn't stand it any longer, the heat subsided and the wind died down. She was so exhausted that she nearly went to sleep right there in the yard. Somehow, she found the strength to dump the water and drag herself back to the house. Going up the stairs was another challenge. All she wanted to do was get into bed and go to sleep. She sighed the moment she rolled into bed, her last conscious thought, hoped the spell would work.

Erin could have slept the entire day, but Fae had other plans. He walked over her, meowed, and licked her nose with his rough tongue until she got up. She threw a pillow at him, just to show him how angry she was, which he dodged easily and sauntered off, tail high. She heard the phone ringing downstairs and groaned again. Who in the world would be calling her this early?

"Hello?" Erin answered.

"Oh I'm sorry... did I wake you?" It was Caelan. Erin was instantly awake.

"No, it's alright," Erin said quickly. "Has something happened to Moira?"

"It's a miracle!" Caelan exclaimed. "She's awake and finally getting better! The doctors still have no idea how, but I don't care. They want to keep her for a few more days, just to be sure, but they said that if everything keeps going the way it is, Mum will be able to come home!"

Erin had to use the wall to hold herself up as her knees gave out over the good news. She told Caelan that she would head to the hospital as soon as she could. When she hung up the phone, she wondered if Moira's miraculous recovery had something to do with the spell that she casted last night, or if it was just an enormous coincidence. Either way, the important thing was that Moira was awake and on the mend.

Erin was greeted by the best sight in the world when she finally got to the hospital. Moira was sitting up in bed with her grandchildren piled around her, laughing with her family. Everyone had smiles on their faces. You wouldn't have known that a few days before they had been preparing for the worst. When they saw Erin standing in the doorway, they shouted in joy and ushered her into the room. She smiled brightly, intent on enjoying the moment.

"Well Mum," Barry said after a while. "I think it's time to get the babes home and let you get some rest." The kids complained. Moira let out a week chuckle.

"Don't worry, duckies," Moira told her grandchildren, "I'm not going anywhere."

"You promise?" Aiden said.

"Yes, I promise." Reluctantly, the children gathered their belongings, and with final hugs and kisses, walked out with their parents. "Erin, could you stay for a bit longer, please?" Moira asked. Erin nodded and made herself comfortable. Murphy placed a kiss on his wife's forehead and then left.

The two women sat in silence. Moira had closed her eyes and lay back in the bed. For a moment, Erin thought that she had fallen asleep again. Erin was about to leave when Moira's hand shot out and grabbed hers.

"I knew you could do it," Moira boasted. "I just knew it."

"I didn't do anything," Erin replied stubbornly.

Moira laughed, but it turned into a cough. Erin got her some water. "I suppose you'd like an explanation?"

Erin was about to say that she had no idea what Moira was talking about, but then she saw the look on the older woman's face. Erin sighed. Slowly she nodded. Moira readjusted herself so she was more comfortable, before she started to speak.

"I'm sure, by now, you've noticed some strange things about your house and your family?" Erin nodded slowly. "Your gran should be the one to tell you all of this. But since she's not here, I guess I have to." Moira closed her eyes and sighed. "Your family has magic in their blood, Erin. And with that magic, they protected Dorshire and the people who live on its lands." Erin stared at the woman in the bed like she had lost her mind. Moira mentally sighed. This was going to be more difficult than she thought.

Moira steeled herself before she continued. "A long

time ago, another family, similar to yours but evil, came to these shores and started making all sorts of trouble. Your ancestors tried to defeat them, but failed. The fighting is still going on. Your gran, tired of all the fighting, wanted more for her children. That's the real reason why she fled to the states. She only came back once, just after her parents died. It was during that last visit that she locked away your family's book and placed protections around the house. She hoped that with the book safely locked away and her nowhere to be found, the dark family would lose interest and leave her and her descendants alone."

"Why did she send me there then?" Erin asked. This was the one thing that she was having the hardest time understanding. Why would her grandmother send her somewhere that she would be in danger?

"She hoped that they would honor the pact," Moira sighed. She saw Erin's confused look. "During the Witch Trials, your family and the dark family came to a sort of truce," Moira explained. "In order to prevent the Inquisitors from crashing down on them both, they agreed to not harm anyone who didn't know the families' true identities and about the war."

"So are you a witch too?" Erin asked. Moira started to laugh heartily, much to the confusion of Erin.

"No, I'm no witch," Moira laughed. "I *made* your grandma tell me her secret when we were younger."

"You were willing to put yourself in danger for

gran?"

"Of course," Moira replied. "Although, I didn't know I was putting myself in danger at the time. I just knew that your gran was keeping something from me. She is my best friend. It doesn't matter that we're not in the same part of the world or that we haven't seen each other in years. She is my soul friend and I am hers. I would walk through Hell itself for her, and I know that she would do the same for me."

Erin was taken aback by the conviction in Moira's voice. Erin sat in awe of the older woman's devotion to her grandmother.

"The new head of the dark family, however, is ruthless and that's the reason why he came after me. He's been testing you from the moment you arrived. I suppose he wanted to see how much you knew. Since I already knew the whole story, it meant that I was fair game."

"But why?" Erin asked. "Why go after you? Why not just come and attack me outright?"

"You're protected," Moira replied simply. "Your house and the land it sits on are protected by your grandmother's magic, not to mention your ancestors'. He couldn't touch you, even if he wanted to, and he does. He attacked me in hopes of exposing you, and therefore, drawing you into the fight."

Erin cursed her luck. She was the only person she

knew who was so unfortunate that, while trying to escape a bad situation, would end up stumbling into a worse one. She really couldn't be too surprised though, given her current track record. She sighed and ran her hand through her hair.

"Moira, who is it?" Erin asked. Moira debated the question. She was under strict instructions from Elise not to tell Erin anything. But with all that was going on...in for a penny, in for a pound.

"Connor," Moira stated finally. "Connor Ferguson."

Seven

rin stared at the woman on the bed. Moira had to be mistaken. Connor was the last person that anyone would suspect of being a witch, or anything supernatural. There was nothing about him that screamed 'evil villain mastermind' either. Then again, whenever he was around, she always felt on-edge. Amara didn't like him, neither did her sister, and they were usually good judges in character. Erin shook her head. It was just too much for her to take in.

"You're joking," Erin accused.

"Oh, how I wish I was," Moira scoffed. "It's the truth, and you know it. I can see it in your eyes."

Erin leapt from the bed and paced around the

room. Over and over in her mind, she kept telling herself that Moira was still recovering from an illness. That she didn't know what she was talking about. But when has this woman ever led her astray? When has she been anything but precise? Moira watched Erin carefully, her eyes full of concern. She wanted to say something, but felt it would be better if the young woman came to her own conclusion.

"You're not thinking clearly," Erin told Moira. "The doctors have no idea what happened to you. You're still recovering from a deadly illness. Your thoughts are all muddled. You're doped up on painkillers and what not." Moira sighed and gave Erin a stern look.

"You can't keep denying what is right in front of your face," Moira told her. "You're being drawn into a war that your grandmother tried to save you from. I wasn't quite sure why she sent you here to begin with, but now I know that this is your place. I'm sorry for exposing you to all of this, but I was afraid of dying. I didn't want to leave my family. I didn't want to leave you."

Erin sat hard on the couch. Everything she knew was wrong. She wasn't safe here. This wasn't her home, no matter what Moira had just told her. She would never be able to escape from those who wanted to hurt her. She felt herself beginning to crumble under the weight of it all, when something inside her rebelled. All of this was just too ridiculous to be true. There are no such things as witches, light or dark. There cannot have been a war that raged for centuries without someone noticing something, anything, by now.

"I think you should get some rest now Moira," Erin coolly stated. "You've only just waken up and you shouldn't exert yourself. I will see you tomorrow."

"Erin —please wait!" begged Moira. "Don't run from it. You can't run from it. It's a part of who you are. Please believe me!"

Erin ignored Moira's pleas and walked out without looking back. She wasn't about to let the addled mind of an elderly woman, no matter who she was, destroy what little peace she had in her life. Erin had been through too much and suffered for long enough. Moira's fantasies would fade in time and she would probably be embarrassed by them, once she regained her wits. Erin made up her mind to never speak of what she had heard to anyone, ever again.

Erin never made it back to the hospital the next day, or the day after that. A week had passed before she even allowed herself to think about what had happened between her and Moira. She knew from Caelan that Moira was steadily getting better. The doctors where still wary about letting Moira go, however, since they still had no idea on the cause of her illness. She also would occasionally have minor relapses, all which meant an even longer stay for the elderly woman. Caelan asked Erin repeatedly when she was going to come for another visit, because Moira was asking for her, almost frantically.

Moira hadn't told her daughter what it was about, which made Erin grateful, but Moira was insistent all the same to see Erin again. Erin made her excuses, but promised to stop by on the weekend. She meant to keep her promise, even though she still had some reservations about facing Moira. She hoped that Moira would apologize for freaking her out, but a small part of her knew that wouldn't happen.

The night before she planned visit, Erin kept herself busy in the kitchen, whipping up a batch of lavender scones for Moira and her family. Erin had to work a mid-morning shift the next day, so she wouldn't have time to cook beforehand. This also meant that she had a good excuse to cut the visit short if need be. Once the scones were out of the oven, she was ready for bed.

For some reason, she felt uneasy as she climbed into bed. Something was wrong, but she couldn't figure out what it was. All the doors and windows were locked. All the lights were turned off. She hadn't left anything on in the kitchen. She sighed as she rearranged the pillows. It reminded her of when she waited anxiously for her ex-husband to come home after work. Sometimes he would be in a good mood, but more often than not he burst through the door like a storm cloud, destroying everything in his wake. Erin tried to ignore the feeling, but it lingered like a bad scent.

Fae picked up on it too. His green eyes scanned every inch of the bedroom, while his tail swished madly about. To Erin, it looked like he was hunting for something. She sighed again, tucking the covers up around her face. She figured that she was just uncomfortable about seeing Moira tomorrow. *Yes,* she thought, *that's why I'm so wound up. Well, there's nothing I can do about it. I just need to go to get over it.* She reached out to pull Fae in close. Even though she had rationalized her fears, the warmth from Fae helped her to relax enough to finally fall asleep.

It was in the dead of night when Erin sat up in her bed, drenched in a cold sweat. She could have sworn that she had heard something crash —something enormous. She would even swear that she felt her bed shake. Fae must have heard it too, because he was up as well, staring intently at the corner of the farthest end of the room. His tail twitched and he hissed.

"What is it?" Erin whispered.

Fae yowled, launching himself at the corner. Erin thought that she saw something move in the shadows, but she couldn't be completely sure; it was just too dark. Fae lunged again, and this time, Erin knew that she had seen something move. It looked like the shape of a man. Her heart jumped up into her throat. The first thought through her head was *Oh god, he found me.* Despite her grandmother's reassurances, Erin always carried the fear that her ex would find her. Amara and Laura had; who's to say that John couldn't? While Erin had enjoyed their visits, it had proved to her that she wasn't as hard to find as she liked.

Erin threw the covers back as she rolled out of bed. She crouched behind her bed, terrified that the shadow in her room was her ex-husband. In that moment, she had reverted back to the abused housewife. All her strength, confidence, and defiance flew right out the window. She watched as Fae attacked the shadow man over and over. As she watched, she noticed that something was off about the fight between Fae and the shadow man.

Fae's claws seemed to pass through the shape more often than not. If it was John, he would have at least shouted once by now. But the shadow man was unnaturally silent as the cat repeatedly attacked him. He also kept to the shadows. John would have made his presence known the moment he arrived. The shadow man didn't even seem to notice Fae at all. He swatted at the cat as if it was a nuisance. The shadow man was more interested in looking around the room —searching for something, or someone.

"Who are you, and what are you doing in my house!" Erin demanded, braver than she felt. She was grateful her voice didn't shake as much as her body. The intruder apparently wasn't her ex-husband, but it was still an intruder.

The shadow man turned towards Erin. He took a step towards her, which caused her to back up, keeping the same space between them. He took another couple of steps towards her. She backed up as much as she could, until she felt her back press up against the wall. She spared a quick glance towards the door. Lightning fast, the shadow man was between her and the door. Her jaw dropped. There was no way that any living man could move that fast and that quietly. What the hell was in her room?

Fae leapt across the bed to place himself in front of Erin, hissing at the thing that threatened his mistress. Much to Erin's surprise, Fae's eyes started to glow a vibrant green. *As if my night couldn't get any stranger*, she thought calmly. Erin received another nasty shock when Fae's glowing eyes irrupted into emerald flames that spread to cover his entire body. Erin and the shadow man screamed at the same time, but his scream didn't remotely sound human. She wasn't sure if she had actually heard it with her ears or in her mind. Regardless, she covered her ears, trying to make her body as small as possible, but she could feel the creature's roar in her bones.

Fae seemed to be perfectly fine, despite being on fire. The light from his flames illuminated Erin's room. She could see the shadow man clearly, and it confirmed her doubts about the thing in her room being human. It looked like someone had cut a man's shape from pure darkness, but did so poorly. It had an overly large head, but no neck. Its arms and legs were too long for its short but stocky body. It had no facial features at all, but that didn't stop Erin from feeling its eyes on her, nor stop her from hearing its roar. The creature roared, taking a swipe at the cat. Fae quickly jumped out of the way, but was caught by the creature's other arm.

Fae's light dimmed when he hit the wall. It then flickered out, leaving Erin in darkness once again. She watched as her cat's body slumped to the floor, lifeless. That sight filled her with a self-righteous rage. This creature had broken into her house and attacked her cat. Fae had been her companion since the day she had arrived. He was *her* cat, this was *her* home, and no one messed with what was hers —not anymore.

"Leave him alone!" Erin shouted. The creature turned its head towards her and laughed so cruelly that she started to sweat. It lunged at her so fast that she swore she never saw it move. The creature's hands wrapped around her throat and slammed her against the wall with enough force to crack the wall. She tried to free herself, but it was no use. Her hands just passed through it like a shadow. Lights danced in front of her eyes, and it was getting harder for her to think clearly. Just when she thought that she was going to pass out, the creature threw her across the room.

Erin hit the wall hard enough to dent it. The impact also knocked out what little breath she had. She slumped to the floor, gasping for air. She just laid there, too stunned to move, while the creature lumbered slowly towards her. *Get up!* yelled a voice in her mind. *Get up now or you **will** die.*

Erin shook her head and tried to crawl away but the

creature lunged at her again. This time it hit her with its fists. The creature pummeled her again and again, until her lip split and her nose bled. The creature picked her up once more and threw her to the other side of the room. This time, she tried to get away, but no matter how quickly she moved, the creature was always faster.

The creature was relentless in its attacks. Erin barely had time to catch her breath, let alone attempt to defend herself. She cried out when the creature broke her arm, and she thought that a few of her ribs had broken as well. She wished that she had a neighbor to come to her rescue, but on the other hand she was glad she didn't. What would that neighbor do against a creature that was made of shadows and inhumanly strong? Maybe once she was dead, the creature would disappear leaving her spirit to haunt the house like the rumors had said.

"Please stop," Erin begged. The creature tilted its head. for a brief moment, hope flared in Erin. That hope was crushed when the creature advanced towards her again. She heard the unmistakable sound of a sword being drawn. The creature raised the sword high above its head, and then lowered it slowly until the tip of the sword was pointed directly at her. She closed her eyes and readied herself for her inevitable death. She mentally told her family that she was sorry for disappearing without a word, and that she loved them. She forgave everyone who had ever done her wrong, even her ex-husband. If she was about to leave this earth, she would do it with a clear conscience, nothing to hold her back.

As the creature poised for the final blow, a blinding, white light erupted, filling the room. Erin closed her eyes against the light, but they still stung. She heard the creature roar again, but also thought that she heard a man scream as well. She briefly wondered if someone had, in fact, come to her rescue. She heard the sword clank as it hit the floor. She strained her ears trying to hear what, if anything was happening but heard nothing other than the sound of her own breath. Slowly, the light began to dim enough for her to open her eyes.

The source of the light was the bracelet on Erin's wrist —her grandmother's farewell gift. The creature was gone, but she wasn't alone. Dozens of people were standing in her bedroom. She thought they looked like ghosts. She struggled to get to her feet and realized that she felt no pain. A quick check of her body told her that some, if not all of her injuries had been healed. She looked around her room as she stood up. Miraculously, or magically, her room had been fixed as well. Not one item was out of place and the sword that the creature had dropped was gone. Fae meowed weekly as he limped over to her. Erin cried as she picked him up, bringing him close to her heart.

Erin stood to face the ghostly people. They didn't appear threatening, but after what she had just been through, she wasn't going to take any chances. The ghosts met her stare without flinching. They seemed to be waiting for her to make the first move.

"Um…thank you," Erin ventured. The ghosts smiled. "Not to seem rude or anything but who are you?" The ghosts laughed without making a sound, which freaked her out, if truth be told. One of the ghosts, a woman, walked forward, stopping a few feet from Erin. Fae leapt out of Erin's arms and trotted up to the ghost woman, rubbing his body against hers purring loudly. As Erin stared at the ghostly woman, she felt a chill run up her spine. She felt like she had seen the woman before.

"Yes you have seen me before," the ghost woman said, as if she had read Erin's mind. "I am your great-grandmother, Clara," she stated with a smile. "I must say that I love what you've done with my old home. I was sad when my daughter, your grandmother, abandoned this house. I knew that it wouldn't be long before it started to decay. Well, that's what happens when a house sits. Which is odd when you think about it; an empty house decaying faster than an occupied one? But I suppose what keeps a house standing is the life force of those who dwell within its walls." One of the other ghosts cleared its throat. Clara blushed. Erin didn't know that ghosts could blush. "That aside, you asked who we are and the answer is this: you are us and we are you."

"Okay…" Erin said slowly. Clara chuckled a bit and waved her hands in front of her chest, murmuring words that Erin couldn't make out. A ball of red light formed in the middle of Clara's chest. The light stretched to Erin's chest, and then spread to each of the ghosts. Erin's eyes widened once she understood. "You're my ancestors!" she exclaimed. The ghosts smiled and nodded their heads. Another ghost walked forward to stand beside Clara.

"My name is Kieran," the ghost informed Erin. Erin's jaw dropped. This ghost was supposedly the one that her family descended from.

"Many centuries ago I had a terrible vision about the destruction of my family and everything I held dear," Kieran told Erin. "The threat was a family like ours, but who chose to walk the dark path. However, when that family finally came, I had already passed from this world.

"This is the way of visions," Kieran said with a shrug. "Time is always unclear, however, none of that matters right now because this war stands at a crossroads. You have to learn how to use the abilities that bless our bloodline, or everything we fought to protect will be destroyed, and my vision will come to pass."

"Connor is part of this dark family," Erin stated, wanting confirmation. Kieran nodded. Erin slumped to the floor again, only this time it was due to shock, rather than exhaustion. "I can't," she mumbled.

"You must," Kieran commanded. "If you do not, everyone you love will die: your mother, sister, grandmother, and even your father. Connor will not leave any member of your family alive."

"Why *now*?" Erin moaned.

"The barriers that protected you and this house have been broken. The magic that placed them has faded. If you do not do something soon, Connor and his kin will steal our family's heritage. This attack was only the first..." Clara explained. "I know this is a lot to take in right now..."

"No kidding," Erin muttered.

"You only have two choices: run or fight," Kieran stated. "We cannot tell you what to do, only guide you."

To Erin, it seemed like she only had one choice. Her ancestors were trying to urge her into a fight that she wasn't in the slightest bit prepared for. She really wanted to deny it all, run away, and never look back. She shook her head. She knew that she couldn't do that. After what had just happened, she knew that it was better to face it head on instead, of running like she always had. But she was scared. She didn't know how to deal with this, or even where she should start.

"Use the book," one of her ancestors offered, as if he had read Erin's mind. "It will show you what you need to do."

"Trust in your own strength," said another. "You are stronger than you realize."

"Learn from the past," spoke Kieran, "to safe-guard the future."

Erin nodded her head, but inside she was seething.

She wanted answers, not cryptic messages. What she really wanted was for it all to go away. She wasn't in a position — mentally or physically— to get tangled up in a fight. She sighed, wishing that her ancestors would leave, giving her the peace to sort through this on her own. They may be family, but ghosts were ghosts, and therefore, unnerving.

Whether the ancestors saw Erin's thoughts, or had finished their business, one by one, they faded away, until only Kieran and Clara remained. The two seemed to be having a silent argument. Erin suspected this because of the way they moved their hands and the expressions on their faces. Kieran sighed and faded as well, leaving Erin with her great-grandmother.

"You must forgive Kieran and the others," Clara said, shaking her head. "They lived during the height of our family's power, and Kieran has always been quick to fight. I know that this is a lot to take in right now, but the choice is still yours. You don't have to fight, but you *do* need to be able to protect yourself." Clara's words comforted Erin. Protecting herself she could do. "Could I ask a small favor of you?"

"Sure," Erin replied.

"I understand why my daughter made the choices that she did. I too wanted to save her from this life, but this isn't something that you can run from —not for long. When you speak to her, please let her know that I love her and that I forgive her."

Erin was surprised. She had figured that Clara would have been angry with her daughter, not understanding. She studied her great-grandmother's face. It was serene and sad. Clara missed her daughter, and didn't care that she had turned her back on everything that she knew. That gave Erin hope that she and her own mother could one day repair their bond. She gave her great-grandmother a small smile, which Clara returned.

Clara started to fade, but then stopped, as if she had remembered something else she had to tell Erin. "I have one more piece of advice to offer you. Learn to love again, Erin. Love will help to ease the burdens of this life. Open your heart to those who want to be in your life. Also, take good care of Fae." Erin tilted her head, confused. "Consider him a house warming gift... although, I think he would be here whether we asked him to or not."

Clara walked up to Erin and placed a kiss on her forehead. The kiss filled Erin with so much love and peace that it brought tears to her eyes. Clara bid farewell to Erin once more, then faded away, leaving Erin alone. Fae rubbed up against her, purring, letting her know that she wasn't entirely alone. She wondered what other surprises he had in store for her. She realized that she didn't care whether or not he was supernatural. He had come to her defense. He also was her friend. He welcomed her home at the end of the day, and comforted her when she needed it.

Erin bent down to pick Fae up. She looked around her bedroom again; everything looked as it should. Her mind was still reeling from the night's events. Now that she had her peace and quiet, she wasn't sure what to do next.

Too wound up to go back to bed, Erin walked down to the kitchen. She made herself a cup of coffee and opened several cans of tuna for Fae. He had earned them. She smiled at the sounds he made as he devoured the cans. Watching her pet eat, Erin was reminded of how close she came to losing him and her own life. Her rage came back in full.

If Erin's family had been fighting for this long, why hadn't they found some way to win? One would have thought that by now *someone* would have done something to end it. Why did it fall to her now, and more importantly, just how in the world was she supposed to accomplish what generations of her family could not? She slammed her mug down on the table, ignoring the burning sensation as hot coffee splashed on her hand.

Erin wanted answers and she was going to get answers. Her ancestors hadn't given her any, not really, not the ones she wanted right now. There was only one person who could give them to her. She yanked the phone off the wall and angrily punched in the numbers. She waited impatiently for the person to pick up on the other end. She glared at the phone, daring the person not to pick up. The phone continued to ring. She twined the cord around her fingers. Finally, the ringing stopped as the person finally picked up the phone.

"Hello Erin," her grandmother said calmly on the other end. "I figured you would be calling soon."

Eight

How could you!" Erin shouted into the phone. She didn't care that her grandmother answered like she knew it was her who was calling. Her grandmother was a witch, so why shouldn't she be able to tell who was calling her? "You told me that I would be safe here. You said that no one could hurt me here. You said that I could start over!"

"I'm sorry," Elise calmly replied.

"You're sorry?" Erin repeated, "For what, huh? Sorry that you sent me here without knowing how to protect myself against Connor and his messed up family? Sorry that you never told me, or my mother for that matter, that we're witches? Or maybe you're sorry that you ran away, leaving your *granddaughter* to clean up *your* mess!"

Erin breathed heavily, waiting for her grandmother to say something, anything. She heard Elise sigh heavily. "I never thought that they would have gone after you. By our laws, you should have been left alone, especially since you don't...didn't know anything." Erin remained silent. She didn't quite trust herself to not start yelling again. Plus, she wanted answers. "I felt the barriers break. Tell me what happened."

"I don't even know where to start," Erin snorted.

"Start with tonight," suggested Elise. Erin took a deep breath and then told her grandmother about the strange feeling she had had before she went to bed and why she had woken up. She described the creature that had attacked her and how Fae had tried to protect her. She ended her tale with the ancestors showing up and what they had told her. The whole time she spoke, her grandmother just listened, not interrupting her once. For that, Erin was grateful. It felt good to unburden herself.

"Tell me more about Fae," Elise prompted, when Erin had finished.

"Well, I found him shortly after I got here. And according to great-grandma Clara, they sent him to me."

"Other than tonight, has he shown any other signs that he's not what he appears?" Erin looked at her pet, who was fast asleep, and told her grandmother no. "I can't be sure until I see him, but I'm fairly certain that he is fae."

"That's his name," Erin replied lamely.

"That's not what I mean, Erin, and you know it," chided Elise. "I think he's a fairy cat."

"You can't be serious," choked Erin.

"Like I said, I can't be sure until I see him for myself. Even if he's not, you should take good care of him, because he is most definitely your familiar." Erin looked at Fae again, who was now watching her intensely. "You should start paying more attention to how he reacts towards the people around you. Honestly, he should go everywhere you go."

"Gran I can't do that," Erin said. "For one, people would say something, and two…"

"Who cares what people will say?" Erin's grandmother snapped. "Until you learn how to defend yourself, Fae is the only one who can stand up to whatever Connor sends your way. If he hadn't been here tonight, you would be dead."

Erin stared at the phone. Her grandmother never yelled, especially at her. "Well then, how do I defend myself?" Erin demanded. No matter what her grandmother called Fae, Erin was not about to place her life into a cat's hands —or paws. Her grandmother sighed on the other end.

"The first thing you need to do is set protection wards around yourself and the house. The ones I laid are gone. To do this, you need to enter the astral plain."

"The astral plain?" Erin repeated.

"It is the space between this world and the other world," Elise explained. "It looks like a land made of mist."

"No!" Erin shouted into the phone. "I won't go back there!"

"What in the world do you mean 'back there'?" Elise demanded.

"You know that Laura came to visit me a while back? I showed her the book, and Laura being Laura, wanted to try something. We did this meditation thing to talk to our ancestors, or whatever, and ended up in the astral plain." Erin shivered just thinking about it. "We got attacked by something. I never really saw what it looked like. It stayed under the mist. Luckily, I was able to bring us back... somehow." Erin shuddered again, "So, like I said before, I'm not going back there." Her grandmother was silent. Erin could almost hear the wheels turning in her head through the phone.

"Erin, I want you to listen to me carefully," Elise said slowly. "Magic isn't how it is in the movies or on TV. It's more subtle than that. Our gifts are meant to work alongside nature, and it takes a lot out of us." Erin nodded, remembering how tired she felt after she did the spell to heal Moira. "It takes time and skill to be able to channel magic on this plain without tiring out, but you don't have time for that. The astral plain will help you learn faster. It's easier to call and channel magic there."

"But we were attacked there," Erin pleaded.

"There are ways to protect yourself," Elise told Erin. "You can create a 'safe place' there to practice." Erin's grandmother paused. Erin found herself holding her breath. "But you are right about one thing...I should have handled this before now."

"Gran..." Erin whispered.

"At least now I can do something to correct my mistake. I don't want you going after Connor, Erin," Elise said.

Erin snorted. "Fat chance."

"You never know," Elise commented. "Just learn enough to keep yourself —and those you care about —safe until I can get to you. I have to do a few things first...it may take a while."

Erin could hear the uncertainty in her grandmother's voice. "Gran, it's okay," Erin said. "I think I can manage until you can get here. I have Fae. I have the book; and I have Moira."

Erin heard her grandmother laugh. "Alright, Erin. Hold down the fort until I arrive."

"Do you know how long you'll be?" Erin asked.

"I'm not sure," Elise replied. "But do not hesitate to call me if things change."

"I won't," Erin promised. She was about to say goodbye, when she remembered something. "Gran, wait...great-grandma Clara wanted me to tell you that she doesn't hate you for what you did. She said that she would have done the same if she could've."

Erin felt her grandmother freeze on the other end of the line. She could almost see her gran raising her hand to her mouth, tears forming in her eyes. "Thank you Erin," Elise said softly, and then hung up.

Erin stood in her kitchen trying to process everything that had happened over the past few hours. She realized that she had forgotten to ask why Connor and his family were trying so hard to kill her and her family. She almost called her grandmother back, but didn't. She really didn't want to know —at least, not yet.

"One problem at a time," Erin told herself. As she glanced out the widow, she noticed the soft light of dawn. She groaned.

"I'm too wound up to sleep anyway," Erin said, rubbing her burning eyes. "I guess there's no time like the present." She quickly made a pot of coffee, and then headed out to the study to collect her family's spell book. She still balked at the idea, but she was too worn down to keep fighting it.

Erin placed the book on the kitchen table. But she didn't open it. She took her time making her coffee. She stared at the book as she sipped. Part of her didn't want to open it, but another part, the larger part, was not about to turn up anything that could help her, and her family's, survival.

Erin ran her hand over the cover, feeling the ancient leather. She opened it and flipped through it, not really looking for anything. *So witches are real,* she thought, *and I'm one of them.* She wondered how many more were out there in the world, living seemingly normal lives. How many every-day people were hiding the fact that they were witches? Not the neo-pagan variety, but real spell-casting witches? She wondered if there were any who lived near her. She hoped so. She stopped flipping through the pages when she came across a section dedicated to familiars. She glanced at Fae from the corner of her eye. He was up on the counter watching her.

"So you're my familiar?" Erin asked. Much to her surprise, Fae nodded his head. She had to sit down. "Can you talk?" Fae nodded *and* shook his head. "Which one is it: yes or no?" He sighed and leapt to the table. He walked over to her and sat down. He patted the book with his paw. "OK I get it," Erin said, smirking in spite of herself.

"'Familiars are a witches greatest asset,'"," Erin read aloud. "'They serve as guides, teachers, protectors, and companions. Familiars choose whom they wish to serve; although, a witch can summon a familiar for help...'"

Erin spent the rest of the morning reading about familiars. She was actually surprised at the amount of information the book held. Familiars, apparently, were a big deal for witches. There was a whole page detailing how familiars should be treated by their masters; it made her head spin. Fae had crawled into her lap to read along with her. As she petted him, she found that she was glad to have a familiar. He had already proved himself to be an ally and a friend. She really needed both of those right now.

Several hours later, Erin sat back and rubbed her tired eyes. Her mind was swimming with all that she had learned. "I think I should take a break." She got up and made another pot of coffee; she had emptied the other long ago. As she waited for it to brew, she realized that she was starving. She was prone to forgetting to eat when she delved into a new subject. Her roommate in college often had to drag Erin away from her books just to get her to eat.

Erin reheated some left-overs and let Fae out. She sat at the table, munching tiredly, and continued to flip through the book. She was still trying to get a feel for what the book contained. She found the 'charm' section particularly interesting because, according to the book, charms and talismans required less of a witch's power. What made them even more appealing to her was that they could be used more than once. She felt like a freshman all over again. There was so much that she had to learn.

Strangely, Erin was excited. She always had a love of learning. She loved it when she discovered something that changed the way that she looked at the world. If learning that magic and witches were real didn't change the way she looked at the world then nothing would. She felt foolish for denying this fact for so long, especially after Laura's visit, but she was stubborn to a fault. None of that mattered anymore. Erin had a plan of attack, so to speak. She just needed to learn enough to survive until her grandmother arrived, and then she could go back to...Erin had no idea how to finish that thought. She couldn't go back to how she had lived before— not really. A whole new world was open to her now and that made her feel surprisingly hopeful.

Erin squeezed in a shower and a much needed nap before she tackled the challenge of protecting not only herself but those she cared for. She was still wary of entering the astral plain again, no matter what her grandmother had said. She chose to experiment with charms instead. It was rather easy to gather all the supplies; she had most on hand already. She made a trip up to the attic to see if there was anything in the chest where she had found the book. She found various stones and what not at the very bottom; with these she was able to create the charms.

The charm for protection was quite simple. It

consisted of a clove of garlic from her pantry, a pin, and a tiger's eye stone. The ingredients were placed in a white cloth and bound with red thread. Erin made three: one was for her, another for Moira, and the last one to place in Haven. She wasn't sure if Connor would leave her place of work alone, but she figured it would be better to be safe than sorry.

Fae watched as Erin made the charms. She swore that he looked disappointed. "I'm not ready yet, Fae," she told him as she tied each sachet up. "Can't you just give me some more time?" He blinked slowly. She took that as an acceptance. With the last of the sachets tied up, all that was left was to charge them. This was the part that made her nervous. If she didn't do it properly, the protection charms would be weak— or not work at all.

Erin took a deep breath before she placed her hands on the first charm. If she did this, she would be taking her first steps towards accepting her role as a Guardian. She didn't count the spell she had done for Moira, because that was done out of desperation and not a conscious choice. If she did this, there would be no going back. She closed her eyes and focused her thoughts on the small bundle. She focused on what she wanted the sachet to do. She was surprised when her hands began to heat up and tingle. She kept focusing, pouring as much of her will into the sachet as she could. The burning sensation left her hands, and left her head aching.

Fae mewed. "I'm ok," Erin said, shaking her hands.

Erin did the same for the second sachet, only this time she had to grab the counter to steady herself once she had finished. She had to wait for the room to stop spinning before she attempted the last one. Fae's tail twitched madly. She took a deep breath and charged the last charm. She fought to keep her focus. Once she was done with the final sachet, her legs gave way. She fought to keep consciousness.

"I'm okay," Erin said over and over again.

After a few minutes, Erin's world stopped spinning and she was able to pull herself up. She was exhausted, but excited at the same time. She had done it. She had taken her first steps towards becoming a Guardian. She hadn't realized until this moment that she actually wanted to be one. All of her life, she had looked out for people. She was the friend to call if you were in trouble. She was the sympathetic ear and the giver of advice. She finally saw that, even though her grandmother had tried to break free, she had failed. Protecting people was in their blood. No matter what they did in life, Erin's family would always put themselves in danger to protect others.

Erin spent the rest of the day lazing about. She barely had the strength to do anything else. As soon as she was able to move without feeling like she wanted to vomit, she got in her truck and drove to the hospital. The sooner she gave Moira the protection sachet, the better. Not surprisingly, Moira knew something was up the moment Erin walked in.

"I really don't want to talk about it," Erin said, holding her hand up. She collapsed into a chair. She reached into her bag and pulled out a small, white pouch. "Here," she said, holding it out for Moira, who looked both happy and sad.

"Erin," Moira whispered, holding the sachet close to her chest.

"You're right. I can't fight it anymore," Erin said calmly. "I talked to my gran." Moira's eyes widened. "She said she'll get here as soon as she can, but until then..."

Moira's eyes started to water. "Thank you." Erin waved her off. Even though Moira had willing placed herself into the line of fire, she felt responsible for her. If anything were to happen to Moira, then it would be her fault. While she sat with Moira, she had fallen asleep in the chair. Moira let her, even though she had a thousand questions of her own. She figured that Erin would tell her in her own time. Until then, Moira had to focus on getting better.

Erin's next stop was Haven. Stephen smiled as she walked in. "Lord, girl,, he said, "you look terrible!"

"Hello to you too," Erin shot back. Stephen blushed. "I just had a rough night," she explained. He tried to apologize, but Erin waved him off. She was anxious for him to leave. She needed to stash the protection sachet somewhere that no one would find it. Thankfully, he left for a few hours shortly after she had arrived.

Erin walked around the bookstore, looking for the best place to hide the charm. She needed to put it in a place where Kayle or Stephen wouldn't discover it accidentally. Erin also wanted to put it where Connor wouldn't be able to even enter the shop at all. Ideally, she would have just hung it over the door, but that would raise too many questions. Behind the register was definitely off limits, and so was the office and the break room. She thought about putting it on top of a tall bookcase, but Kayle was adamant about dusting everything. Erin sighed as she pushed a rolling cart laden with books towards the door. She was just about to stick it behind a picture or something, when the cart crashed against something, causing several books to fall.

As Erin placed the books back, she discovered the cause for the crash: a stone that was against the outside of the bookstore had come loose and had shifted. She smiled. She had found a hiding place. It was actually perfect. Since she couldn't hang it over the threshold, the next best thing would be to bury it next to it. It didn't take her long to pull up the loose stone and dig a small hole underneath it. She dug the charm out of her pocket, placed it in the hole, and then placed the stone back. She stepped on the stone, pressing it back down into the earth.

As Erin dusted her hands, she looked down the alley

and froze. Standing at the opening, looking very dapper in a tweed jacket and cap, stood Connor. He was smirking at her. The more she stared at him, the greater her anger grew. If it wasn't for him, she would be living a normal life. She noticed another man walk up next to Connor. She noted the resemblance between the two. The other man was shorter, but he had the same hair and the same eyes, which bore an identical expression to Connor's.

Erin swallowed her fear and tilted her chin up daring, Connor to say something. But he never did. He just tipped his hat to her and sauntered on. The other man smiled toothily at her and licked his lips. She showed no emotion and watched as the man followed Connor. When they were out of sight, she quickly went back inside and closed the door. It was only then that she allowed her fear to wash over her.

Erin's body trembled, and she was drenched in a cold sweat. She wondered who the other man was. He clearly was related to Connor in some way. She shook her head. It didn't matter who the other man was, because, judging by the look he had given her, he was on Connor's side. She began to question her decision about delaying putting up the wards. She was still scared of the astral plain, but there were beasts on Earth's plain too, and they wouldn't be stopped by a few measly charms.

Erin was so tense by the time she got home that she

felt like a feather could have shattered her. Fae was there to greet her, but his demeanor showed that he was as tense as she was. His tail twitched madly. She groaned, dropping her bag by the door.

"I know," Erin told him. She rubbed her eyes frustrated. "Will you help me with the wards?" Fae nodded his head, and then lead her to the kitchen. He jumped up on the table and patted the book with his paw. Curious, she followed. Under his paw was, according to the book, the easiest way to enter the astral plain. She gulped, and with shaking hands, touched the passage. This was it. She was going to enter the astral plain again.

Erin knew she needed to calm down before she attempted to cross over. According to the book, if she didn't want to, then she wouldn't. It took a long bath, a light meal, and several shots of liquor before she felt like she could brave the astral plain.

"You'll be with me?" Erin asked Fae again. He nodded and settled down in her lap. She exhaled and tried to clear her mind. Easier said than done, but after what seemed like hours, she found herself standing in the familiar mist-filled plain. She looked around nervously for Fae and for any signs of an attack, growing more anxious by the second.

"Not bad at all." Erin jumped when she heard the deep, lilting voice behind her. She let out a startled shout when she felt something brush against her legs. Relieved, she saw that it was only Fae. She quickly bent down to pick him up.

"I think there's someone else here," Erin whispered to Fae.

"No, it's just the two of us," Fae replied. Erin was so startled to hear him speak that she dropped him.

"You can talk!" cried Erin. She briefly wondered when she would stop being amazed.

"Ye didn't have to drop me," Fae said indignantly, shaking himself off. "But to answer yer question, I can, but only here."

"Why?"

Fae shrugged. "That's just the way it works. Donnat ask me." Erin crossed her arms over her chest. He waited patiently by her feet. She swore that he was laughing at her. This made her angry. He had no right to laugh at her when she was obviously new to this world. She let herself relax a little, determined to show him that she could handle it.

"So how do I do wards from here?" Erin asked finally.

"In due time, love," replied Fae. "I think you better make yer mark first." Erin looked confused, but he didn't give her a chance to ask questions. "Close yer eyes and picture a place where ye feel safe. It donnat have to be perfect...just get the gist of it."

Erin obeyed, but nothing came to mind. Her first thought was her parent's house, but she hadn't felt safe there in a while. Her current home came up too, but she no longer felt safe there. Suddenly she had a place...from long ago. It was the one place that hadn't been tainted by her divorce, her current situation, or anything else. Memories of her time there flowed freely, bringing a smile to her lips. Once the images faded, she opened her eyes and gasped.

Instead of the open field with the mists, Erin stood in front of a cabin, deep in the woods. It sat a little way up on a hill. And even though she couldn't see it, she knew that there was a river just a few minutes' walk from it. The air smelled of summer: the sun, growing things, and the wet earth.

"Not bad at all," Fae commented as he surveyed the land. "Why this particular place...if ye don't mind me askin'?"

"I used to come here every summer with my family when I was little," Erin explained. "My sister and I used to pretend that this cabin was in the fairy world and that the woods protected us from monsters." Fae tilted his head. "It really felt that way. This place would be magical to any child." The smile on her face faded. "But there's no protection here."

"Oh, I wouldn't say that," Fae commented.

"And why is that?" Erin asked.

"Not all protection is stone and mortar," Fae stated. "Sometimes it *is* an enchanted forest. This will do nicely."

Fae trotted up to the door of the cottage and pushed it open with his paw. Erin rushed to follow. Inside was just as she had remembered it. There even was the smell of cookies that her mom had always baked. She walked slowly, touching everything. She understood that it wasn't really there, but it still felt so real.

"Fae can I ask you a question?" Fae, who had jumped on a table, nodded. Erin bit her lip and asked, "Why is Connor's family so adamant about killing mine? What do we have that they want so bad?" He regarded her solemnly, but then broke out into a huge grin. Or at least, she hoped it was a grin.

"I knew ye were smart, lass," Fae boasted. "I knew that once things settled a bit, ye'd start askin' the big questions." He continued to grin at her for a while, and then got serious again. "He wants yer power, darling, and the only way he can have it is if yer dead."

"What?" Erin said, stunned, and sat down.

Fae sighed. "Yer magic is connected to yer soul. Witches like him only want one thing— more power. But to get that, they have to kill. When ye die, yer magic goes back to the world, and it is at that time that it can be stolen." Erin nodded. "He can also use yer magic to tap into yer family's, and that would cause them to also die."

Erin paled. She was glad that she was already sitting down. "And our book?" she ventured.

"He'd take that as well and use yer family's spells for ill."

Once again, Erin nodded. Gaining power was something that she understood, even though she didn't strive for it. Her father was a businessman, and he was always on the lookout for new ways to get a step-up on the competition. Both of her grandfathers were businessmen as well. The community that she grew up in was filled with people who either had quite a bit of power or were constantly trying to get more. She had seen these people do terrible things in order to obtain it. Connor may be magical, but his desires were purely worldly.

"Well, we can't have that can we?" Erin remarked coolly. She was rewarded with another smile from Fae. "I have a lot to learn and not much time to do it. So, let's get the wards set and be on our way."

"Let's start with the house," said Fae. "Basically, all ye got to do is place these stones, in opposite colors, around the area that ye want to be protected."

Erin was about to ask him what he was talking about, when she noticed a replica of her house sitting on the table. Next to it were two piles of stones, one black and the other white. She was about to ask where those things came from, but stopped. What was the point of asking? She had to learn to roll with the punches and only ask questions when she really needed to.

Erin walked up to the table and saw that her yard, the barn, and the study were all included as well. She picked up the stones and placed them so that the house and the study were enclosed in the circle; although it was more of a square. She wondered if she should do more, but she didn't want to overexert herself.

"Now just picture a while line going from stone to stone," Fae instructed. "Once ye do that, hold that image and create a dome."

Erin tried, but couldn't manage to hold both images at the same time. Fae encouraged her, until finally, she was able to. When he told her it was done, she opened her eyes and saw that what she had envisioned was mirrored by the model. More importantly, she wasn't tired. She couldn't stop herself from smiling.

"Is there anywhere else ye like to set a ward?" Fae asked.

Erin didn't even question it, and no sooner than she had thought about the places, their models appeared. There was Moira's hospital room and house, and Haven. Erin repeated the process for each, and was only a little dizzy from her effort.

"Now comes the hard part," Fae said calmly.

"There's more?" Erin cried. True, she wasn't as tired, but it wouldn't take much to push her over the edge.

"Oh yeah," Fae said somberly. "Now ye got to tell the wards what they're protecting ye from. Ye got to be as specific as ye can. Otherwise, things will get through."

Erin's first thought was to keep Connor out, but that wasn't nearly enough. The past few days showed her that not only could he summon creatures that could do harm, but he had allies as well. She had no idea how many, or who they were. She bit her lip again. Clearly, this was the most important part, and she desperately wanted —no needed— to get it right.

Erin placed her hands on top of the dome that held her house, and just let her feelings take over. She wanted protection from those who would harm her —both mortal and supernatural. She wanted a safe haven for all of her friends and family. But most important, she wanted to have peace.

Erin felt a ball of heat form near her heart. The heat flowed down her arms to the model. There was a small flash of light that caused her to close her eyes. When she opened them, the dome was gone, but she knew that the ward had been set. Fae beamed at her, which let her know that she had made the right choice. She did the same for the other models. By the time she was finished, she was struggling to keep her eyes open. She wondered what would happen if she fell asleep in the astral plain.

Erin closed her eyes for just a second. When she opened them again, she was happy to see that she was back in her house. She smiled and slowly made her way upstairs. She didn't bother getting undressed. She just pulled back the sheets and crawled in. Fae leapt up and snuggled next to her, purring loudly. He was proud of her. She was proud of herself. She kissed the top of his head and then drifted off to sleep.

Nine

Erin woke up the next morning feeling like she had the worst hangover in the history of hangovers. The sunlight burned her eyes, her head pounded, and on top of all of that, her whole body hurt. When she tried to sit up, a wave of nausea hit her. She fell back down. She would have to call in sick, if she could get to the phone that is. She groaned, pulling the blankets over her head. Hopefully she'd feel better after a little more sleep. The next thing she knew, someone was calling her name.

"Erin, wake up." Erin opened her eyes to see an extremely distraught Caleb standing over her. "Thank god," Caleb exclaimed, bowing his head. It took her a few moments to register the fact that he was in her bedroom. Once she did, Erin sat up so quickly that she and Caleb banged heads. She had been holding on by a thread, and that pushed her over the edge. She made a mad scramble for the bathroom. She barely made it to the toilet before throwing up.

Caleb didn't try to come to her aid— something that she appreciated tremendously— but he was there with a glass of water when she came out. Her throat felt like sandpaper. The water helped to clear her head enough to question his presence in her bedroom.

"What are you doing here?" Erin croaked.

"Making sure that you hadn't die," Caleb replied. "No one's heard from you in three days."

"Three days!" Erin cried. Caleb nodded and helped her back into bed.

"But after what I just saw, I'm not surprised." Caleb smiled a little as he said that, but Erin was too worn out to feel embarrassed. "Have you eaten anything lately?" She shook her head. "Alright, you just take it easy. I'll let everyone know you're alive and fix you something, if you think you can handle it."

"Thank you," Erin said. She really meant it. As much as she hated being weak as a kitten, she was glad that there was someone she could count on. Caleb tucked the blankets around her. She was already falling back to sleep, so she couldn't be sure if he really did kiss her forehead or not before he went downstairs.

Caleb woke Erin sometime later. He helped her to sit up. Once she was comfortable, he placed a tray on her lap. She offered him a weak smile. He had made soup. Actually, it was more like broth with some bits in it. Either way, she was happy to have it. She carefully spooned the broth into her mouth. It was delicious. She stared at him, wide-eyed, with her spoon still in her mouth. He gave her his trademarked smirk, but said nothing. He waited until she had eaten before he said anything.

"It's not surprising that you got sick," Caleb commented, taking Erin's bowl. "The weather here bounces back and forth a lot." She knew that wasn't why she was sick, but she wasn't about to correct him. It was safer to lie, even though she hated doing it. "I already called your job to let them know. Kayle said to come back whenever you feel up to it."

"Thank you," Erin said, reaching for Caleb's hand. He rubbed his thumb over the top of her hand. She felt her cheeks heat up. Blushing, she slowly lifted her head and met his eyes. Big mistake. She wasn't ready for the emotion behind them. He wanted her, but he was holding back for her sake, giving her the room to make up her own mind. She tore her eyes away and that was when she noticed that something— someone, actually— was missing. "Where's Fae?"

"He ran out the door as soon as I opened it," Caleb said sitting back. The moment was gone much to her regret and relief. She wasn't sure which emotion was stronger.

"I'll go see if he's back and then finish supper." Erin knew that he was disappointed, even though he hid it well.

As soon as he closed the door, Erin buried her face in her pillow. She wanted to get closer to Caleb— truly she did. He was a great man. But she knew that she couldn't— not really. She couldn't tell him about what her family was. What she was. Not only would he probably freak out, but it would put him in danger. But you can't keep things hidden from someone you're in a relationship with; at least, she couldn't. Maybe, once things had settled down, she would tell him everything. She just hoped that he would still be around for her to do that.

Groaning, Erin got out of bed and heading once more, towards the bathroom. What she really wanted was a hot bath— something to ease her aches and pains, and something to give her time to think before she headed downstairs. As she waited for the tub to fill, she added bath oil and salts. She eased herself into the steaming water, sighing as her tight muscles relaxed. She tilted her head back so that it rested on the rim of the tub, closed her eyes. She just let her mind empty. She didn't allow a single thought to flit across it. The bath felt wonderful.

Erin was startled when Caleb knocked on the bathroom door. "Just letting you know that supper's ready whenever you are." Had she fallen asleep again? She figured that she must have. It was easier to move now, and the water was cool. She toweled off and pulled on sweats and a tank. She grabbed a light sweater, pulling it on before she headed downstairs.

Whatever Caleb had cooked smelled delicious. It made Erin's mouth water. She could hear him in the kitchen, humming. When she rounded the corner, it took everything in her not to laugh. He was wearing her frilly apron and dancing around the kitchen as he cleaned up a little. Fae sat on a stepstool, watching the large man with obvious amusement. When Fae noticed her, he meowed, causing Caleb to turn around.

Instead of being embarrassed, Caleb just smiled and motioned for her to sit. Fae jumped up into her lap, purring. He clearly approved of Caleb, which made her feel better about her attraction to him. She petted Fae, smiling, as she watched Caleb filled her plate. The food looked just as good as it smelled. Pan-seared lamb chops with potatoes and other veggies. She dug in at once. She didn't even need a knife to cut it; it was that tender. Flavors exploded in her mouth, causing her to close her eyes.

"Where did you learn to cook?" Erin asked in between mouthfuls.

"My mum," Caleb replied, setting down his own plate. "I was always in the kitchen, trying to steal bites. So one day, my mum handed me a spoon and said that if I was going to be underfoot, I should at least make myself useful." Erin chuckled.

"You learned your lessons well," Erin joked, taking another bite. Caleb toasted her and they fell into an easy silence. She tried to help clean up afterwards, but he brushed her off. She wasn't sure how she felt about being ordered about her own home, but he seemed to enjoy looking after her, so she figured there was no harm in letting him. If truth be told, she was still wobbly on her feet.

Caleb joined Erin in the living room to give her a cup of water and two pills. She faked taking the pills and handed the glass back. When he went back into the kitchen, she spit the pills out and hid them in the couch cushions. It wasn't that she didn't trust him. In fact, she trusted him greatly, but since she was little, she had been told to never take any medicine that she didn't need. She turned when she heard him coming back, and was sad to see that he was getting ready to leave.

"I guess I should be getting on," Caleb said, rubbing the back of his head anxiously. She wondered what caused the sudden change. Up until now, he had been carefree and silly, but now he seemed to be upset over something.

"Thank you for coming here and taking care of me," Erin told him. "I really meant it Caleb. I owe you one"

Caleb suddenly had a wicked gleam in his eye. "Well, you could always come over and have dinner with me." Erin was shocked and could only sit there with her mouth slightly open. Whatever she had expected him to say, definitely wasn't that. "My mum has been pestering me since she met you that one time...and since you owe me..."

Erin busted out laughing. "Alright," she said once she caught her breath, "to save you from your mother, I'll have dinner with you." Caleb smiled and said goodbye. She watched him leave from the window. She still had a smile on her face and shook her head. Men. They act all big and bad until their mom turns on the heat. She yawned and figured that she might as well go back to sleep.

Erin curled up on her bed and let herself laugh once more over Caleb. She thought it might be nice to just see where this road would take them. She could always tell him later about her uniqueness, if they became something serious.

Erin felt like a band spanking new woman when she woke up. She actually had a smile on her face, which was something in and of itself, because she was not a morning person. The first thing she did was call into work to apologize for dropping off the face of the earth for three days. Kayle told her that it was alright, and that she and Stephen could cover things for a while. She just wanted Erin to focus on getting better. Erin almost told her that she was alright, but decided that she could take a few days to get a better handle on her newfound abilities.

The wards were holding; that much Erin knew for sure. The house felt calm and safe. Fae yowled for his breakfast. She wished that she could talk to him in the physical world the way she had in the astral world. She shrugged. It was what it was.

Erin took the book back to the study. It made sense since most of her family's history was located in that building; plus, it helped her to keep her supernatural life separate from her normal life. She wasn't sure how she was going to manage the two or if she would be able to blend them. She made another trip to carry the pot of coffee she had made, as well as plenty of pencils and paper. Once everything was set up, she sat at the desk, unsure of what to do next. Sure, she could start learning spells, but she really didn't want to cast without really understanding the principles behind it, especially when she had just recovered from the last casting.

Erin flipped past the first few pages in the book, since she had read them already. She really wished that someone had put in a table of contents or at least an index. The book didn't seem to have any organization at all. It looked like someone— several of them in fact— just wrote whatever they thought would be useful, whenever they felt like it.

Erin sighed, leaning back in her chair. She was just about a third of the way into the book and still hadn't found what she was looking for. Sure she had looked at several spells, but nothing that would help her to understand the basic principles of magic.

Fae rubbed his head against Erin's leg. "You would think that my ancestors would have at least written one page about the basics," she said, picking him up. "I mean I guess it makes sense that there isn't one, when you think about it. Until me, they were all brought up in this world." She sighed again, cursing her luck. Fae jumped up onto her shoulder and pointed his nose towards the bookcase behind her. "You think there's something there?" He nodded.

Together they browsed the shelves until Fae meowed, pointing to a small, blue book. Erin picked it up. "*Walking through the Hidden World*," she read out loud skeptically. Fae nodded and pawed at the book. Erin shrugged and sat back down. When she opened the book, she noticed that the author had written something on the inside of the cover.

To my dearest friend Clara,

Without your help, I would still be half blind to the world around me. I hope you are not too angry with me for sharing what you have taught me. I believe that this book will not only help us mere mortals, but others like you, but who do not have such a wealth of family history to fall back on.

Your faithful student,

Charles Bentley

Erin's eyes widened and she quickly flipped to the table of contents. Sure enough, the author covered everything that a novice witch— or guardian— would need to know. The book touched on basic concepts, visualizations, and many do-it-yourself projects, like creating your own spells. Erin broke out into a huge grin. This was the book that she needed, and it was so conveniently travel sized. It really was no larger than any other book, but it held a greater wealth of information. Erin wasted no time. After she refilled her cup, she turned to page one.

Erin sat at the kitchen table eating leftovers. Instead of making her feel better, Bentley's book only proved that she was painfully ill-equipped. She had so much to learn, so much to master, just to be able to do the bare minimum of what was required of her. She had been lucky so far that none of her spells had gone wrong. She had completely forgotten that she wasn't going to accept her family's role. She had forgotten that she was just trying to survive. She had become too absorbed by the new world springing up around her. She felt alive, and her academic half was demanding more.

Charles Bentley's book was an easy read; although he did like to use flowery language. Erin had read the book twice already. The first time was just to see what it held; the second time to take notes. She also wrote in her family's book. It was nothing fancy. She just made a small note at the end of the family history, referencing Mr.

Bentley's book and what it held. Not that she needed the reminder. It was for any future members of her family who would have to walk the same path that she was.

"I have so much work to do," Erin told her familiar. "I could study for the rest of my life and only just scratch the surface." She sighed and looked at her notes. "I guess I don't have to learn it all," she mused. "Maybe I should see what the rest of my family did. Maybe they only focused on one thing?" Fae tilted his head. "I guess I should look into that." The clock chimed and she yawned. "But that is a task for tomorrow. Let's go to bed."

The next morning, Erin had her morning coffee on the back porch. She kept her mind blank and just focused on what she felt. She was attempting to tune in to the energies around her home, just like Mr. Bentley suggested. According to his book, the world was full of energy and those who used magic could tap into those energies to manipulate them. He suggested meditating three times a day: morning, noon, and evening. The earth's and a person's energies were different at these times, and by meditating, one could get familiar with how they felt.

Erin closed her eyes and breathed deeply. She felt the cool morning air rush inside to fill her lungs. She did this a couple more times, but didn't notice anything in particular. Disappointed, she slumped in her chair. *Rome wasn't built in a day*, she mentally told herself, and tried again. This time, she tried to focus more on what she could feel. Again, she noticed the morning air— cool and refreshing. The wind was gentle but warm. As she focused on the morning breeze, in her mind she noted that it took the form of a silver mist, but not like the mists in the astral plain. It looked like starlight and dew swirling around; making everything it touched shimmer in the morning light. It was all very relaxing and pretty to look at in her mind's eye.

When Erin opened her eyes, she felt more awake than she normally did first thing in the morning. She didn't feel hyped up like she would with coffee, just charged and ready to take on the day. Elated, she breathed deeply again, this time savoring the smell of the wet earth. She allowed the smell to filter through her body. Looking inward, she observed that her own energies were the same shade that she had witnessed earlier. Opening her eyes, she smiled at the day. Not bad for her first time.

Erin called work and told them that she would be in on the next day she was scheduled. She originally planned to take a few more days off, but finding Mr. Bentley's book made her realize that there are other sources of information out there. Haven was sure to have a book or two that might be able to help her.

Fae had disappeared right after Erin's morning meditation. She didn't mind. She really didn't expect him to hang around all day. He may be her familiar, but he was still a cat and needed to do cat things. Besides, once she was in academia mode, she really wasn't good company.

Erin flipped through her family's book again only this time, she looked at it more critically. As much as she hated to admit it, she was dying to try a new spell. She wanted to see if there would be any change, now that she knew a little more. She caught herself. *No*, she told herself, *it's better to go slowly.* She stared wistfully at the spells on the page one last time, before she closed the book.

Erin took a break around lunchtime. She grabbed a quick bite, and then went back outside to do her afternoon meditation. She stood in the yard, closed her eyes, and took slow, deep breaths. The heat from the sun was the first thing that she noticed. She also birds singing in the trees. Unlike the morning meditation, she strongly felt something: life. The deeper she delved, the more life she could feel. Forest creatures and even the plants themselves —she could feel them all. As she stood, reveling in life, she felt someone walk up behind her. When she opened her eyes, she saw Fae trotting up to her.

"I felt you coming," Erin whispered, amazed. Fae twined around her legs. She stooped down, picked him up and cradled him against her chest. "I felt more this time," she told him. "I could almost see every living thing." Her face broke out into a gigantic smile. Without another word, she walked back to the study. Her first steps towards becoming a Guardian were going smoothly.

The rest of the day, Erin flipped through some of her ancestors' journals. Although the book had explained what her role was as a Guardian— somewhat— she still didn't have an idea of how to go about it. While the journals didn't provide her a clear answer, they did show her that there was no right way. Her grandmother had volunteered for various charities. Her great-grandmother dispensed herbal remedies to people who couldn't afford doctors. And another ancestor had helped to raise money for schools and public buildings. As long as Erin did something that benefited the lives of the villagers, she was on the right track.

Erin also discovered that as the years passed less, and less of her family were born with magic abilities. But then again, as the world transitioned more towards science, the need for magic became less and less. *Who knows*, she thought as she put the journals away, *maybe one day there wouldn't be any need for people like me.* The thought made her a little sad. From what she was learning, there was so much good that she could do. Sure, people nowadays didn't need spells and charms like they did in the past, but a world without at least some magic would probably be a little empty.

Erin was about to place the family book back in its locked drawer, when suddenly she dropped it. Slightly cursing, she bent down to pick it up. She stopped when she looked at the pages open to her. She smiled as she read one the pages. It was a very special type of charm, and one that she was excited to try. Placing the book back on the desk, she quickly wrote down the items required to make the charm. Still smiling, she tucked the paper into her jeans, and locked the book up for the night.

Erin was glad to see that the wards around Haven were still holding up. She was also glad to still feel the protection sachet under her feet. As she walked in, she inhaled the smell of old books and lemon wood polish.

"Be right with you!" Kayle called out from somewhere in the back.

"Don't worry. It's just me," Erin replied.

Kayle jetted out from the back and gave Erin a bone-crushing hug. "When Caleb told me how sick you were, I was so worried," Kayle cried. "Are you sure you're feeling better? You don't have to come back on my account."

Erin laughed. "I was over the worst of it by the time he came around," she reassured her friend and boss. "If I start to feel bad, I'll go straight home. I promise." Kayle narrowed her eyes as if she thought that Erin was lying.

"We got some new books in today...well, new for us," Kayle stated, walking back to the office. "I'm not sure if we'll keep them. We already have several *older* books on the subject. But hey, they were free. Maybe I could donate them to the library or to Ravenswood?"

"Ravenswood?" Erin asked, tilting her head.

"It's a posh boarding school outside of town," Kayle

explained. "Most of the students there are supposed to be geniuses, or something like that, although they do take in underprivileged kids from time to time." Erin nodded and followed Kayle into the office.

The office looked completely different from the first time Erin had seen it. While there were still several boxes and bags that were waiting to be sorted, they were stacked neatly. She noticed a box sitting on the desk.

"That's it?" Erin asked. Kayle nodded.

"I've gone through some of it," Kayle stated. "But I guess you can finish it. I really need to tackle the accounts. I need to see if we can even afford to buy that empty space next door."

The buildings that made up the shops were constructed so that the front and back of the building could be used. The buildings at the end that formed the alleys often had smaller shops in between the front shops and the back. Haven was the middle shop. The front shop was "Long Feet"— a cobbler, but the back shop was vacant. Kayle had been trying for several years to save up money to purchase the vacant shop, but hadn't been able to. Mainly because she spent more time in the bookstore than acquiring and selling antique books— her real money maker. The vacant shop was also in dire need of a construction crew, which would cost even more money than the shop itself. If she did purchase the vacant shop, all the books would be able to be displayed and would hopefully sell.

With Erin employed, Kayle was finally able to devote a large amount of her time to that venture. Now, she and Stephen could both be gone, and the shop could remain open. The sales of antique books may bring in the most money, but the shop was steady revenue. While Kayle's plan would be too grand for a simple farming village, the boarding school nearby made it well worth the effort.

Kayle remained in the front so she could balance the accounts and keep an eye out for customers. Erin turned on a small radio, making sure the music wasn't too loud, and pulled out the first book she reached. It was a horticulture book. She flipped through the book, noted its condition, and saw that the majority of the plants listed in the book were local. Most of the book was about how to get one's plants to grow properly, but it also told the uses that the plants had. She noticed that some cooking herbs also had magical properties; although the book stated that it was all superstition. While she entered in the book's information, she thought back to her home— more specifically, the bookcases. She hadn't really paid any attention to what books they held. Could there be other books there that could help her learn more about her craft? She thought that there just might be.

"Hey Kayle," Erin called out. Kayle grunted. "If you're going to get rid of these books, do you mind if I get a couple?"

"Why not," was Kayle's reply. Erin smiled and went back to work.

That night after dinner, Erin asked Fae to accompany her to the astral plain. The cabin and the woods surrounding it looked the same. She paused for a moment to see if she could sense anything or anyone; they were alone. Once inside, she asked Fae if he could take a seat on the couch, which he did. He tilted his head, curious.

"I just wanted to tell you how grateful I am that I have you for my familiar," Erin began. "I know I'm probably not the best choice, but I'm trying."

"What's on yer mind lass?" Fae asked.

Erin reached into her pocket and pulled out a green collar with a silver tag. Fae stilled, his eyes pinned to the collar. "I want to make a contract," Erin said carefully. Fae looked at her startled, and then back to the collar.

"You don't have to say yes right away," Erin rushed on. "I just wanted you to know..."

"I want to," interrupted Fae. "Yer smart, kind, and a quick learner." Erin smiled. She sat on the couch next to Fae, and held the collar up.

"With this symbol," Erin said, repeating the words that she had read earlier in the day, "I make known my desire to form a contract with this being called Fae. I will not seek to be his master, only a friend. I will never to ask him to do something that goes against his nature or his will.

I vow to treat him with the respect that he deserves and listen to any advice he may offer. Do you accept?"

Fae walked forward and dipped his head. "I accept and I, Fae, promise to never seek to lead you down a path that you do not wish to tread. I will always be a friend and confidant to you, Guardian Erin."

Erin fastened the collar around Fae's neck. It flashed gold, and then returned to normal. Now he had extra protection, should he have to fight. This protection would only get stronger as she became more skilled. They would also be able to communicate in the physical world. However, it would only be telepathic, not verbal. Fae purred loudly as he rubbed himself against Erin. She had tears in her eyes. She knew that she had made the right choice. Now she had someone to turn to help her along as she tried to find out who she was supposed to be.

When they returned to the physical world, Erin was pleased to see that she wasn't as tired as before. She barely felt anything at all. She and Fae were up late into the night, getting to know each other better. She hadn't forgotten about Connor and their fight, but for one night she pushed all dark thoughts and worries from her mind. Who knows how much longer she'll be around to enjoy life's little pleasures?

Ten

It was September before the doctors finally let Moira out of the hospital. They still had her coming in regularly for checkups and put her on bed rest. Her mysterious illness still had them confused, and concerned as well. For all the doctors knew, it could be only a matter of time before she had a relapse. Only she and Erin knew it would never happen. They often smiled and laughed about it when no one else was around.

"For years, I've told myself that I should take a vacation," Moira joked. "Looks like I'm finally getting it."

Erin smiled and shook her head at her elderly friend. She filled Moira in on the happenings and reintroduced her to Fae. Moira wasn't able to understand him, so Erin had to serve as a translator. She didn't mind though. It was good to finally have some people that she didn't have to hide anything from. She even told Moira about her upcoming dinner with Caleb. Moira was beside herself with happiness.

"I knew from the moment I saw you two that you would end up together," Moira said with a sly grin.

"We're not together, not really," Erin sighed.

"Why not?" Moira demanded.

"How can we be together when I'm hiding a large part of who I am?" Moira patted Erin's hand, but couldn't offer any words of wisdom. If Erin told Caleb about her abilities, it would open him up for attack. But keeping such a big secret would definitely prevent their relationship from blossoming.

Erin had other things to worry about. Since the day she placed the sachet at Haven, she hadn't seen Connor at all. It was like he had dropped off the face of the earth. He wasn't trying to break her wards, nor was he trying to go after Moira. Erin was completely in the dark and hated it. She had a sneaky suspicion that he was planning something particularly nasty, and Fae agreed with her.

There's not much we can do about it now, Fae told Erin when she voiced her concerns. *We just need to keep an eye out, and keep on with yer studies. That way, if he does try something, we'll be ready.*

More than ever, Erin was glad that she had had made the contract with Fae. It really helped to be able to talk to him at all times. They were also spending more the in the astral plain. He was helping her to learn spells— mostly protection— and to tune in more with energies around her. He kept telling her that she was making good progress, but she felt like she could be doing more.

"Why don't we try of offensive spells," Erin asked one day. "I remember coming across a few I think I could do."

"You're not ready for that yet," Fae remarked sternly. "Your defensive spells are not where they need to be. I can still break through one out of three attacks."

"That's not half bad," Erin countered, crossing her arms. "I may not always be able to block an attack. If my defenses fail, I need to be able to fight back." Fae eventually relented, and offensive spells were added to her lessons.

Erin was learning in the physical realm too. As it turned out, she already had many books on magic and folk practices in her possession. There were also books about different cultures and their practices. She added them to her reading list. She knew that Connor and his family had traveled all over the world. There was no doubt in her mind that they had picked up a trick or two along the way. All in all, it was a busy time for her. So consumed with learning, she completely forgot about her date with Caleb, until he called her one evening.

Apparently, the rest of his family had found out about Erin coming over for dinner, and they all wanted to meet her. They had been trying for years to get Caleb back out into the dating world and for years had failed. He tried to offer her an out, but she turned him down. She reminded him that she made a promise and she always tried to keep her promises.

"What's the worse they could do?" Erin told him over the phone.

"You have no idea," Caleb snorted.

On the day of their date, Erin dressed casual, but still nice. She wanted to make a good impression. She really liked Caleb, and if it wasn't for Connor and the war, she wouldn't have any second thoughts about opening up to him completely.

Every few minutes, she looked out the window to see if Caleb had pulled up. When he did, she let Fae out for the night and trotted out to meet him. He was obviously nervous as they drove. His fingers tapped against the steering wheel and he changed the radio often. She couldn't help but smile. She was nervous too, of course. Her stomach was full of butterflies, but she did a better job of hiding them. The fact that he was nervous made her like him even more.

Caleb's parents house was similar to Erin's, only it

was a little larger. The driveway and yard was full of cars.
Dozens of people were milling about, and a horde of
children were running rampant. Caleb stopped at the end
of the driveway. He was gripping the steering wheel so
tightly that his knuckles were white.

"Oh god," Caleb cried. "It looks like the whole clan
is here." He gave Erin an apologetic smile.

In truth, Erin was surprised to see so many people.
She hadn't expected what was supposed to be a quiet
dinner to turn into a family reunion. She half wanted to tell
Caleb that she had changed her mind, but when she turned
to tell him, the look on his face made her stop. She met his
eyes. Erin suddenly could see into his mind.

Caleb liked her— *really* liked her. He believed that
they could have a good life together. He was also afraid.
He was afraid of getting hurt again and afraid that his family
would drive her off before they even got a chance. It was
that mix of longing and fear that gave Erin the courage to
lean over and give him a kiss on the cheek. He relaxed a
little and pulled the rest of the way into the driveway. Once
stopped, Erin got out of the car quickly. She didn't want to
waste what was left of her courage. She smiled once more
at Caleb, then took his hand; in for a penny, in for a pound.

Caleb's family let out a cheer when they saw the
two walk up hand in hand. An elderly man, who turned out
to be Caleb's grandfather, assessed Erin intently. She
blushed as the old man looked her up, then down, then up

again. Caleb didn't complain, but scowled at his grandfather. While Erin was uncomfortable, she understood somewhat that the old man in front of her would largely dictate how she would be received by the rest of the family. Caleb's grandfather broke out into a smile. Erin heard Caleb exhale. Whatever the old man saw in her, he approved.

"So this is your new lass?" the grandfather asked Caleb. When Caleb nodded, the old man stuck his hand out, which Erin took. "Glad to see his taste has improved." Erin didn't know what to make of the comment. Caleb's grandfather gave her a smirk that was identical to Caleb's, then said, "I can be available if you'd rather have a man with some miles on him."

"Okay, granda," Caleb said, quickly taking Erin by the arm. "Nice to see you too." Erin was too shocked to say anything. She let Caleb lead her towards the house, deaf to the laughter behind her.

Caleb's mother snatched Erin away, as soon as she entered the house, to drag her off to the kitchen. His mother put Erin to work, chopping vegetables. A few aunts and cousins were busy in the kitchen as well. They asked Erin so many questions that she barely had time to answer one before another was asked. It was all good-natured though. They asked about where she grew up and what the United States was like, how she was enjoying Ireland, and so on and so forth.

"It is lovely to see you again, Erin," Caleb's mother said during a lull in the questions. "I do hope that you come by around the holidays. From what Caleb's told me, your family's back in America?"

"They are," Erin said. "I talk to my gran often, and my sister came for a visit over the summer."

"What about your mum?" one of Caleb's aunts asked.

Erin frowned. "We're not exactly on speaking terms right now." The kitchen fell silent. Caleb's relatives didn't want to pry into an obviously tender subject.

Caleb managed to free himself from the rest of his family to rescue Erin from the kitchen. He led her to the family room. As soon as she sat down, several children clamored to climb into her lap. She was startled at first, but then she started laughing. One little girl with blonde pigtails tugged on Erin's sleeve.

"I really like you," she told Erin with the confidence that only a child could possess.

"I like you too," Erin replied with a smile.

The little girl smiled. "You made Cousin Caleb smile again." Erin was stunned. The little girl gave Erin a kiss on the cheek, then skipped away. Erin heard someone laugh and she laughed too, shaking her head at the boldness of a child. It was hard to not get swept up in the excitement that filled every inch of the house.

Soon, Caleb's family fought amongst themselves in an attempt to tell Erin the most embarrassing stories they had on Caleb. Caleb, at first, was irritated and a brilliant shade of red. Erin shared a few embarrassing stories of her own, and from the corner of her eye, she saw Caleb relax and the grateful smile he gave her.

Dinner was an informal affair. People just grabbed plates, filled them, and then found a place to plop down and eat. Erin ended up sitting on an ottoman, while Caleb sat on the floor next to her. In between, bites the conversation continued, although it was a bit more subdued. Caleb's mother kept piling food onto Erin's plate, telling her she should eat more. However, as soon as his mother's back was turned Caleb scooped the food onto his plate. Erin gave him a grateful smile, amazed at the amount of food he could eat.

Erin was too stuffed to eat dessert, not that his family paid any attention to her protests. She ended up giving hers to the children. She then went outside for some fresh air. The night air carried the first hints of fall. She noticed a rope swing and sat down. She closed her eyes and tilted her face towards the sky.

"They have this effect on people," Caleb said, coming up behind her.

"No they're wonderful," Erin insisted.

"I bet your family's nothing like this." Erin's face fell, and Caleb grimaced.

"No they're not," Erin remarked. "We never have gatherings like this. My family's small. The only parties we have are for my father's business."

"You miss them," Caleb observed.

"Yes and no," Erin shrugged. "I miss my gran and my sister, and sometimes my mom. I never really had a relationship with my father. He's all about work." Caleb placed his hand on her shoulder, giving it a reassuring squeeze. "But it's alright," she said brightly. "Not every family is close."

"Well, whenever you feel lonely you can borrow my family," Caleb joked. Erin laughed and got off the swing. Caleb put his arm around her and together they walked back to the house.

Erin dozed off on the way home. She had a full belly and a light spirit. Caleb gently shook her when they arrived. She stared at her dark, empty house, suddenly sad. She wanted what Caleb had— a loving family. She was tired of being alone.

"Caleb, what are we?" Erin asked, softly still staring at her house.

Caleb opened his mouth a few times, but nothing came out. "I'm not sure," he finally replied. "We've only just started out on this road."

"I'd like to find out," Erin said, turning to look Caleb in the eye. She watched as his face changed from confused to a shy smile. His smile lit a small fire in her chest.

"Me too," Caleb said, leaning in close. Erin closed her eyes and leaned in as well.

Caleb's lips brushed gently against Erin's. She reached up to grab the back of his head and pulled him in closer. He responded by deepening his kiss. A small fire started to form in the center of her body. Its heat poured into the kiss, until the two were gasping for air. Caleb tried to apologize, saying he didn't mean to, but Erin cut him off with another kiss. When they parted again, she bid him goodnight and got out of the car. Every bit of her demanded that she invite him in, but she didn't. It was too soon for that. Erin watched as Caleb's car pulled away, with a smile on her face. It was too soon, but not impossible.

Erin's training continued as she learned to love again. She still was concerned about hiding her magic from Caleb, but it was for the best that she didn't tell him anything. She hoped that he would stay, once he learned the whole truth. Until then, she allowed herself to bask in Caleb's affection. He treated her the way that women should be treated. He was courteous, but didn't treat her like she was made of glass. The time that they spent together was always enjoyable, but he also gave her space. What she liked the most was that, even though he had just as much baggage as she did, he let her set the pace of their relationship. This meant that, at the end of their dates, he didn't invite himself over for the night.

This frustrated Erin to no end. She wanted Caleb to make the first move, but was glad he didn't at the same time. It was maddening. She had been alone for a long time. She wanted someone to share her bed with. She wanted someone to love her. The fact that she wanted him so badly scared her. The last time she felt that way about a man she married him, and look how that turned out.

The leaves were just starting to change when Erin started to mix defensive and offensive spells. She and Fae were in one such training session in the astral plain, when she felt a tingle in the back of her mind. At first, she ignored the tingling, but the feeling only got stronger. Finally, she had to stop.

"What is that?" Erin asked. Her eyes scanned her surroundings, looking for the source.

Fae tilted his head and listened. "Someone has crossed the boundaries of the ward," he answered.

"Is it someone dangerous?" Erin asked.

"No," Fae replied, shaking his head. "If they were, the wards wouldn't have let them through. It seems like the wards don't know what to make of the person though.

We'd best get back."

Back in the physical world, Erin looked out the front window. She didn't see any cars in the driveway. Instead of opening the front door, she walked to the back. When she rounded the corner, she saw a woman with blond hair knocking on her door.

"Can I help you?" Erin called out. She saw the woman stiffen. When the woman turned around, Erin knew why. It was her mother, Jessica. It was Erin's turn to freeze. The two women stared at each other for a long time, neither willing to look away. It was Erin who finally broke the silence.

"What are you doing here?" Erin demanded.

"Is that any way to greet your mother," her mother replied, "especially after the way you've treated her?"

Erin heard just the barest of a quiver in her mother's voice, but she knew that her mother was more upset than she let on. The one thing that Jessica prided herself on was her ability to control her emotions.

"Seems right to me," Erin snapped. "Again what are you doing here?"

Erin's mother sighed and reached into her coat pocket to pull out a crumpled piece of paper. "I was washing some of the clothes that your sister left behind, when I came across this ticket. Imagine my surprise seeing the destination. Laura never mentioned that she took a trip to Ireland. She was supposed to be in Paris." Erin kept her face blank, but mentally reminded herself to kill her sister when she saw her again. "And then I remembered my mother talking about the house where she had grown up. Then I realized that this *could* be the place where you were hiding."

Erin crossed her arms and continued to glare at her mother. Her coming could only mark the beginning of the end to Erin's happy life in Dorshire. "Well, as you can see, I am alive. So you can just turn around, get back on the plane, and forget that you ever came here."

Erin turned and started to walk towards the back of the house. "Now, wait just one minute, young lady!" Jessica shouted. "You come back here this instant and explain yourself!"

That was the final straw. Erin turned, fuming.

"No I won't!" Erin shouted at the top of her lungs. "I don't have to explain myself to you, or to anyone else. This is my life and I will live it as I damn well please! I don't want anything to do with you, father, or *John*!" Erin's mother stood there on the steps with an amazed look on her face.

"Furthermore," Erin continued. "You will not— I repeat, *will not*— tell that sorry excuse for a husband where I am. I divorced him, mother. I don't want him in my life. What part of that don't you understand!" Erin's mother opened her mouth to scold Erin, but she cut her mother off.

"More to the point, if you were a *decent* mother you would have known. You would have understood. You would have been there for *me*! But no, you were too wrapped up in your own little world, where everything is perfect. You treat me like I'm some willful child. I'm not. I'm not even the same Erin who you thought you knew. She was killed at the hands of a man who was supposed to love and protect her!"

Erin was shaking with anger. She watched as her words cut her mother down to size. Jessica finally lost her composure, breaking down into tears. Erin tried to hold onto her anger, but the sight of her mother weeping cooled the flames. Erin sighed and walked towards her mother. She didn't offer her any comfort, but she did open the front door to let her in.

Erin's mother, sniffling, picked up her overnight bag and entered. When Fae saw Erin's mother, he hissed and ran out of the house as fast as he could. Erin just shrugged. She would ask him what his problem was later. Right now, she had to deal with her mother.

Erin told her mother to sit in the kitchen. She then went about making a pot of tea. She used the time to get the rest of her anger under control. By the time she placed two cups on the table, Erin was able to hold a civil conversation. Her mother had regained control as well. Other than her puffy eyes and red nose, there was no evidence that, only a few moments ago, she had broken down.

Erin sipped her tea, waiting for her mother to speak first. She felt a little guilty about shouting at her mother, but only a little. The air between the two women was so thick that it could have been cut with a knife. Erin started to fidget. The only thing she wanted was to get her mother back on a plane and out of her life. When Erin saw her mother's shoulders stiffen she braced herself.

"Why did you leave the way you did, Erin?" Jessica asked, not looking up.

Erin sighed and slumped in her chair. "If you have to ask, Mother," she replied, "then you'll never understand."

Eleven

J essica's eyes, so like Erin's locked onto her daughter. Erin and her mother engaged in a silent battle for dominance. In the past, Erin always conceded to her mother's desires, but not this time. This time she wouldn't push her own feelings aside just for the sake of peace. Her mother must have seen this, because she was the first to break eye contact with a sigh.

"You have changed," Erin's mother whispered, delicately sipping her tea.

"You have no idea," Erin mumbled. The two fell into silence again.

"You look like you've put some weight back on,"

Jessica commented. Erin quickly stood up and walked towards the laundry room. If her mother was resorting to small talk, then Erin would need to keep her hands busy. For some reason, this was the only way she could talk to her mother without giving in or blowing up. "Erin, come back here!" her mother commanded.

"I have things to do," Erin replied coolly. "You can't expect me to put my life on hold for you and your problems. You sure as hell didn't." Her mother started to tear up again, but stopped herself. This only made Erin angrier. For once, she wanted her mother to lose control and not hold everything in. Instead, she followed Erin into the laundry room.

"Please tell me you aren't wearing these in public," Erin's mother asked scornfully. "I know dressing 'retro' is the fashion these days, but that doesn't mean you have to wear your grandmother's clothes."

Erin bristled. "Actually, they're *your* grandmother's clothes. Not that it's any of your business, but no, I'm not wearing them. I'm washing them so I can give them to a thrift store, and some are going to Laura."

"I just don't know what I'm going to do with either of you," Erin's mother sighed. "One of my daughters is throwing her life away, and the other is lashing out for no reason."

"I am not throwing my life away!" Erin said indignantly. "I'm actually trying to improve it!"

"What...oh, not you dear," Jessica said with a wave of her hand. "I mean your sister... wanting to be a fashion designer." Erin stared at her mother, eyes wide. "It's such an impractical profession."

"She loves it," Erin countered, "and that's what important. It's better to be poor and doing what you love, than to be rich and doing something you hate."

"Why can't you have both?" Erin's mother retorted. "Why does it have to be one or the other?"

Erin sighed, running her hands through her hair. "That's not what I mean and you know it." She slammed the dryer close, and then turned to the pile of clean clothes that needed to be sorted. She could feel her mother watching her intently. She knew that her mother was looking for any weakness she could use to twist Erin to her will. The phone rang.

Erin swore. She had completely forgotten that she was supposed to go to the movies with Caleb tonight. Walking quickly, she skirted past her mother to get to the phone first.

"Hey you," Caleb said cheerfully on the other end. "Ready for the movies?"

"I can't make it tonight," Erin said softly. "Something came up."

Caleb knew from the sound of Erin's voice that

something was wrong. "Is everything okay?"

"Just a little family drama," Erin replied. "My mom showed up."

"Do you need reinforcements?"

Erin laughed. "No, I'll be fine. She won't be here long. I'll call later. Bye." Erin cringed as she hung up the phone. Taking a deep breath, she turned to see her mother smirking, arms folded over her chest.

"And who was he?" Jessica asked in a motherly tone. Erin fought not to roll her eyes. She was a grown woman and didn't have to explain any aspect of her life to anyone.

"A friend," Erin said quickly. "When are you leaving anyway?"

"Tomorrow," Jessica replied. "Even with the pictures, I wasn't sure if you were here or not."

Erin felt her stomach drop. "What pictures?!" she demanded.

Jessica was startled by her reaction. If she didn't know any better, she would have thought that her daughter looked frightened. Slowly, she reached into her purse to pull out a large manila envelope. Erin snatched it from her mother and tore it open. She pulled the first picture out, confirming her suspicions.

It was a picture of Erin from the May Day Festival.
She had her arm around Moira's shoulder, laughing. Erin
collapsed in a chair. She turned the envelope upside down
and dozens of pictures fell out. With shaking hands, she
touched every one. It looked like someone, and she had a
good idea who had stalked her from the moment she had
landed.

There were pictures of Erin walking around
Dorshire, working in her yard, and even setting out books in
front of Haven. Indignation burned fiercely in her chest.
She wanted nothing more than to burn the pictures, throw
her mother out of her home, and go confront Connor. She
was just about to follow through with her violent thoughts,
when she heard Fae yowling outside to be let in. She had
forgotten all about him. Pushing her dark thoughts aside,
she went to let her familiar in.

"You have a cat," Erin's mother commented calmly.
Erin, however, knew that the comment was meant to be
derogatory and glared at her mother. Fae stared at Jessica,
growling softly, until she attempted to pet him. Then he
yowled and slashed at her hand. He broke free from Erin's
hold, taking off into the night again.

Erin stared after Fae in disbelief. *What was he
playing at*, she wondered. "I should go after him," Erin said.
She walked out the door without waiting for her mother to
argue or offer to come. She walked straight to the barn,
knowing that she would find him there. She had some
words for her familiar.

Sure enough, Fae was waiting for Erin inside the barn sitting in front of the door. She closed the door and crossed her arms. *Now don't be mad at me*, he told her.

"I'm not," Erin reassured him. "I'm angry at Connor. *He's* the one who took those pictures and sent them to my mother." Fae closed his eyes, relieved. "Do you not like my mom, or was all of that just an act to get away?"

A little of both, Fae said sadly. She *doesn't mean ye harm, but there's something not right about her either.* He shook his head. Erin stooped down and picked him up. She knew he was doing the best that he could. *There has to be a reason why Connor's doing this... there has to be. He may be trying to shake you up, or he could just be trying to make you leave.*

"Well, we can't let him can we?" Erin said, smiling. Fae nodded in agreement, and together, they made their way back to the house.

Erin's mother had left the kitchen and was standing in front of the fireplace, running her hand over the mantel, just like Erin had done on her first night. The Guardian and the familiar remained silent, watching. Her mother's eyes were closed, and a small smile graced her face. Erin thought that her mother looked peaceful, as if all the stress in her life had faded. Erin knew that some of her mother's stress was her fault, but she knew that she had to stand her ground. Fae meowed and the moment was gone. Her mother's face hardened, but this time, her eyes looked livelier.

"I can see why you like it here," Jessica told Erin. "It's calming. This house is old, which you always loved." She smiled lovingly at Erin. "And as much as I hate your methods, you do look better...more like your old self. What type of mother would I be if I didn't support that?"

Erin was shocked. The woman in front of her was not the same woman she had let into her home or had left a just few minutes ago. Tears formed in Erin's eyes. It was like she had her old mother back. Not wanting to let the moment pass, she released Fae and ran to her mother. Mother and daughter embraced for the first time in years and it felt good, really good.

Erin pulled her mother towards the couch. Her intuition told her that now was the time to explain to her mother why she had made the choices that she had. If her mom still didn't understand, then all hope was lost.

"I'm better because, for the first time I'm not living in fear of John showing up," Erin said. "For the first time in a long time, I have the space to just be me, without risking his wrath." Her mom opened her mouth to argue, but stopped when Erin held up a hand. "I just need you to listen to me," she said. "Just listen to what I'm about to tell you, and then you can speak." Erin took a deep breath. The memory was still fresh in her mind as if it had just happened.

The world outside the car was awash in reds and golds with splashes of green here and there. Erin loved going to the country. It was like a different world when compared to the city. It looked different. It smelled different. It felt different. Not any better or worse than the city, mind you, just different. She looked over at John, who was focused on not missing their turn. She still wasn't sure about coming back, but a part of her still loved him. With a silent sigh, she turned back to her window, watching the trees speed by.

They were on their way to a small dinner party with one of his clients. All sorts of people were invited: musicians, politicians, artists, professors, and business owners. Although the event was supposed to be for fun, John was going purely for business. He had a limited number of days to get a contract signed, and that's why Erin was accompanying him. Her role this evening was to charm his client's wife so that she would pressure him into signing the contract. Erin really didn't want to, but things were still very tense between them. She only agreed because John had promised her that, if the deal went through, they would go on a vacation— just the two of them— and work on rebuilding their marriage.

Erin tried to steel herself as they turned up the gravel road that would take them to the house where the party was being held. A valet took their car around back, leaving Erin alone with John. He took her hand and gave her a large smile. It was the same smile that she had fallen in love with while they dated in college. She found herself smiling as well. Things would get better.

"Don't worry," John reassured Erin, "we'll be fine." The smile faded as they walked up towards the house. He had switched from the boy she had fallen in love with to the ruthless businessman so fast that it made her head spin. Which was the real John?

Sounds of music and laughter greeted them the moment they crossed the threshold. A woman took their coats, while a server escorted them towards the party. Erin stopped for a moment to take it all in, but John scanned the crowd looking for one man. With a firm hand, he guided Erin towards the perspective client and his wife.

John introduced Erin, then wheeled the client away to talk business, leaving Erin alone with his wife. The woman was beautiful in the way that movie stars were in the fifties. She regarded Erin with a ruby-red smile. Erin knew, without saying a word, that she would get no help from this woman. She knew why Erin was there.

Erin shrugged. "My husband is relentless when it comes to business."

The woman laughed handing, Erin a drink. "That he is. I do hope you enjoy yourself all the same." Erin accepted the drink gracefully. She toasted the woman, and then walked into the crowd.

After thirty minutes, John still hadn't returned. Erin tried to not get angry, but she wanted to spend some time with him.

"Erin?"

She turned around and let out a cry of delight. It was Thomas Greenly, her study partner from college. They weren't exactly partners in the traditional sense. He majored in Anthropology, she in History, but they often sat together in the library because they used many of the same materials for their studies. Thomas was sporting a tan that he never had while in college.

"How was India?" Erin asked. She vaguely remembered that he was part of a team that worked towards preserving the ancient temples around the world.

"Hot, humid, and I nearly got eaten alive by insects," Thomas replied dramatically. "What about you? Torturing students with countless wars and empires yet?"

Erin felt self-conscious. Because of the problems with her marriage, her life's dream of teaching History got put on the back burner. "Not yet," she said shyly.

Thomas gave her a crooked smile and gratefully didn't press the issue. The two soon found themselves in a quiet corner, talking about their lives after college. Well, Thomas did most of the talking. Erin was laughing, enjoying herself tremendously, until John appeared out of nowhere, scowling.

"Here you are," John growled. His eyes briefly flipped towards Thomas, taking in everything about him. Erin suddenly felt guilty. "I've been looking everywhere for you."

"John, this is Thomas Greenly. We were study partners back in the good ol' days. You remember, don't you?"

John glared at Thomas, then gripped Erin's arm so hard that she knew she would have bruises later. A dark cloud settled over John's face, and Erin knew she was in for it later. Bewildered, she allowed John to drag her out of the party without any resistance. She didn't know what brought this darkness out of him. She, John, and Thomas often went out together. They were all friends— or had been.

John didn't say anything to Erin as they waited for the valet to bring their car around. Nor did he talk during the long ride home. She kept peeking at him from the corner of her eye. Her palms were sweaty and her body shook with nervous energy. She had been in this situation enough times in the past and knew better than to utter a sound. If she did, John would lash out and strike her. It was better if she remained silent and then fled the moment they got home.

Erin opened the door as soon as John parked the car in the garage. She heard him turn off the car and get out. She tried to make it inside without looking like she was running away, but she wasn't that lucky. He quickly came up behind her, grabbing a fistful of her hair. He pulled hard, swinging her around. She stumbled into a wall, but before she could gather herself, he reeled back and struck her in the face. Her head bounced against the wall. When she touched her lips, she found blood.

Afraid, Erin looked up— big mistake. This was a version of John she had never seen before. There was no sign of the boy she had fallen in love with, or the temperamental husband she had come to know. This John was deadly. His eyes were filled with such contempt and rage that she froze— much like prey does when a predator is close and they don't want to attract its attention. But Erin wasn't so lucky. This predator had her in his sights and there was no escaping.

John yanked Erin back to her feet, staring right into her eye as if he was daring her to defend herself. She was crying, silently pleading with her husband to let her go. He sneered, and then began his assault anew. Fists, elbows, knees, and feet all struck her mercilessly. His attacks came so fast that she couldn't even protect herself from the blows. She screamed; she begged. But nothing reached him. He grabbed her hair again. This time, he dragged her into the house. She dug her nails into his hands, but his grip was unbreakable. She tried to use her feet to find a purchase, but the delicate heals of her shoes snapped. She continued to scream and shout, but knew that it was fruitless.

They lived at the end of a street in a secluded neighborhood. Their nearest neighbor was within shouting distance, but they were holding a party. Erin could hear the music, even inside her home. There would be no help for her.

John threw Erin into a corner of their kitchen. Erin, free from his grip, quickly pulled herself up. "Why?" she cried. "Why?"

John's only response was to backhand Erin so hard that she fell into the sink. Dishes from the day were still sitting in the drainer. A few got knocked lose, fell to the floor and shattered. Instinctively, she reached out to catch the dishes, and just barely caught the cast-iron skillet her grandmother had given her as a wedding present. She glanced over her shoulder to see John pulling knife after knife out of the wooden block. Her blood ran cold. He meant to kill her.

John's back was to Erin; as if he knew that she was too pathetic to attack him back. The fear that had frozen her melted, with her own rage. How dare this man treat her like she was nothing more than dirt beneath his feet! How dare he turn his back on the vows he took when they became man and wife! She slipped her ruined shoes off her feet, creeping silently towards him. She tightened her grip on the handle of the skillet, slowly raising it above her head. She stopped a few steps from him, and then swung the skillet down.

It sounded like a gong when the skillet hit John's head. He went down and didn't get back up. Erin hit him again for good measure. She stood over his body, breathing heavily. For a brief moment, she was afraid that she had killed him, but she noticed the rise and fall of his back. He was just unconscious. Knowing the animal she would have to face, should he wake up, she tore through the house, grabbing a change of clothes, her purse, and car keys. She ran back to the garage, got in her car, and tore down the street.

Erin drove without thinking. It took her a few moments to realize that she was heading towards her parents home. She pulled into a gas station, putting her car into park. She needed to think. She couldn't go to her parents. Time after time, they took John's side. She saw no reason why this time would be any different. There was only one person she could turn to. She needed to get to her grandmother. She put her car into gear and drove off into the night.

"Gran hid me for two weeks. She helped me file for divorce and file a restraining order. She helped me resettle every time I had to run away from John. When it looked like I would never be free of him, she got everything ready for me to leave the country," Erin told her mother. "Once that was settled, I got on a plane and never looked back."

Erin had watched her mother's face the entire time

she told her story. At first, Jessica was calm, and then her façade crumbled. Now, tears fell freely. Once she realized that Erin was done speaking, she pulled her into another embrace.

"I am so sorry sweetie," Erin's mother cried. "I'm so sorry that I didn't believe you. I'm sorry that I wasn't there for you when you needed me. And most importantly, I'm sorry I wasn't the one you thought you could turn to when you were in need."

By this time, Erin was crying herself. For so long she yearned to hear her mother say those exact words. Her mother responded by pulling her in closer, almost as if she was afraid that Erin would disappear if she didn't hold on tightly enough.

"I promise that John will never find out where you are," Jessica promised. "Your father doesn't even know that I'm here. He thinks that I'm in Florida visiting friends. He won't ever know any different."

"Thank you," whispered Erin. Her mother smiled weakly, running her fingers through Erin's hair. "You can stay here," Erin said. "I'll drive you to the train station in the morning."

"Alright baby."

The next morning, Erin woke up feeling exhilarated

and anxious at the same time. On one hand, she had finally gotten the response she wanted from her mother— even if she had to share her darkest story first. But on the other hand, she wasn't sure how long that would last. What if her mother got home and reverted back to her old ways? What if she let it slip, somehow, that she knew where Erin was?

Breakfast was tense. Erin knew why and she guessed her mother was feeling guilty. They ate their meal in silence. Erin cleaned the dishes while her mother showered. *If breakfast was this nerve-racking the car ride would be ten times worse*, she thought, frowning into the sink.

Erin was right. Neither she nor her mother uttered one syllable on the two-hour drive to the train station. To make matters worse, the train was delayed. Erin couldn't leave until she was sure her mother got on the train safely. Call it whatever you like— a daughter's duty; a chance to ensure her secret— Erin was not leaving the station until the train had.

Jessica sat on a bench, looking just as uncomfortable as Erin felt. She looked like she was on the verge of tears. Erin's heart went out to her mother. The whole situation was hard on her too.

"Maybe after things have settled a bit, we can fix things between us," Erin offered, sitting next to her mother.

"I'd like that," Erin's mother replied. "I know I don't deserve another chance, not after what I did to you, but I'm grateful for it. I promise that once things have settled, we will work on us. I miss you." Her mother whispered the last part. Now it was Erin's turn to cry.

Fifteen minutes later, the train pulled into the station. The platform was soon filled with people disembarking and boarding. Erin didn't notice any of them. The only person who mattered was standing right in front of her. She helped her mother board, and then waited for her to find her seat. Mother and daughter smiled at each other through the glass. A whistle blew and the train heaved forward. Slowly at first, then faster, the train pulled away. Erin's mother opened her window and waved goodbye. Erin waved until she could no longer see the train.

Erin was strangely at peace. She knew that it could take years to repair the damage between herself and her mom, but they had already taken the first tentative steps towards that. Erin couldn't help but smile as she started her car. *One problem down and one to go*, she told herself grimly. Things may be better on the family front, but there was still the little matter of Connor trying to wipe her family off the face of the earth.

Erin's mother's surprise visit actually proved to be a good thing after all. Now there was a future that Erin wanted to protect, not just her own survival. As she drove home, she swore to spend as much time as humanly possible learning to control her magic so that, when her gran arrived, they would be able to kick Connor's sorry tail out of Ireland, and their lives for good.

Twelve

Before Erin realized it, fall had arrived. The trees shed their rich, green leaves for scarlet and gold. Gone was the warm summer night, replaced by evenings that were crisp and carried the scent of wood smoke. She already missed summer. She missed the warm breezes, the long days, and the way the world seemed to be bursting with life. The arrival of fall only meant one thing: winter was on its way. Every living creature went into a frenzy as they did their last minute preparations for winter. Although winter was still a few months off, any dallying now could mean misfortune once the snow arrived.

Erin was just as busy as the woodland creatures. There were leaves that needed to be raked and disposed of. She also stocked up on candles and batteries, because according to Moira, power outages were common during the winter storms. Erin bought these items a little at a time, often adjusting her lists as she talked to the locals, taking their experiences into account.

Speaking of Moira, she was finally allowed to work again. Her doctor cautioned her against taking things too fast but his words fell on deaf ears. As soon as she was given the green light, she reverted back to her old ways becoming the powerhouse that Erin had come to love.

Moira complained for days that the nursery had descended into chaos during her absence. She harried the staff relentlessly as the nursery shifted gears towards the fall and winter season. Now was the time to bring in the harvest and prepare for next year. The rest of Moira's family was glad to see her back to her old self as well. They still watched her like a hawk, searching for any signs of weakness. But as the weeks passed, they relaxed and everything went back to normal.

The roads became hectic, with truck after truck bringing the year's harvest to the markets. In the pub, farmers claimed that this was the best harvest they had in a long while. Erin wondered if it was because the village Guardian had returned. She tried not to think about that too much; it always made her feel conceited. There were good years and bad years, when it came to farming. It just so happened that her arrival coincided with a good one— or so she kept telling herself.

In addition to purchasing candles, Erin also stocked up on food. Being from the northern region of the US, she knew how to drive in snowy conditions, but preferred not to if she could help it. Why ask for trouble? She knew what the winters were like back home, but she had no idea how they would be here. For all she knew they could be harsher. It always paid to be prepared.

As busy as Erin was, she still made sure that she made up for the date with Caleb that she had to cancel when her mother had showed up unexpectedly. Erin procured a TV and cooked spaghetti. It wasn't going to be anything special, just lounging about the house, but she was still excited. Her feelings for Caleb had only grown stronger over the past few months. It was getting harder and harder for her to deny the way she felt when he was around. The more they spent time together, the more she wanted to open up and let go. Every now and again, she would catch a gleam in his eyes that told her that he felt the same. It elated and frustrated her at the same time.

When Caleb arrived, he held up a bottle of wine and a bouquet of flowers. He gave Erin no explanation for the gifts, just that crooked smile of his that made her heart speed up and her knees go weak. He handed her the flowers, then went into the kitchen to open the wine. She pretended to smell the flowers to hide her blush. The bouquet was beautiful and it did smell nice, but she was happier over the gesture than the actual bouquet.

Erin placed the flowers in a vase, and when she

turned around, Caleb was behind her, holding a large glass of wine. "To fixing things with family," he toasted. "'Cause if we don't, they can make our lives miserable." Erin laughed accepting the glass. She toasted him, and then took a large swallow.

They talked and laughed over dinner, but Erin was only partially there. Every time Caleb lifted his wine glass, she couldn't help but notice how gentle his large, calloused hands handled the delicate glass. She wondered what it would be like to have those hands on her body. She pushed the thoughts away, trying not to blush. Thoughts like that were just too much for her to deal with right now.

After dinner, Caleb and Erin curled up together on the couch to watch a movie. She was only partially aware of the images on the screen. She was more aware of the heat coming from Caleb's body as she snuggled into his side. His arm seemed heavy but comforting, wrapped around her. He laughed at something in the movie. She felt it rumble in his chest, then work its way out. She turned her face towards him, drinking in everything. Feeling her gaze, he turned his face towards her, still smiling. Before her mind could stop her, she leaned in and kissed him.

To say Caleb was startled would be an understatement. He didn't move an inch, his eyes wide. Erin shifted, taking his face in her hands and deepened her kiss. For a second, she was afraid that he was going to stop her. Instead, he let out a small groan, pulled her into his lap, and started to kiss her back. Oh, the things his kiss was doing to her. Her whole body felt like it was on fire. Her heart was beating so hard that she felt like it would burst soon, but it wasn't enough. She wanted more— more of him, more of this feeling, just more. When they finally came up for air, she reached for the ends of her shirt.

"No," Caleb said gruffly, holding her hands down. Erin didn't pretend not to be hurt by his refusal. "Not like this."

"I want you," Erin stated, calmer than she felt. "I've wanted you for a while now. It's time for both of us to let go and live again— to love again." She took Caleb's face into her hands again, looking directly into his eyes. She willed her eyes to convey all the feelings that were raging in her heart and soul. He must have seen it, because he started to kiss her again, only this time slowly, savoring her.

Suddenly, Erin found herself being carried upstairs. She let out a squeal. She popped Caleb when he laughed at her. When they got to her bedroom, he put her back down. She strode into the room, but he remained in the doorway. He still looked uncertain. She crossed the room and took him by the hand. She led him to her bed.

"We don't have to," Erin told Caleb, meaning every word. She may be all hot and bothered, but he was a more controlled individual. She would have to let him decide. She knew that if she went ahead, he would give in, just because he wanted to please her, but that wasn't what she wanted. She wanted him to want to. So she waited. She didn't have to wait for long.

Caleb pulled his shirt over his head and threw it towards the door. He then kicked off his shoes and removed his socks. Erin swallowed. He looked even better standing there just in his jeans. Erin had always loved that look on a man. As he walked towards her, she scooted back, taking her shirt off as she did. In a matter of moments, they laid naked under the blankets, content to run their hands over one another's body.

Caleb shifted, putting himself on top. He waited, giving Erin one last chance to change her mind. She fell completely in love with him in that moment. Smiling, she wrapped her arms around his neck and pulled him in. There was no turning back now. It was time for them both to let go of their baggage from the past and start a new chapter in their lives and they were going to do it together.

The next morning, Erin was surprised to find that she was alone in bed. Startled, she sat up pulling the blanket close to her chest. She listened, hoping to hear the sound of Caleb somewhere in the house, but heard nothing. Just as panic started to set in, she heard a grunt and the sound of wood splitting. She wrapped her robe around her to look out the window. What she saw made her smile. Caleb was in her back yard, chopping some of the larger pieces of wood from the pile. She stayed at the window enjoying the manly spectacle taking place below her. Caleb

noticed her, when he straightened back up, and waved.
Erin waved back, turning from the window, shaking her
head slightly. She pulled on some sweats before heading to
the kitchen and was greeted by the aroma of coffee.

"Well then," Erin said out loud. Wanting to do
something for Caleb, she made breakfast. She heard the
back door slam, but didn't turn around. She felt Caleb's
presence the moment he entered the kitchen, but still she
didn't turn around. Her pulse sped up when she heard his
footsteps. He wrapped his arms around her from behind.
Erin closed her eyes and leaned into him. He smelled
distinctly male, with a hint of crisp morning air. He kissed
the sides of her neck, sending shivers down her spine.

"I was gonna take care of that," Caleb said, meaning
breakfast.

"Well, you looked busy this morning," Erin laughed.
Caleb made himself a cup of coffee and sat down at the
table, smiling at her as she finished breakfast. They ate in a
comfortable silence. Words were not needed between
them now. Caleb looked at his watch and groaned.

"I have to go," Caleb said. "Work."

"You could always call in sick," Erin suggested.
Caleb laughed.

"I thought about it," Caleb said. "But you know
what they say about too much of a good thing." Erin
laughed and gathered the plates. "You should look into

getting more wood for winter," Caleb said as they cleaned up. "I know just the guy for it too."

"Why am I not surprised?" Erin laughed.

Caleb left Erin with another kiss, and a number to call later to order more wood. As she watched him pull out of the driveway, she realized that everything had changed— once again— for her. She now had a man who was kind, sweet, and not too bad to look at either. She knew, as sure as she knew her name, that he would only ever treat her with respect and love. He would go out of his way to make her smile, and surprisingly, she felt the same way. She was filled with a glow that only comes in the early days of a relationship. She was still worried about keeping her secret, but she felt that after so much suffering, she more than deserved a bit of happiness.

The season, and Erin's relationship with Caleb, weren't the only changes going on. The house was changing too. Slowly, she started to put more of herself into the house. The walls still had pictures that belonged to her great-grandparents, but now they also bore pictures of Erin and her friends. She even replaced the books on the shelves beside the fireplace. She didn't get rid of the books. She just placed them in plastic storage bins and put them up in the attic.

Moira was the first to notice the changes. "You're making this place your own," she commented, when she stopped by for a visit.

Erin shrugged. "I don't know when, if ever, I'll be able to return to the states," she explained. "I guess I got tired of feeling like a guest here. It's become more of a home for me."

"Good to hear it," Moira said, beaming at Erin over her tea. Erin laughed.

"Actually, I have a favor to ask of you."

"Oh?" Moira said, raising her eyebrow.

"Yes," Erin said, becoming serious. "I've been learning what it means to be a Guardian, and there is something that only you can help me with." Moira stared at Erin, curious. "My gran may have told you that a Guardian's power comes largely from their connection to the land. That's why so many of my ancestors were farmers or had their hand in farming in some way."

"So you want to start a farm?"

Erin chuckled. "Nothing so complicated. I was hoping you would help me start an herb and vegetable garden." She watched Moira's face trying to judge her response. At first, she seemed to be confused, but then her face broke out into a huge grin.

"Of course I'll help you!" Moira exclaimed. "I'd help you even if you weren't a Guardian."

"Thank you," Erin said smiling.

"You asked at the right time too," Moira stated digging into her oversized purse. "This is the best time to start preparing for next year. You can lay the ground work now so that everything will be ready by spring. Now, what exactly do you want to plant?"

Moira talked Erin's ear off during the following weeks; not that Erin minded. Moira told her which plants would do the best and how they should be planted. She helped Erin pick out the best location for her future garden which, incidentally, was where her great-grandmother had had hers. Moira gave Erin every bit of gardening information she had. She also encouraged her to join the gardening club in the spring for even more support.

Erin's head was spinning from it all. She had no idea how much went into getting things to grow. Sure, she had an idea, but she was a city girl, with most of her knowledge was gleamed from references in books or from the media.

In addition to the harvest, Dorshire was also gearing up for the Samhain festival. Which Erin found out later, was an ancient pagan holiday that would later become Halloween. At first, she was confused as to why the village would be celebrating a pagan holiday. Caleb chuckled when she asked him about it.

"That's how villages like this are," Caleb explained. "There's always a bit of pagan mixed in. Most of the farmers figure it's safer to keep some of the old practices around. Old man McGrearty has always said that the pagan rituals have been a part of this country for so long that to abandon them now would just be rude."

Erin didn't know what to make of that. Of course, she knew that there was some truth to pagan rituals, but she had never come across such a mix of old and new in her life. She was even more confused when she learned that Halloween wasn't really celebrated in this part of the world. Back in the States, every kid couldn't wait for Halloween, but in Europe, there was nothing special about the day at all. The only ones who seemed to follow the traditions were the farmers and the pagan practitioners.

Erin laughed at the difference between countries and plunged head first into her own preparations for the holiday. She volunteered to do the window display for Haven. She had everything planned out. It was going to look like a witch's work table. She rummaged around in her attic and came up with a rich, red velvet cloth, an assortment of interesting looking bottles, and even a crystal ball. She also removed a few of the herb bundles to add to the display. She purchased some fake cobwebs and a smoking cauldron. The final touches came from Haven's stockpile of unique books. It took her about a week to get the display ready, but it was worth it. Kayle loved it, telling Erin it was the best one they had ever had, and then set about making a new sign— just for Samhain— to draw in customers.

When Moira saw the display, she could only laugh.

"Leave it to a witch like you to embrace your heritage on Samhain."

"What can I say?" Erin shrugged. "It's about time I had some fun with all of this."

"True," Moira conceded. "Well, since you finished yours, you might as well help me with mine." Erin laughed, but agreed all the same. Inspired by Erin's display, Moira decided to make her display look like an apothecary shop.

Erin was helping Moira complete the finishing touches to the display, when the phone rang in the office. Moira left to answer it. Erin heard her greet the person on the other end warmly, and then there was silence. At first, Erin paid it no mind, but then something shifted in the air. Erin turned towards the office and knew that the call meant bad news. Her suspicions were confirmed by the look on Moira's face when she came out of the office. When Moira wouldn't meet her eyes, Erin's throat tightened.

"It's your grandma," Moira whispered.

Erin dropped everything and sprinted to the office. Moira went back to the display to give Erin some space. She would need it.

"What's wrong?" Erin demanded, the moment she put the phone to her ear.

"Did your mother show up in Dorshire last month?" Elise asked. Erin could hear the tears in her grandma's voice.

"Yes," whispered Erin, gripping the phone tightly with both hands. "She isn't back home?"

"No," came Elise's reply. Erin sat down hard on the chair, her blood turning to ice. "Are you sure she got on the plane?"

"No," Erin whimpered. "I just saw her to the train. She had no reason to stay here." Erin bit her thumb. "Maybe she's just with friends. We sort of came to an understanding. Perhaps she's just giving herself some time to work things out?"

Erin heard her grandmother choke back a sob, "We called all of her friends. No one has seen her. I fear that she never made it to her return flight."

"That doesn't make any sense!" Erin protested. "If she is still here, then why hasn't she come back to my house? She doesn't know anyone here...does she?"

"I don't think so," Erin's grandmother said uncertainly. "You said that you two came to an agreement. Did anything else happen?"

"Yes," Erin said. "It turns out that Connor has been photographing me since I got here. He sent the pictures to Mom. That's why she came here in the first place."

"Why didn't you tell me about this sooner?" Elise demanded.

"There wasn't anything you or I could do about it," Erin told her grandmother. "I destroyed the photos and Mom let it go." Her grandmother was quiet on the other end. Erin bit her thumb again.

"I'm afraid that Connor has your mother," Erin's grandmother said softly. "He's most likely got her under a spell; otherwise he wouldn't be able to keep her."

"Where?!" Erin growled. Messing with her was one thing, but no one messed with her family without paying for it, and dearly.

"I know what you're thinking and don't," Elise ordered. "Even if you were fully grown into your powers, it would be suicide to confront Connor on his territory."

"Why?"

"No matter who you are, the rules that govern our world remain the same," Elise explained. "The place where you live gives you more power than anywhere else. It will be best if you fortify the defenses around the house, and wait for me and your sister to arrive."

"What's Laura got to do with this?" Erin asked.

"The more of us there are, the more power we will be able to draw upon," Erin's grandmother said. "Your sister may not know much, if anything, but the same blood runs through her veins. We will need all the help we can get, if we are to save your mother and push Connor back.

Until then, do *not* go to his home. Keep Fae close to you, and wait for us." Erin glowered. "Promise me, Erin", she pleaded. "If he has taken your mother, then he is getting ready to make a play. You must wait."

"I promise," Erin said through gritted teeth. She heard her grandmother sigh with relief on the other end.

"We'll be there soon. I promise," Elise said, and then hung up.

Erin slowly put down the phone. Outwardly, she was cool and collected, but inside she was a firestorm. Connor has taken her mother. Yes, their relationship was shaky right now, but that didn't mean that they didn't still love each other. The thought of her mother at the mercy of his hands was enough to make her shudder. She didn't know much about him, but it was enough for her to not wish that on her worse enemy.

"Sorry gran," Erin said. "Not gonna keep that promise."

Ye know this is crazy, Fae told Erin for the hundredth time. *While I admire yer drive, ye have to know ye can't possibly win a fight with him.*

"I'm not going to fight," Erin replied coolly. Fae snorted. "Honestly, I'm not. I just want to see." Fae continued to grumble as Erin drove towards the one place she wasn't supposed to go to.

During Erin's first meeting with Connor, he had told her where he lived. There weren't that many old castles around Dorshire, so his home was easy to find. When she had told Fae where she was going, he protested, but eventually relented when Erin told him that she wanted him with her.

Erin was glad that Fae had agreed to come with her. Her initial anger had simmered down and she was afraid that if she went alone, she would have lost her nerve. She wasn't exactly sure what she was going to say to Connor when she saw him. She tried to prepare as she drove, but her mind came up blank. She kept seeing her mother strapped down to some medieval torture device in a dark, dank dungeon, screaming for mercy. Erin tried to dispel the image. She told herself that, even though Connor was an evil prick, he didn't have a dungeon or torture devices...probably.

In what seemed like no time at all, Erin found herself at the end of a very long, gravel driveway, looking up at a decent sized castle. Her doubts about Connor having a dungeon were quickly fading, but that wasn't important right now.

Taking a deep breath, Erin got out of her truck. She stood there with Fae, taking in everything. The sun's light seemed weaker here. The air was heavy and still. She also noticed that she didn't hear a single bird; in fact, she felt no life around the castle at all. The only thing that she felt was suffering, rage, and despair. She wrapped her arms around herself in an attempt to protect herself from these feelings. Fae brushed up against her leg, lending her his strength until Erin got it under control.

Erin was amazed at how far the aura reached. Technically, she was still in the street— neutral territory— but she felt like she was right in the thick of things. She took a few tentative steps towards the driveway. What she felt earlier became stronger with each step. She gritted her teeth and continued up the driveway. She had only gone a few feet before she had to stop. She wondered how in the world someone could live in a place like this.

"You have some balls; I'll give you that." Erin was so preoccupied with fighting the dark energy around her that she didn't notice that someone had walked up. It wasn't Connor but the young man she had seen with him when she buried the protection sachet at Haven. "Allow me to introduce myself. The name's Zander and I will be assisting my brother in the destruction of your family." He bowed slightly, smirking. Erin just glared at him.

"My brother says I'm not allowed to touch you, but since you're here..." said Zander, straightening. He took a step towards Erin.

"Enough Zander," Connor commanded from behind Erin. To her credit, she didn't jump. She just shifted until she could see both brothers. Connor regarded her with a smirk that mirrored the one Zander had given her. "Go back inside," he told his brother, scowling. Zander sighed, but obeyed. Erin didn't watch him leave. Her attention was focused on the bigger predator in front of her.

"I don't know if you're brave to come here…or foolish," Connor said. "Probably the latter. What can I do for you?"

"Where is my mother?" Erin demanded.

"I have no idea what you are talking about," Connor replied sweetly. "Has she visited this country? I was unaware of that. The two of you should come by for dinner."

"Where is she?!" Erin demanded again. "If you harm one hair on her head, I swear, I will hunt you down to the ends of the earth, and end you!"

"You are quite a creature," Connor commented, reaching for her. She quickly stepped back, slapping his hand away. His eyes hardened. "Little girls shouldn't go around poking things that should be left alone. It could be quite dangerous." He sneered at her. "That doesn't matter though," he said. "This will all be over soon. Do tell your grandmother and sister I said hello."

Dumbfounded, Erin watched as Connor got back into his car— once again she hadn't heard it— and drove towards his home. She stood there and watched until he waved from the front door. She couldn't take it anymore.

As calmly as she could, she returned to her truck and sped away.

Zander watched from the window as the truck disappeared down the road. He smiled cruelly as his brother came up beside him. "It's nice to have someone worth playing with," Zander said. Connor didn't return his brother's smile. Instead, he spun around quickly, striking his brother. Zander fell to the floor his hand to his face.

"She is *not* your plaything," Connor growled. "When she falls, it will be by *my* hand and no one else's. Do you understand?"

"Yes brother," Zander whimpered. "Forgive me. I forgot myself."

Connor ignored his brother and turned his attention back to the window. A hollowed-eyed servant appeared, carrying a silver tray with a single glass. Connor took the glass and sipped slowly. Unobserved, Zander slowly got to his feet, fighting back tears. "The prize that our family has sought after for generations is almost in our grasp."

"What about the old lady?" Zander asked. "She's powerful."

"Her powers are fading." Connor laughed. "Soon, she won't be able to even light a candle, let alone stand up to me. The younger sister isn't any threat either. No one is in that family. They are just a minor obstacle. It's quite a shame, almost anticlimactic after all of these centuries of fighting."

Connor sighed, then turned and smiled at his brother, who flinched. "Perhaps, I will let you play with the younger sister, once everything is said and done. She is a spirited young woman, and I know how you do love to break them in."

Zander broke out into an evil grin. "Thank you, brother."

Connor nodded. "Soon, we will be able to put this behind us and continue with our plans. There will be no one to stand in our way."

Thirteen

S tupid. Stupid. Stupid," muttered Erin as she
slammed her hand against the steering wheel. Her
little trip down insanity lane had done nothing but
prove to Connor that she was a scared little girl. Her
driving was so erratic that Fae dug his claws into the seat.
He didn't say a single word to her. He knew exactly how she
felt, and she didn't need any commentary from him.
Eventually, she slowed down and drove normally. "I really
screwed up, Fae?"

Not entirely, mistress, Fae told her. *It took guts a*

plenty to go there like ye did. Yes, they know that ye are afraid of them. But they also saw that wouldn't stop ye from standing up to them.

Erin reached over and stroked her familiar. While she didn't entirely believe his words, they were still reassuring. She had underestimated the whole situation, and what was worse, she was still treating Connor and his family like they were normal. Once more, she had forgotten that she was dealing with a whole new world that had its own rules.

As Erin sped home, she became aware of the growing darkness around her. She wondered if it was natural, or something that Connor and his brother had concocted to scare her more. Either way, she sped, up wanting to be home before the darkness completely settled.

Erin nearly cried with relief the moment her headlights shone on her house. Quickly, she turned her truck off, and bolted towards the door, Fae hot on her heals. She kept glancing over her shoulder as she fiddled with her keys, convinced someone was coming after her. After a few, heart-stopping minutes, she threw herself through the door, slammed it shut, and bolted it. She pressed her forehead against the door in relief, but an old, familiar fear crept back in. The darkness of the house pressed in on her, making her see shapes that weren't there. In a panic, she tore through the house flipping every light switch as she went. For the first time in a long while, she slept with every light on in the house. Everything that could be locked was locked, and she placed the poker from the downstairs fireplace next to her bed.

Erin hardly slept at all. Every time she fell asleep, she would hear something and wake up, heart pounding. Fae tried to comfort her, but he was just as on-edge as she was. They were only able to catch a few minutes of sleep, just as night gave way to dawn. She called in sick. There was no way she would be able to work, even if she had gotten a full night's sleep.

Erin tried to spend the day catching up on her sleep, but she was too worried about her mother. Her gran was supposed to double check and make sure that her mother never made it back to the States, but that was just a formality. Both Erin and Elise knew that Connor had gotten to her. Erin paced around her home, anxiously waiting for the call that would let her know when to expect reinforcements.

Her heart started to race when she heard someone pull up into her driveway. She only relaxed when neither Fae nor her wards sounded the alarm. She heard the front door open, but she didn't bother to see who it was.

"Erin?" Caleb called from the hallway. Erin hurried towards him. He turned when he heard her. His face mirrored what she felt inside. Before she could stop herself, she broke down. Caleb wrapped his arms around her, pulling her in close. She hid her face in his chest both ashamed and grateful.

Normally, Erin tried to avoid crying in front of men. She knew that, as a whole, they couldn't handle seeing a woman cry, and some women exploited that fact. But Erin wasn't trying to get something from Caleb. She was just so stressed out that she couldn't take it anymore. If she had to cry in front of someone, she was glad it was Caleb. Inside his arms, she felt a small measure of safety and she desperately clung to that. He patted her back and rubbed her hair. But he was still male, and therefore, uncomfortable.

"Moira told me," Caleb said, once Erin's sobs subsided. Her head shot up, surprised. *Moira told him?* "I'm sure they'll find your mother soon." Erin put her head back down to hide her relief. She hadn't really thought that Moira would tell her secret; well, not unless she felt like she had to. Erin already had a lot on her plate and didn't want to add to it, if she could avoid it.

"Gran's checking with the airlines back home," Erin said, sniffling. "We're trying to find out where she went missing."

"When are you leaving?"

"I'm not," Erin stated. Caleb leaned back so he could read her face. "If she never made it back to the States," she explained, "that means that she's still in Ireland somewhere. I can start the search here, while my family makes arrangements to come."

Caleb nodded, guiding her towards the kitchen. With a gentle hand, he urged her to sit. She complied. He then set about making her something to eat and a cup of tea. She allowed herself a small smile. Typical guy behavior— avoid an emotional situation by handling problems you can fix with your two hands. She allowed him to take charge. It made both of them feel better.

"Thanks," Erin said when Caleb returned to the table bearing a sandwich. While she hadn't eaten anything since yesterday, she only picked at it. She just didn't have an appetite. She did manage a few bites; although, they were more for Caleb's sake than her own. He gave her a reassuring smile, and poured tea for them both.

Caleb stayed for the rest of the day. They didn't talk much, but that wasn't what Erin needed. Instead, they curled up on the couch and watched old movies. He cooked dinner and cleaned up afterwards. They stayed up until Erin could barely keep her eyes open, then they went to bed. With him there, she didn't feel the need to sleep with the lights on. Instead, she slept curled up on his chest, listening to the rhythm of his heart until she fell into a dreamless sleep.

It was nearly noon when Erin finally woke up. She stretched first, before curling up into a ball. She heard the TV downstairs, meaning Caleb was still there. Despite everything, she smiled. It was nice to have someone to lean on. With a sigh, she got out of bed, washed her face, and brushed her teeth. After debating with herself, she ran a brush through her hair as well. She then grabbed her robe and went downstairs to join Caleb.

"How'd you sleep?" Caleb asked when she joined him on the couch.

"Better," Erin replied.

"I hope you don't mind, but I called Kayle and she told me to tell you that you don't have to worry about coming in." Erin shot Caleb a look. "She said if you want to come in, that's fine," Caleb went on, "but it's all up to you." Erin was glad that she decided to brush her teeth before she came down. She leaned in and gave him a kiss.

"What would I do without you?" Erin said, smiling.

"Wallow in despair," Caleb joked. Erin kissed him again.

Caleb stayed over another night, but went to work the next day. He promised to stop by later. He told Erin to call him if she needed anything, or heard any news. She agreed. She forced herself to smile until he was gone. Her smile fell when she couldn't see him. She remained at the window, frowning. She brought her thumb up to her mouth and chewed on the nail. What was she going to do? Until her gran called her back, all she could do was wait. She wondered if she should go to work, just to keep her mind busy. But just the thought of getting ready and dealing with customers— or just people in general— made her shudder.

Waiting is always the hardest part, Fae told Erin. *Once we know more, we can form a plan. Ye will feel better then. Until then, there's still work to be done here.*

Erin knew he was right. Connor may try something now that he knew that she, and her family, were on to him. And thanks to her ill-advised visit, her confidence in her defenses had dwindled. She fortified each ward around herself and her friends. The rest of her day consisted of practicing defensive and offensive spells, in the astral plain and in the real world. All of the extra work completely drained Erin. She nearly fell asleep in her dinner. Yawning, she crawled into bed and snuggled up to Fae. She was so tired that she didn't even remember to turn on the lights.

For two days, Erin reminded in her house. It didn't take long for her boredom to override her fear. She could only clean her house or practice the limited number of spells she knew, so many times. She was nervous during her drive into town. She kept checking her rearview mirror, convinced that she was being followed. However, the moment she crossed the threshold of Haven and breathed in the scent of old books, tea, and furniture polish, all her fears faded away. Haven was her territory just as much as her home was. Everything within its four walls was familiar to her. Within them she was safe.

"Erin," Kayle cried when Erin entered the office. "I thought you were taking some time."

"I need to be busy," Erin explained. "If I have to sit at home another day, I'm going to pull my hair out." Kayle gave her a knowing smile, relinquishing the desk to her. Erin plunged into work like someone who wished to banish everything else from their mind, which she did.

Erin worked every moment that she could. Hundreds of books passed her desk were cataloged, categorized, and stored. She was the first to arrive and the last to leave. As she worked, she wondered if her father was doing the same thing. He had always been career driven, often at the expense of his family. She wondered if he even realized that his wife was missing. She shook her head and tried not to think about it. It was too depressing.

A week went by with no word from America. Erin tried to not let her worries take over, but the longer she went without hearing anything the worse her imagination became. So when her phone rang one evening, she launched herself at it.

"Hello! Gran?" Erin stammered into the phone.

"It's me," Laura said on the other end. "So we have good news and bad news."

"Just tell me," Erin urged.

"The good news is that the airline finally got back to us with the bad news that Mom never made it onto her return flight. She disappeared after you put her on the train."

Erin slumped to the floor, still holding the phone to her ear. Her sister's words echoed in her mind. "When are you getting here?" Erin whispered.

"Soon," Laura replied. "Gran's getting the tickets right now. I'll call you once we have a date and time."

"I'm picking you up," Erin said. The tone in her voice told her sister it would be useless to argue. Connor had already snatched up one member of her family. She'd be damned if she'd let him do it again.

"Okay," Laura replied. Erin heard Elise speak in the background. "Okay, Gran. She wants me to tell you that we will be there in two days."

Erin wrote down their flight and arrival time. She said goodbye to her sister and hung up the phone. She grinned. In just a few days, she would have her own backup, and then things would get real interesting. Feeling better, she called Moira to fill her in, and then Caleb. The part of her life that involved Caleb was normal and that was something that Erin cherished, especially now. It helped to keep her grounded.

Erin kept her eyes glued to the screen that kept track of flight times for incoming and outgoing planes. The plane that had carried her grandmother and sister had landed ten minutes ago, but they had yet to arrive. She knew that going through customs could be a lengthy process, but the wait was grating on her nerves. Finally, she saw Laura's bright blue hair. Erin let out a sigh of relief before she ran to greet her family, fighting back tears. She hadn't realized how much she had missed them. Yeah, her sister had paid her a visit over the summer, but it wasn't enough. Plus, with everything else going on, she felt better facing it with her family by her side.

"Sorry about the wait," Elise said. "They were having problems with their computers."

"Don't worry about it," Erin replied, waving her hands. "Let's just get your bags and head home." They walked to baggage claim, arm in arm, and for the first time since finding out about her hidden heritage, Erin felt hopeful. Maybe, just maybe, everything would turn out alright.

It was a tight fit, but the three women managed to fit into the cabin of Erin's truck. With their luggage carefully stowed in the back, they left the bright lights of the city behind them. They rode in silence for the first few miles, tension building, until Erin thought the truck would explode.

"So what's the game plan?" Laura asked, unable to take it anymore.

Elise sighed. "First things first, we have to get your mother away from Connor. As long as he holds her, we are vulnerable."

292

"He won't kill her, will he?" Erin asked terrified. Laura's eyes widened.

Elise shook her head. "I don't think so," she said; although she sounded doubtful. "He could use her as leverage to get what he wants."

"So how do we get Mom back", Laura asked.

"We have to somehow break whatever hold he has over her, and to do that, we have to be near where she is."

"He's probably got Mom at his house," Erin said, biting her lip. "It's actually nice looking if you can get past the overbearing sense of despair that hangs around it." Both Elise and Laura stared at Erin.

"I thought we had agreed that you were not to go near him?" Elise said sternly.

Erin shrugged. "I lied. Besides, I didn't go far, just a few feet up the driveway. I met his brother too. He's even creepier than Connor."

"You have some balls, sis," Laura said with feeling. Elise, however, shot Laura a look, then turned her disapproving gaze towards Erin.

"That was a very foolish thing to do," Elise reprimanded.

"I know," Erin sighed. "But I had to see it for myself." Elise's scowl softened and she reached for Erin.

"I know, sweetie," Elise whispered, "I know. This is all my fault." Erin and Laura tried to tell her that it wasn't, but she waved them off. "It is. If I hadn't hidden our heritage, then you two and your mother would have been better armed. Connor wouldn't have been able to even lift a finger against us. I hope that one day you girls can forgive me. I just wanted a normal life for myself and my children." Elise started to sniffle. Laura dug around the glove box and handed her a paper napkin. Elise dabbed her eyes.

Laura and Erin reached out and took their grandmother's hand. This brought a weak smile to her face. The past was the past and there was nothing anyone could do about it. Their energy would be better spent tackling the problem at hand and not worrying about things that could not be changed.

It was late by the time the three women made it to their family home. They all agreed that it would be better if they waited until morning. Erin offered the master bedroom to Elise, but she declined, saying that she wanted to stay in the room that had been hers growing up. Laura wanted to bunk with Erin.

"Do you think Mom's alright?" Laura asked as they crawled into bed.

"I hope so," Erin replied. Her sister's face fell. Erin reached out and pulled her in close. Laura was trying to hold back her tears. She was trying to be brave. "Don't worry about Mom," Erin told her sister. "I would worry about Connor. Once Mom is herself again, she'll give him one of her long lectures about how men are supposed to act."

The mental image of their mother scolding Connor made Laura laugh. For years the two of them had been subject to a number of their mother's lectures about how ladies are supposed to act. They were used to it, but Connor would most likely end up trying to stuff books into his ears to block it out. Erin kissed the top of her sister's head then closed her eyes. She needed to sleep so that she could keep her wits about her. Things were going to move a whole lot faster now that Elise was back. Connor probably already knew, and they needed to be ready to make their move before he made his. The time for reacting was over. Now it was time for them to go on the offensive.

Instead of diving right into the matter, like Erin had expected, Elise took on the role of a teacher. Erin knew quite a bit already, but Laura knew nothing. However, she was a quick learner, especially with help from her sister.

"We can't go in there half-cocked", Elise explained. "The more the two of you know, the better our situation will be. Plus, I'd rather not attempt anything until Halloween."

"Why?" Laura asked. Erin was curious herself. She wanted to go after Connor now. She wanted her mother back where she belonged, with them.

"It will give us a power boost," explained Elise. "And believe me, we will need it. If there was some way to make Connor come to us, I would do it. But I highly doubt he'll give up the advantage of home field. On Halloween, we will be able to call upon our ancestors for help."

"Won't he be able to do the same?" Erin asked.

"Yes," replied Elise. "We just have to hope that our ancestors are more powerful than his." Erin wasn't too happy with their plan. It seemed like it relied too much on luck, and her track record wasn't that good.

To give herself a distraction from the looming battle, Erin continued to work. She found herself shaking her head more and more as the days progressed. The village continued to take on a festive look and feel. Here she was, preparing for the biggest fight of her life, and everyone else was looking forward to a good time. It was ironic and unfair, and Erin mentioned it to her grandmother after a training session.

"That's the way it is I'm afraid," Elise sighed. "I suppose it was easier in the old days, because magic— and the families who wheeled it— were more common." Elise sighed again. "But that's not the case now."

"How come?" Erin asked.

"We're dying out."

"What?" exclaimed Laura.

"Each year, among the families, there are fewer people born who have the ability to use magic. To make matters worse, there doesn't seem to be any new families popping up. Some think it's because of technology, while others think our time is fading. There aren't many questions in the world today, and most people have an easy life."

"What about us?" Erin asked. If this was true then maybe her future children— if she lived long enough to have any— would be free to live their lives without the burden that had been placed on her shoulders.

"Your children may have the gift," explained Elise, "or they may not. It may skip them and your grandchildren may display the skills. But we have a more pressing issue in the present." She flipped through the family book. "Now, let's try manipulating flames."

The closer they got to Halloween, the harder Erin and Laura's grandmother worked them. Erin suspected that it was to keep them from over-worrying themselves. It worked. From the moment that Erin and her sister opened their eyes, to the moment that they went to bed, their grandmother drilled them on spells, charms, and everything else.

"Despite your late start," Elise said one evening over dinner, "you girls are doing well. Given a little more time and training, you two could easily become the most powerful Guardians in our family." Erin was shocked, because she didn't feel like that at all. Laura, on the other hand, got a mischievous gleam in her eye.

"Don't let it go to your head," Erin joked. Laura stuck out her tongue at her sister and the table erupted into laughter. Their grandmother's comment may have given Laura a boost in confidence, but Erin was still uneasy. Elise was aging and her magic wasn't what it used to be. Laura could only work magic in the astral plain. The only magic Erin could work in the physical world was a few shield spells. She reminded herself to have faith in her family's strength, because right now that was all that they had.

Halloween— D-Day— the point of no return. All of this flashed through Erin's head the moment she opened her eyes. Were they prepared? What evils would Connor throw at them? Would they succeed? All of these questions raced through her mind without pause. She groaned and covered her face with a pillow. She mentally demanded the questions to stop and leave her alone. She would have the answers soon enough. When she uncovered her face, she noticed that her sister was also awake. Laura's eyes were filled with uncertainty and fear. Erin reached out and took Laura's hand. She gripped Erin's hand with white knuckles. Erin tried to give her a reassuring smile, but it came out more like a grimace.

"Good morning girls," Elise said from the doorway.

The sisters turned and offered small smiles. "I made breakfast. I know you may not have the stomach for food right now, but trust me, you'll need the strength."

Breakfast was a quiet affair. Erin picked at her food and so did her sister. If it wasn't for Elise's urging, the girls wouldn't have eaten a single bit. They cleaned up in silence, and then stood around the kitchen, unsure of what to do next. Normally, there would have been lessons but the book was nowhere to be seen.

"There's nothing we can do until nightfall," Elise told her granddaughters, filling a kettle with water. "I suggest you take this time to prepare yourselves. Read, take a bath, sleep... do whatever you feel is required."

Erin and Laura stared at their grandmother in disbelief. They were just supposed to find something to fill the time between now and tonight? Laura wanted to argue, but after seeing the look on their grandmother's face Erin stopped her. Their grandmother was miles away.

Erin took her sister to the attic, showing her the boxes and chests of clothes that she still had. Soon, her sister was absorbed by the vintage clothing. Erin retreated to the study. She pulled down a couple of journals to read. Maybe she would find something that would help her, or maybe not.

Around noon, Erin decided that she was going to take a nap. Her eyes were tired and sore from reading. She hoped that she would be able to sleep the rest of the day away, sparing her from working herself up too much. Apparently, Laura had the same idea because she was sprawled out in the third bedroom. Watching her sister sleep, Erin's heart swelled. Her sister looked so young when she slept. Erin said a silent prayer to her ancestors that they would get through this night in one piece.

Sleep evaded Erin. She tossed and turned for hours. She watched the sunlight make its journey across her walls. The shadows had just started to lengthen when she finally gave up. The house was quiet. She tip-toed downstairs, hoping that the rest of her family was getting some rest. Elise was still sitting in the kitchen, sipping tea and stroking Fae who had curled up in her lap.

"Couldn't sleep?" Elise asked. Erin shook her head. Elise gave her a knowing smile, before Erin turned towards her coffee maker. As the coffee brewed, she took a seat across from Elise. They didn't say anything. They just looked out the window and watched as the daylight faded.

Laura eventually came down, looking terrible. She grunted a greeting and made herself a cup of coffee, joining in the watch. Erin's unease steadily climbed the darker it got. She started to twist the knot work bracelet around her wrist.

"Oh," Elise exclaimed when she noticed Erin's bracelet. "I can't believe I forgot about that."

Elise stood and beckoned the girls to follow her. Together, they climbed into the attic and went straight to the chest where Erin had found the book. Their grandmother dug around the jewelry, picking up and putting back pieces. She gave Laura a silver necklace with a pendant, and a bronze armband that fitted just below Laura's elbow. Erin received a necklace as well, only this one had amber beads. Their grandmother placed a ring on her finger and a torque around her neck.

All three of the women relaxed as the pieces, filled with the energy of their ancestors eased their souls. It felt as if they were surrounded by loved ones. Fae rubbed his head against Erin's leg offering her his own brand of comfort. Erin reached into the chest, digging around for something for her familiar. He would be joining them—combining his strength with theirs. It was only fair that he should have something too. Erin found a small pendant with a wolf motif and attached it to his color. Fae's eyes shone with gratitude first, then with power.

The wind had picked up and night had fallen. The three women looked at each other— solemn, but calm. "It is time," said Elise, closing the chest.

Erin and Laura nodded. Erin bent down and picked up Fae. Slowly, they made their way downstairs, stopping only to pick up the supplies that they would need to free their mother from Connor's hold. Erin felt a tingling in the back of her head, but pushed it aside. It was most likely nerves. The tingling got stronger the closer she got to the front door, until it turned into a dull ache. She was about to say something to her grandmother, but when Laura opened the front door, she found the cause.

Connor stood at the end of the driveway, but he wasn't alone. Standing next to him was Erin's and Laura's mother. She wore the same clothes that she had been in when Erin had taken her to the train station. The wind whipped Jessica's hair and clothes about, but she remained still, unaware of her surroundings. Laura took off running, followed closely by Erin and their grandmother.

"Well, would you look at this..." Connor sneered, "an old crone and two fledgling witches. I have my work cut out for me." He laughed mercilessly. The three women shivered at the sound. Erin was surprised that Connor had come alone. Did he really think that they weren't a threat to him? She hoped that his arrogance could be used to their advantage.

"Shut up!" Laura shouted. "Mom! Mom?"

Erin reached out and grasped her sister by the shoulders, partially to keep her from getting any closer to Connor, and partially to hold her up. Yes, their mother was standing in front of them. Yes, she didn't look like she had been harmed. But when they looked into her eyes, they were vacant, soulless.

"Mom," Laura cried, crumbling. "What did you do to my mom?"

Connor's usually handsome face had been replaced by one that was twisted and evil. The more that Laura cried, the crueler his face became. He relished their suffering. Erin tried to stay focused on him, but she found that her eyes kept shifting over to her mother. Erin hoped to see some sign of her mother's soul, but her eyes remained vacant, her face expressionless. Connor noticed Erin's quick glances and grinned.

"As you can see your mother is the picture of health," Connor said, gesturing.

"What did you do to her?" Erin demanded, moving her sister behind her. Connor laughed.

"Just a simple binding spell." Connor laughed. "*Very* simple actually... beginner level, if truth be told. I knew that you didn't know much about magic, but I didn't realize that you knew nothing." Connor looked at Elise in disgust when he said it, as if she was the foulest creature on earth.

"I wouldn't be so sure," Erin snapped angrily. Without stopping to think, she cast a protective circle around herself, her grandmother, her familiar, and her sister. Erin felt better within the circle, but her mother was still Connor's captive. He smiled at her, like a teacher who sees a promising student. It made her blood boil. Elise placed her hand on Erin's shoulder.

"Not now," Elise said quietly. Erin groaned, but released the circle to allow her grandmother to step forward. "Connor Ferguson," Elise said clearly. "Release my daughter and we will allow you to leave with your life." Erin and Laura glanced at each other from the corner of their eyes, wondering if Connor would buy their bluff. They fought to keep their faces blank when he started to laugh.

"I have to admire your spirit," Connor laughed, wiping his eyes. "Really I do. Between the three of you, I highly doubt that you could follow through with that little threat." He stopped laughing, turning the full power of his gaze on them. "It is time for this to be over. For centuries, your family has been a thorn in my family's side —but no more."

"If you're so powerful," Laura jeered, "then why has it taken you this long to make a move?" To Laura's credit, she didn't flinch when Connor turned his dark gaze towards her. Instead, she lifted her chin and met his eyes. Erin was proud of the courage her sister displayed. Erin wished she had a fraction of her sister's strength.

"Other things were more pressing," Connor replied coldly. When they didn't react, he sighed and then went on. " Magic is fading from this world. When someone who carries magical blood dies, their power returns to the Universe. Normally, it gets shifted around, but not recently. Soon there will be no more. It's survival of the fittest ladies. I will save what little magic that is left from those who would ignore its full potential, like your family." Connor shook his head. His face hardened. "We were once gods among men. We will be again...well I will. I would have succeeded sooner, but Elise here disappeared long before I was born, and my simpleton of a father had no inclinations to search for her. Unfortunately, it took me years to track down your lovely grandmother here. I watched your family for years, trying to figure out whether or not you had the gift. Finally, I got tired of waiting."

"What do you mean," Erin asked, with a sinking feeling.

"I think you know," Connor offered with a sneer. When Erin didn't respond he shrugged. "It didn't take much really...a little manipulation here and there. I needed to push you in the right direction. It was quite fun."

To say that Erin was shocked would be an understatement; she was floored. Connor noted her expression and laughed mercilessly. While she appeared calm on the outside, inside she was raging. This rage drove the rest of the world away, until the only thing she could see was Connor laughing at her. He had caused her so many problems since her arrival at Dorshire, but he had done so much more that she hadn't been aware of. All of the humiliation and pain she had experienced at the hands of John came rushing back to her. It had all happened because of the laughing man in front of her. This man had played with people's lives to suit his needs. The sanctity of life meant nothing to him. He was the lowest of the low and needed to be put down like a rabid dog.

Power began to radiate off Erin— although, she wasn't aware of it. Connor just thought it was her anger over being duped, but her grandmother knew better. She had told Erin and Laura that they had the possibility to be the strongest Guardians in their family, and now Elise knew that Erin would be, without a doubt, the strongest of them all. All the while, Connor continued to laugh.

"But I am nothing if not fair," Connor said once he had stopped laughing. "Given how far your family has fallen, I am willing to allow this little battle to happen on your land. Here are the terms. If you can manage to break my hold over your mother, you can have her. No tricks. It was been so long since I had a decent fight, and I think you might provide me with a little entertainment before the end. What do you think?"

Erin's grandmother remained silent, trying to figure out if they could in fact win. Laura realized that the whole situation was out of her league, so she deferred judgment to her grandmother and big sister. Erin, on the other hand, was still too shocked to realize what Connor had offered them. Connor took their silence for fear and smiled. In his mind, he had already won.

"Oh, this is perfect," Connor chuckled. Once again, he started to laugh. Fae, fed up with him laughing at his mistress and her family, leapt onto her shoulder. Connor caught the movement, and was surprised for only a moment.

"I had forgotten you had a fae cat for a familiar. But he won't be of much use." Connor shifted his pale blue eyes to Fae. "Tell me, fae, just how many of you are left? A hundred, ten...just you?" Fae jumped down and hissed, eyes blazing. Connor just shrugged nonchalant, "Do we have a deal? I don't have all night you know, and neither does your mother."

Fae leapt back onto Erin's shoulder, and his weight brought her back to reality. She was disturbed that her grandmother hadn't given him an answer yet. Fear started to trickle in, then Erin heard a voice. *Accept,* it urged her. *Family bonds are stronger than any magic. Accept and save your mother.* Bolstered, Erin stepped forward.

"Deal," Erin said. Her grandmother and sister stared at her in disbelief. Connor smiled again. "If we free my mother, you leave," she said. "But if we lose, we'll give you our book and our power."

"Erin!" exclaimed her grandmother, but Erin ignored her. If they failed tonight, Erin would rather be done with it once and for all.

"Agreed," Connor said. His acceptance was accompanied by the sound of rolling thunder. The wind picked up and the air became charged. He may have scoffed at their diminished state, but he wasn't going to make it easy for them.

Erin closed her eyes, took a deep breath, and stepped forward. She looked deep inside herself, to the place where her magic dwelled. Slowly, words formed in her mind. She took another deep breath, and started to chant. The language was one that she wasn't familiar with, but it didn't matter. The words poured out of her mouth.

Her grandmother stared at her, amazed once again, but only for a moment before she joined in. Laura joined in a few moments later, taken over by a power that she was only just beginning to be aware of.

As the three women chanted, the air around them began to spark. If Connor was surprised or impressed with this display, he kept it to himself. Unfortunately, this didn't seem to have an effect on the sisters' mother at all. She didn't move from her spot, and her eyes remained vacant. Connor placed his hand on Jessica's shoulder. Erin could feel his power working against hers. Briefly, she wondered if their battle was having any effect in town. The wind tore at the trees, making them creak and groan. Branches fell, unable to withstand the maelstrom that surrounded Erin's home. Lightning flashed in the sky— though there wasn't a single cloud.

Erin chanted the ancient words, pouring more and more of her strength into them. Fae glowed with his pale green light adding his power to hers. Erin felt her grandmother's and sister's power behind her— calm and reassuring. But Erin's main focus was on the man in front of her. She locked her eyes with his.

But Erin noticed that around her was becoming misty, almost like the astral plain. Terrified, she realized that she was crossing over and was just about to throw herself back into the physical world, when something familiar came into view: a red thread. The thread connected Erin to her grandmother and her sister. It also connected her to her mother, but that connection was frayed.

Strengthen the bond, the voice urged Erin. *I don't know how,* she argued. An image of her mother smiling flashed before her eyes. *The ties that families make are stronger than any force in the world. They are stronger than death, distance, and Connor.* More and more images and memories flashed before her eyes. She saw her mother baking in the kitchen. She saw the care her mother put into decorating the Christmas tree. She saw her mother sprawled out on the beach, basking in the summer sun. Faster and faster the memories came. Each time her heart fluttered. *Love,* she realized, *love binds families together. It's what allows them to forgive each other and is what makes them go to the ends of the earth for each other.*

Erin poured her love for her mother into the torn thread. She loved her mother. She forgave her for not seeing her hurt. She told her mother that she wanted her back, wanted things the way they used to be. She poured everything she had into mending the thread and breaking Connor's hold over her mother. Just when she thought she was going to give out, she saw a small tear mend. Elated, she held on, determined. The thread continued to mend slowly, but then it gained momentum.

Connor frowned. He tried to strengthen his hold, to no avail. The scale had shifted and Erin was steadily gaining ground. She reached her hand out towards her mother, still chanting. Her mother shifted away from Connor and took a small step forward.

"No!" shouted Connor.

"Come back to me, Mom," Erin pleaded.

Jessica took another step, and then another, slowly making her way back to her daughters. Laura gripped Erin's hand tightly, chanting louder. Elise took hold of Erin's arm. Together, they let their love of Jessica stream out. When the thread was whole, there was a flash of light that blinded all who were present. Erin saw Connor's hold over her mother break. She also saw that she had broken his hold over John too. She was surprised but pleased. Other people flashed before her eyes, none that she knew. The people shook their heads, confused. Apparently, she had freed many others from Connor's dark grasp. Erin smiled as she left the spirit plain. Her mother was within arm's reach. Quickly, Erin reached out and grabbed her mother.

Erin's mother looked around confused. The last thing she remembered was sitting on the train, heading towards the airport. "Erin?" she said.

"Mom," Erin and Laura cried out, throwing themselves at their mother. Jessica allowed herself to be embraced by her daughters, still confused but delighted.

"A deal's a deal," Elise told Connor, who was still standing at the end of the driveway, with a scowl on his face.

"You may have won this battle," Connor sneered, "but the war still rages on!" He turned his back on them, disappearing into the night like some nightmare.

Erin took Connor's parting words to heart. Yes, the war between their families was still on. But the fear that once plagued her was gone. This small victory had shown her that she actually stood a chance of winning.

"Mom, what's going on?" Jessica asked. Elise took her daughter's face in her hands and kissed her cheeks. "Seriously, someone please explain what just happened."

Erin, Laura, and Elise looked at each other. They couldn't help themselves— they started to laugh. Together, they led a still confused Jessica inside and made a large pot of coffee. The explanation would take some time.

Epilogue

The clock struck twelve, but Erin and her family showed no signs of being tired or having any inclination of going to bed anytime soon. Elise sat in one of the overstuffed chairs, while Erin, Jessica, and Laura were piled on the couch. For hours, Erin and her grandmother brought her mother up to speed on everything. Jessica looked from her mother to her daughter, too stunned for words. The only thing that kept her from running out into the night screaming was Laura holding her hand. Erin had just told her mother everything right up to the point when she broke Connor's hold over her.

Erin fell silent, waiting for her mother to say something, anything. Her mother stared at the fire and slowly sipped her coffee. The only sounds in the house were the ticking clock and the snaps from the fire. Fae was curled up in Erin's lap fast asleep. She stroked his fur lovingly. She didn't begrudge him his sleep. He had served wonderfully and deserved some rest. She would need his strength again soon.

"I guess it makes sense," Jessica said slowly. Erin stared at her mother for a moment. Then slowly, she started to chuckle.

"That's one way to look at it," Erin laughed. Her mother looked confused at first, but joined in the laughter. Soon, they were all laughing, tears falling and gripping their sides. Fae grumbled at them for waking him up. He left them, tail held high, and retreated to a quieter room. This only caused the women to laugh again.

"So what's the plan now?" Laura gasped, holding her aching sides.

Elise sighed and leaned back in her chair. "The only thing we can do," she said, suddenly appearing to age before their eyes. "As much as I wanted to keep you girls out of this, we don't have a choice anymore. Connor has shown us that we will not be safe, no aspect of our lives untouched." She took a long sip of tea. "The only thing we can do, my dears, is fight back." Erin and her sister nodded. Their mother continued to stare at the fire. "But this means that I have to step down as the head of the family and pass it on to my successor."

Erin felt a chill run down her spine and she knew, without a shadow of a doubt, which one her grandmother would choose. She met her grandmother's eyes, confirming her suspicions. She was about to protest, but her mother beat her to it.

"Absolutely not," Jessica said, putting her cup down.

"You don't have a say," Elise remarked calmly. Jessica bristled.

"No say?" Jessica repeated. "They are my children! I am their mother!"

"We're not kids anymore," Laura commented, earning a glare from her mother. Laura shrugged. "I'm eighteen, legally an adult. Erin's even older. We're grown enough to make this choice for ourselves." Jessica stared at her youngest daughter like she couldn't believe what she was hearing. Erin, meanwhile, nibbled on her thumb.

"I'll do it then. I'm your daughter. The burden falls to me," Jessica told her mother. Elise shook her head, but it was Erin who answered.

"You can't," Erin told her mother, who looked at her like she had grown another head.

"I don't choose my successor," Elise explained.

"Then who does?!" Jessica demanded.

"The ancestors," replied Elise.

"And they have chosen me," Erin said. "They led me to the book. They sent Fae to look after me and to teach me. When the wards fell and Connor attacked me, they saved me. They have guided and protected me since I got here." Erin hated meeting her mother's eyes. Her mother knew that Erin was right, that she was the next in line, but she wasn't happy about it— not one bit.

"But you've already had to go through so much. You should be coming home, not staying here," Erin's mother pleaded.

Erin shook her head. "This is my home now. Don't take this the wrong way, but I feel more at home here than I ever did back in the States. Plus, I'm not alone. I have friends, an adoptive family, and a great job."

"Not to mention a hot boyfriend," Laura chimed in. Erin shot her sister a glare.

"Yes, there's Caleb too," Erin sighed. "I belong here. Please understand that and be happy for me." She reached out for her mother, clasping her hand. Jessica looked into her daughter's eyes and saw the truth of her words. What type of mother would she be if she made Erin come back with her, where she wasn't happy? Defeated, Jessica bowed her head. Erin felt bad for her mother— truly she did— but there wasn't anything she could do. This was Erin's life and she had to let her live it.

Elise cleared her throat and pushed herself up. "No time like the present," she told them. They stared at her for a moment, before got up themselves. Elise was right. There wasn't anything they could do but get it over with.

Four cloaked women stood within a circle of candles behind the house. The flames from the candles danced in the breeze. One of the cloaked women stood facing the other three. The scene was not out of place for the Halloween night. A white and red cat sat next to the lone figure, tail twitching.

"It is time," said the figure that held a large, leather-bound book. She stepped forward. The light from the candles grew stronger, and revealing the woman to be Elise.

The woman directly in front of her, Erin, lowered her hood. "I am ready," she replied.

Elise opened the book and began to read their family history. As she did, Erin looked at her mother and sister— the other two cloaked figures. Her mother still looked upset and worried. Erin offered her a small smile, which she returned. Her sister, however, looked excited and gave Erin a 'thumbs up'. Erin nodded to her, almost laughing.

While her grandmother continued to list their lineage, Erin allowed her mind to wander. She thought about everything that had lead up to this point. She was amazed to see how much she had changed in such a short period of time. Eight months ago, if she had been presented with this choice, she would have run for the hills screaming, but now she accepted it. Hadn't she proven to herself that she was strong? Hadn't she proven that she could handle the responsibilities she was about to accept?

Erin had taken herself out of a bad situation and fought tooth and nail for a better life. She had turned her back on everything that she knew, to start fresh. She had made herself a new home, new friends, and even had a blossoming love life. Still marveling over her new life, she turned her attention back to her grandmother.

"Do you, Erin, accept the honor and duties as head of our family? Do you promise to uphold the traditions that we have held dear since the beginning? Will you protect the land, its people, and its creatures from those who walk the dark path?"

"Yes," Erin answered. She would have done it all, even without the blessings of her family or her ancestors. This place had become her home. These people hers. Not to mention, Connor had quite a bit to answer for. She didn't take too kindly to him meddling in her life. She would get justice for herself, and for everyone else he had hurt.

Laura stepped forward, holding out a long knife. Erin held out her hand and braced herself. Her sister offered her an apologetic smile, then cut Erin's palm. Erin gritted her teeth, but didn't cry out. Elise held the family book out, and Erin placed her bleeding palm on the stone in the middle of the book.

Pure power surged into Erin, causing her to gasp. She had never felt anything like this in her entire life. It felt like she was connected to everything that had been, was, and ever will be. It was beautiful. She slowly opened her eyes and let out a small gasp. Her ancestors stood before her, shining softly in the dark.

Each one smiled at Erin, welcoming her to their fold. She looked at her living family and saw that they were crying. Even her mother had tears in her eyes. All doubt that Erin had made the right choice vanished the moment she touched the book.

Filled with love for her family and her new power, Erin mentally dared Connor to do his worst. She swore that she would bring him down and set things right. She was no longer the broken woman she was when she first arrived. She had suffered greatly but came out so much stronger because of it. She now knew who she was and what she was supposed to do with her life. She was a Guardian, and she had work to do.

K. N. Timofeev has been a lover of books for as long as she can remember. Her bookshelf consists of books from many different genres. Her love of the written word has inspired her to become a writer herself. When not writing, or reading, she enjoys spending time with her husband and their two pugs, gardening, and watching historical documentaries.

To see her other works you can visit her at
www. timofeevbooks.com

26669545R00183

Made in the USA
Middletown, DE
04 December 2015